The THIEF AND THE Noble

The THIEF AND THE *Noble*

A ROBIN HOOD REGENCY

DANA LeCHEMINANT

Covenant Communications, Inc.

ACKNOWLEDGMENTS

You know those books that change your life a little bit? For me, this is one of them, and this little story is a testament to a lifetime of dreams come true.

A huge thank-you to my beta readers, who brought out the best in this book and gave me the confidence to actually send it in; Sheri, Sam, and Carolyn, you guys really helped this book shine. And an even bigger thanks to my mom and sister, who have been cheering me on for years and who aren't afraid to tell me when something is terribly written.

I also need to thank the dozens of stories that came before this one. They may live forever on my computer and never see the light of day, but they were stepping-stones leading to a book even remotely worthy of joining the many others that have come through Covenant's doors.

Thank you to my incredible editor, Kami Hancock. You're the reason this book exists. Straight up. And you make me sound like a way better writer than I am, so that's pretty cool.

And finally, a huge shout-out to Robin Hood and the legend that has lived on for centuries. I don't know if you were real or not, but I like to think you were just a guy who wanted to make his world a little bit better and did what he could. We need more people like you.

CHAPTER *One*

LADY MARIAN RUSSELL, DAUGHTER OF the Marquess of Waverly, knew she was making a horrible mistake from the moment she set foot outside that evening, but she had stepped too far into disguise to go back now. Maybe if she had not worked so hard on the accent, she wouldn't have been believed to be of the lower class so easily. But the taverner who ran the Bow and Crown, Mrs. Tuttle, had talked with her less than two minutes before agreeing to take her on as a kitchen maid on a trial basis, so now Marian was finding herself whisked inside through the back door.

It was Will's fault, probably. He had given her too good a recommendation, and the woman had had to listen to his praises for only a minute before she'd realized the girl in front of her was worth more than the wages she was asking for. Marian could see him sitting in a corner, his eyes locked on her notwithstanding the older fellow at the next table over trying to engage him in conversation. Will would likely be watching her all night despite her insistence she would be perfectly safe.

"You don't know those men when they have too much to drink," he had told her multiple times on the walk over. "I trust them only for a glass or two."

Marian did not know why he would keep company with such men, but she kept her questions to herself. Her cousin had spent his life among them, and if anyone understood why she was doing this, it was him.

That did not, however, make her any less nervous. Sure, she had been given the job, but her fate rested on how well she was able to play the part from now on. If anyone realized who she truly was . . .

"You'll be givin' out the drinks," Mrs. Tuttle said as she shuffled through the dingy passage to the kitchen. "And don't be givin' out anythin' until they've paid. I've had too many a leech comin' through lately, and I'll have none of it."

"Yes, ma'am," Marian said. Yet again, she gripped the folds of her skirt and lifted them out of the way of her feet. The maid she had borrowed the clothes from was a good three inches taller than her, and there had not been time to take up the hem. According to Will, the position would not stay open for long, so she couldn't afford to wait until her dress fit properly. Will frequented the pub often enough that Marian figured he knew what he was talking about.

How hard could it be, really, serving drinks? From what she had seen when she first glanced through the window earlier that day, all she had to do was walk around with a tray and provide the right man with the right cup. True, she never indulged herself, so she would not know what drink was what, but as long as she was told what she was given, she could keep track of things. She had always considered herself rather clever, though only time would tell if her self-praise was warranted.

"Now, get to it." Mrs. Tuttle grunted and dropped a tray into Marian's hands.

Was that really all the training she was going to receive?

"Here," a timid voice behind her said, and Marian turned to see another serving girl near her age. "The missus thinks everyone can read her mind. Take this to the table in the corner, and don't let 'em push you around." She handed Marian two cups brimming with something that smelled stronger than anything she'd ever tasted.

"Um, thank you, . . . ?" she said.

"Dinah," the girl said.

"Mary."

Dinah smiled, then gave Marian a nudge.

All in all, the work was not as bad as she had feared. Some of the men had evidently had more to drink than they ought and laughed a little louder than she would like, and others watched her with keen eyes as she made her way around the room, their expressions making her nervous. Will seemed to watch them as closely as he watched her at first, though he got more and more distracted by his companions as the night went on and had stopped nearly jumping to his feet every few minutes to come to her rescue. Marian was glad she did not need her cousin to rescue her, particularly because she had told him over and over that she would be perfectly safe on her own. Besides, if ever anyone got a little too close, Dinah seemed to appear and distract them long enough for Marian to get away.

The worst part was the things the men said. Marian had overheard some of the servants back home talking, and she knew the lower class had varying degrees of lewdness compared to members of polished Society. Most of the men in this tavern were soldiers and dockhands and sailors, and they certainly did not know how to hold their tongues when inebriated as they were. Marian did her very best to ignore them unless they were asking her for another drink, but as the night wore on and the men got drunker, she worried how long she would be able to keep up her charade. Will had not been exaggerating their level of judgment.

"'Ere, miss!" came a man's shout, startling her as she passed a table she had served multiple times already, and she bumped into a sailor as she side-stepped to avoid his friend's wandering hand. Her foot caught on his chair, and she stumbled forward and watched in horror as her tray of drinks slid from her hands directly toward a man in a hat who had only just sat down. As she fell along with the tray, she thought to herself that this was definitely her first and last night as a barmaid because she was most assuredly going to be dismissed.

But the hatted man reached out his hands and deftly caught the tray, balancing the drinks, and he slid it onto one palm so he could reach out and take her by the shoulder to keep her from falling right onto his lap. Only, her momentum kept her moving, and though he tried to steady her, she found herself slipping onto his lap anyway.

She waited for the drinks to spill on top of her, but when her wince of anticipation was met with nothing, she opened her eyes in surprise. The man still held the tray in one hand, and his other was wrapped around her shoulders in a protective hold.

"Easy there," he said, his voice gentle as the tavern erupted into cheers around him. "You all right, miss?" His accent was decidedly lower-class, but he spoke with a softness she had not yet heard during her few hours as a barmaid.

Marian could hardly breathe, knowing what would happen if anyone discovered her in such an intimate position—her cousin, in particular—but she could not find the will to move. She looked into her rescuer's face as he held her, her eyes transfixed as if they wanted to memorize every little detail, from his strong jaw to the shadow of a beard on his dirty cheeks. He wore a wide-brimmed hat that shadowed most of his face, and though she could certainly see more of him than before now that she was looking at him from his lap, in the firelight she could not make out any distinctive features out-side of a crooked grin.

"Er, thank you," she said finally and struggled to get up when she real-ized she had lingered there just a little too long. She found it a miracle that he was not angry with her for nearly dousing him with gin, and she knew her best chance at keeping him in a good mood was to remove herself from his presence as soon as possible. "My sincerest apologies, sir. It's my first day working here." Her voice came out as a mere squeak, but she didn't mind. It probably helped sell the role she was playing.

The man smiled again as she took the tray, the gesture warm and just as soft as his voice. "Pretty lass like you should be more careful," he said and tipped his hat to her before turning to the young man—a boy likely only a year or two her junior—seated at the table with him. Was his companion even old enough to be in a place like this?

Marian could feel the heat of her red face the whole walk back to where Dinah had paused to watch the scene unfold, and she was inordinately grateful to see Will had engaged in a game of cards and was thoroughly distracted. The man had called her *pretty*. No one had called her pretty before, at least not without learning who she was first.

"I wouldn't let Mrs. T. see you cozying up to the customers," Dinah warned, but she was smiling. "Don't think I've ever seen Robin warm to someone like that though," she added, then hurried off to deliver her drinks.

"Robin," Marian said to herself and peeked back at the man out of the corner of her eye. Maybe it was her imagination, but she thought maybe he was looking at her too, and her cheeks blossomed with heat again. It was not as if she would likely speak to the man again, but she enjoyed the idea of a man finding her pretty. Especially a handsome man like him. "Robin," she said again and allowed herself a little giggle before she straightened herself up to get back to business. She had a job now, after all, and Will would give her an earful if she lost it on her first day.

It was a miracle he had not already forced her to leave, and she credited that to his game, which, according to the groans and cheers coming from his table, had become quite intense.

An hour later, though, Marian realized that working an evening shift was more exhausting than she had expected. She'd thought people would go to bed at reasonable hours, but the longer she walked around the tavern and the more her feet ached in her borrowed worn-down shoes, the more she remembered that she had no idea how the lower class spent their time. That was the whole point of all of this. There was a good chance she would work late into the night, but she could not work every night, not when her parents expected her to attend social functions now that the Season was starting.

This little experiment of hers would be short-lived. Based on the number of men who had tried to pull her onto their laps to recreate her encounter with Robin, she was really starting to see that as a good thing.

After the fourth man's attempt, Will finally stood and caught her eye, likely in an attempt to convince her it was time for him to take her home. Before she could agree, a laugh caught Marian's attention, and she searched for the man who owned such a bright and clear laugh that differed so much from the raucous chortling she had been surrounded by all night.

"Of course," she muttered when she realized it was handsome Robin. He and his young companion were both laughing hard enough to draw tears to their eyes, and whatever Robin was saying, it had them both in apparent stitches.

She knew she would do better to mind her own business, but Marian crept closer to their table anyway, eager to learn what could bring such a wide smile to the man's face.

"I think this will be our best one yet," Robin was saying as Marian got close enough to hear over the ruckus of the rest of the tavern's occupants. "I don't think I've ever seen a man hoard so much in one place before. He makes it too easy."

"And the way he looked at you when you warned him what might happen," the younger one said and clapped his hand onto the table. "Looked just like a fish pulled out of water." He mimicked the open-mouthed gaping of a fish.

"A whole lot of people are going to have him to thank for their full bellies come next week," Robin said happily. "And he'll think twice before keeping so much coin in one place after we're done. Do you not think, Miss Clumsy?" He turned to Marian, grinning beneath his hat but hiding his eyes as he kept his head low.

She gulped. "I am sorry, sir," she said and took a step back. "I did not mean to—"

He rose to his feet, towering over her and pulling his hat even lower. He was so tall, though, that she could almost fully see his face as he looked down at her. She most certainly caught the green hue of his eyes, a color she'd never seen before. "Don't fret," he said and took one of her hands, pressing it between both of his. Something cold was between his palm and hers, and alarm shook through her until he smiled again. "It's just a little redistribution of wealth," he said quietly. "Them rich folk deserve a little comeuppance every now and then." And then he tossed a coin onto the table and jerked his head for his companion to follow him out the door.

Marian waited until he was gone before she looked at the thing he had put in her hand, but when she saw several coins in her palm, she nearly dropped her tray. It had to be more than most of these men made in a month. So why would he give it to her?

"Mary!"

She jumped, turning to see Mrs. Tuttle glaring at her from the other end of the tavern with an expression that clearly told her to get back to work.

But Marian had had her fill of being a barmaid, and Will was coming nearer with an expression that said she had better leave before she got herself into trouble. "Sorry," she squeaked and set the tray on a table before darting for the door and into the night.

"I take it you will not be coming back tomorrow," Will guessed when she slipped her arm into his after he joined her. He tensed as soon as they started walking. "Marian, you're shaking like a leaf. What—"

"I am cold," she said, though she drew nearer to him not because of a chill but because she was so unnerved by the whole evening. If that was what life was like every day for a barmaid, it was no wonder being a lady's maid was such a sought-after position. Her abigail, Millie, had never had to deal with wavering hands and leering gazes, and she'd certainly never encountered men like Robin. Or, if she had, she had never told Marian about it.

Will still seemed concerned as they walked back to Aspen House in Grosvenor Square, which probably explained his hurried pace. "I should not have let you do it," he muttered, more to himself than to her. "There are so many things that could have gone wrong, and you're . . ."

"What?" she asked as anger rose a bit in her chest, replacing the fear that had been burning since leaving the tavern. "I am what? Not capable of taking care of myself?"

"That is not what I was going to say," he said through his teeth, which meant he was lying. He threw her a glance, then sighed. "You are barely eighteen, Marian. And the Bow and Crown may have been the tamest pub I could find, but that does not mean the men inside wouldn't . . ." He swallowed the rest of his words and shook his head. "Just promise me you won't do something like that again. Please. I nearly died of worry in there."

She chanced a smile. She did feel guilty for dragging him into her schemes, but she could not have done it on her own. "I told you not to stay with me," she tried, though she was not surprised when he immediately tensed up again.

Will may have been a soldier for half his life, but he had still grown up in polite Society and knew better than to leave a young woman alone, particularly in a place like that.

"You must be out of your mind if you think I will ever let you wander London on your own," he muttered.

"You want to be seen following a serving girl around Town?" she said, hoping she sounded like she was joking. She had to make sure he thought she was perfectly unaffected by the evening's adventure. "What would the *ton* think of you then?"

"I don't care what they think of me," he said rather roughly. He may have been raised among nobility, his father being the younger son of a marquess, but being a second son himself, Will had spent most of his life among the common. Now that he was expected to live among high Society after the unexpected death of his elder brother, George, he was having a hard time adjusting. He had confided to Marian more than once how much he enjoyed being an equal amongst his fellow soldiers. Now that he was heir presumptive to a marquessate, he felt out of place, like an imposter, but returning to his life as a soldier would risk some distant relation inheriting everything instead.

Marian pulled just a little closer to him, glad they could walk under the cover of darkness without being seen. She liked to think she was brave, but she did not particularly want to be seen cowering on her cousin's arm. Even if no one would recognize her as who she really was, dressed as a maid like this. She and Will had practically grown up together, so she had nothing to hide from him, but she wanted the rest of the world to see nothing but confidence now that she was out in Society.

"I know you miss being in the militia," she said after she had calmed a bit, "but I am glad you are here. I don't know if I would survive the Season without you keeping things normal."

"I'm afraid normal might be a thing of the past," he replied. "But you still haven't promised."

"What?"

"To stop doing dangerous things like pretending to be a barmaid."

"I want to make a difference in the world, Will," she said with a sigh, dropping her head onto his shoulder as they approached her family's London residence.

Chuckling, Will gave her a little shove, then gently knocked on the servants' door. "Then you probably should have been born a man," he said just as Millie opened the door. She ushered Marian inside before Will headed back to his flat.

"I've been worried something awful, my lady," the abigail whispered, a candle in hand as she led Marian along the back way to her bedchamber. "You were s'posed to be back an hour ago."

Marian apologized as much as she could, but her abigail was still in a bit of a mood when she finally left Marian alone in her chamber and closed the door behind her. She would be back to her happy self in the morning, Marian hoped.

Curling up in her blankets, she recognized how incredibly plush and warm her bed was. The whole room was warm, thanks to the glowing fire in the hearth. Most people didn't have this sort of luxury—couldn't even dream of affording it—and Marian got to sleep in utter comfort simply because she had been born into the right family.

"It isn't fair," she said to herself. Everyone deserved the basic comforts of life.

Going to the Bow and Crown had given her a taste of lower-class life, which had been her goal, but there was still so much more she needed to see. There was a whole world out there, outside of all the parties and plays and musicales. Marian had never been content to sit for hours and embroider, and she was barely average at the pianoforte and singing. She could put on a good show when forced to socialize with her equals, but like Will, she had yet to feel like she was one of them, and she did not have the excuse of having been abroad among all different ranks. Despite his greater experience, however, Will did not seem to understand that she had good reason for doing what she had.

It had started when she had caught sight of a starving street urchin on the day she and her parents had left for the country last summer, and something had changed inside her. When she'd realized people lived the same way outside of Town, she had become determined to find a way to help them. She had been sheltered by her wealthy life, and she had resolved to change that.

The memory of a charming smile came to mind as if in reply to her thoughts, and she silently repeated Robin's words to herself: *"Them rich folk deserve a little comeuppance every now and then,"* he had said.

Marian wholeheartedly agreed.

CHAPTER *Two*

LORD ROBERT LOXLEY, EARL OF Huntingdon, was utterly and completely bored. It was not a new sensation, but he disliked it immensely nonetheless. He thought he would have gotten used to this part—the parties, the balls, the total disregard for productivity. But eight years in, and he still found himself trapped in the center of attention, listening to Miss Bennett prattle on about something or other. He hardly cared enough to pay attention to any of it. He would have avoided the evening altogether if his sister, Alana, had not begged him to take her to the ball. He had earned himself the nickname the Elusive Earl for a reason.

Rob did not often miss his father anymore, but there were moments when he wished he did not have to serve as his sister's chaperone. He loved her dearly; he did not love how much she delighted in social events.

Alana looked happy, though, her cheeks pink with pleasure as she chatted with her fellow debutantes and giggled as men picked them off one by one to dance. She was meant to live here in Town, and Rob was torn between keeping her and their mother content and retreating back to a quiet life in the country.

"And she has the most beautiful coat," Miss Bennett was saying. She placed her hand on Rob's arm for the third time in ten minutes.

If he had ever planned to show the young lady any interest, he would have done it three years ago when they'd met. As it was, he had heard more about her new horse than he ever cared to know, and he quickly searched for a way to extricate himself from the situation without being completely uncouth. Among the many things Rob abhorred about high Society, the inexplicable number of rules of etiquette was high on the list.

He spotted Henry Felton passing by not far from them, and he jumped on the opportunity. "Mr. Felton!" he said loudly and took poor Felton by the arm; the man had no idea what was coming to him. "I believe you know Miss Bennett."

Felton stammered something that must have been a yes and tugged at his cravat nervously.

Rob resisted the urge to give the man a berating scowl. "Miss Bennett was just telling me about her new mare," he said. "You collect horses, do you not, Mr. Felton?" And before either the bumbling Felton or the suddenly glaring Miss Bennett could protest, he slipped away and made his way to the other end of the ballroom just as a dance started up at its center. It would take Miss Bennett at least ten minutes to get away from Felton, and perhaps another ten to find someone else to escort her across the floor now that the dancing had started. Twenty minutes to himself was not particularly long, but he would take what he could get.

Alana was dancing with Lord Grenton's younger son, a portly man whose given name Rob had never bothered to remember, and she was being a fair sport about his inability to keep time with the music. She was sweet like that, careful never to offer up even the slightest insult, and Rob loved that about her. It would likely get her into trouble someday though. He would have to keep an eye on her now that she had come of age and would be pursued more heavily by the bachelors of London. The sister of an earl would draw in many a suitor, most of whom Rob would have to be cautious not to call out at the slightest provocation. He was rather convinced no one would meet his standards and Alana would just have to endure being a wealthy old maid.

It was not as if she had to marry for money. When their uncle, the late Earl of Huntingdon, had died suddenly and left the earldom to Rob, her subsequent inheritance had been substantial enough that she could live comfortably on her own, if not happily. He had high hopes for a love match for Alana, which would save the whole family a lot of heartbreak and difficulty. In fact, Rob preferred her to meet a poor man of good stock and honest values over a titled one in search of more money and prestige.

He just hoped she would fall in love sooner rather than later, because he had far too many things on his mind to constantly worry about his sister's happiness.

"Yes! Lord Portstone," someone said behind Rob.

He perked up, quickly searching out the small gathering of people listening to the latest gossip.

"You say he was robbed?" one of the matrons asked, completely horrified.

Another woman—Mrs. Finch—nodded vigorously, her jowls wiggling. "I heard the thief came straight into his bedchamber through the window and took his ring right off his finger. No fear at all."

Rob bit back a laugh.

"That is the third robbery in two months," Mr. Salisbury said with some measure of alarm. "Lord Portstone moved all his valuables to a chest in his room to prevent something like this happening. Hid the key and everything."

"A lot of good it did him," Mr. Hewitt said with a sniff. Rob had never liked the man, given the way he had gotten into the habit of eyeing women of fortune a little too closely, but he was good for gossip and couldn't resist discussing the crimes of his fellows to make himself look better. "When he heard of the previous robberies, he fired most of his staff as a precaution as well. Thought they were acting shifty, so he threw them all out and hired new ones."

"Sounds like he deserved what he got, then."

The entire group, Rob among them, turned in surprise at the soft voice at their edge, and the young lady who had spoken turned a brilliant shade of red when she realized she had not spoken as softly as she must have meant to. Now that she had been thoroughly noticed, she stood from her seat at the room's edge and opened up her fan, as if that would distract the group from what she'd said.

"Whatever do you mean, Lady Marian?" Mrs. Finch asked. "Deserved it?"

Lady Marian? This was the Marquess of Waverly's daughter? Rob had heard a rumor she would be making her debut this year, but he had never seen her. She seemed to have been the talk of the *ton* lately—a rare beauty with a fortune and no siblings to share it with, though she had a cousin or something who would inherit her father's title. The description of her beauty was accurate, but Rob was sure her tongue would keep the sharks at bay for a while yet. Few men wanted a wife who gave her opinion so freely, even with a fortune.

Clearing her throat, Lady Marian folded her fan and held her chin high. "A man who can so easily turn people out onto the street with no provocation has no right holding so many livelihoods in his hands," she said rather timidly but with the hint of a challenge in her words. She was young yet, but she had a fiery strength about her that was quite alluring.

Rob found himself grinning as the others in the group exchanged worried glances. Here was a woman speaking against her own kind, almost without fear. "Mrs. Finch," he said, and all eyes turned from the young lady to himself. "If you would be so kind as to introduce me to the charming Lady Marian, I would like to ask her to dance."

Lady Marian blushed crimson again, and once the introductions were made, Rob led her to the edge of the dance floor to wait for the current set to finish. She kept her gaze at her feet, and one glance back at the gossip train told him why. Every single one of them was staring their way with jealousy and confusion and outright offense, and Rob knew what would be headlining the gossip column in the morning: Lady Marian had a sharp tongue, and the Elusive Earl had noticed.

"Thank you," Lady Marian said so quietly that Rob was not sure if she had actually spoken or if he had just imagined it. Only when her gaze flicked up to him did he decide she had said the words out loud.

"For what?" he asked.

"I thought they would call for my head if given a few seconds more."

A hint of a smile crossed her lips, and it seemed to spark a memory in Rob's mind. Perhaps hers was similar to her father's smile. Rob had spoken to him on several occasions in the House of Lords. But whatever was familiar in it, he found he liked her smile quite a lot. A rare beauty indeed. If only she would look at him . . .

"I might suggest you keep your eyes off your feet during the dance," he said gently as he led her out onto the floor for the next set. "It will make you appear confident."

She lifted her head, and a bit of defiance flashed in her hazel eyes. "Would you like me to smile as well, my lord?" she said sharply.

Rob was annoyed that the dance pulled him away from her long enough that he could not offer a quick-witted retort, though there was still a challenge in her gaze when the steps brought them back together. "You are quite headstrong, aren't you?" he asked. "Especially for one your age." He tried to think back on conversations he had had with Lord Waverly about his family. Lady Marian couldn't be older than eighteen or nineteen. She was brand-new to Society, and that only made her outspoken nature more intriguing. Most ladies did everything they could to fit in with the rest.

"Does my opinion displease you, my lord?" she replied when they came back together. There was that bite again. But now she had a different expression mixed with her irritation, like a bit of confusion. What did she see when she looked at him?

Rob allowed himself a chuckle, though he generally did not let himself appear to enjoy dancing; he would be forced into it more often than he would like if anyone thought he was willing. As soon as he got the laughter out of his system, he straightened his countenance and did his utmost to appear uninterested. "I do not particularly believe it matters what I think," he said. "How you act and what you say is entirely in your own hands."

That comment caught her off guard, and she paused for a second too long and had to hurry to catch up with the steps of the dance. "I do not understand you, Lord Huntingdon," she said after a moment's thought. She was a little breathless now, though the dance was not a rigorous one.

"Do you not?" Rob glanced at the gossipers again, pleased to see they had lost interest in the dance and were back to chattering about. "I cannot understand how it would be my place to dictate a woman's actions."

This time Lady Marian stopped completely, staring at him as if he had been speaking German instead of English. He stopped as well, and though the dancers nearest them shot them glares, they moved around the couple and carried on. Causing a scene like this would attract attention, Rob knew, but he was far too intrigued by the young Lady Marian to care.

"Have I failed to speak clearly?" he asked, doing his best to sound innocent.

She shook her head, and then she seemed to realize what she had done and blushed again as she looked at the dancers moving around her. "Oh drat," she muttered.

Rob let out a laugh as the dance finished. He offered his arm, which she took with some measure of hesitation, and the instant they reached the edge of the dance floor where her mother stood gabbing with some of the other Society women, Lady Marian pulled out of his grip and attempted to vanish.

Rob knew he would do well to find his sister and try to convince her to leave early, as he always did, but he found himself watching Lady Marian instead. She tried to keep her head down and hide behind her mother, probably because of the pinkness in her cheeks leftover from their dance, but within moments another gentleman, one Mr. Weston, was at her side and asking her to dance. She did the job splendidly, but Rob felt a burst of pride when Weston did not receive any smiles, and neither did she speak to him. He was a fairly boring fellow, though, who had no ability to carry a conversation, so that bit did not surprise Rob. Hardly anyone talked to him more than once.

The next man who approached Lady Marian was unfamiliar to Rob, and he had a determined glint in his eyes as he made his way through the crowd toward her. For some reason, Rob nearly stepped in and asked her for another dance, but he stopped himself when he remembered that would only draw even more attention to himself. One dance was alarming enough; a second would practically mean he intended to court the young woman.

So he simply watched the unknown man say something to Lady Marian. She blushed, and her partner seemed to search the crowd for something, though everyone nearby was engaged in conversation and apparently unaware of the young couple nearby. Just as the gentleman reached out his hand for a dance, however, a servant slipped in and muttered something to him. He hurried away with a frown and left Lady Marian on her own again.

Rob was tempted a second time to step in and ask her to dance, hoping to experience more of her fiery temperament, but Mr. Tilby beat him to it and whisked her away to the dance floor before Rob had even taken a step. These men of the *ton* certainly didn't waste an opportunity, though Lady Marian seemed disappointed as she searched the crowd for her almost-partner. He must have made an impression on her.

A favorable impression, no less, something that settled heavy in Rob's gut. The girl was too young to know the dangers of Society men, and she would do well to be cautious. She had plenty of time to find herself a good match, though why Rob cared about who she married, he had no idea.

The musicians began their song, and Rob's eyes slid to the doorway just as the unknown man reappeared there with a scowl for Mr. Tilby and a look of interest for Lady Marian as he, like Rob, watched the pair traverse the dance floor. The man lingered for only a moment, and then he turned back the way he had come and disappeared.

Rob felt a rare flutter of sympathy for the poor fellow since his own dance with the lady had left him feeling fuller than he had felt in a long time. For all the effort he put into avoiding the vapid ladies of the *ton*, he could hardly believe he had found one who actually had a brain in that skull of hers.

"Quite the beauty, that Marian," someone muttered just behind Rob.

He turned and fought against the scowl that came on instinct whenever he saw Frank Melbourne. The man was a well-known rake and all-around scoundrel, though he somehow managed to keep himself out of trouble. Rob had been hoping for years to have a good reason to provoke him, and he might have just found one. "That is *Lady* Marian to you, Melbourne," he said, his voice low.

"And how is Miss Loxley these days?" Melbourne answered with a sneer.

At the mention of his sister, Rob curled his fingers into fists, hiding them behind his back. "If you will excuse me," he said and headed straight for the doors. Alana would be angry with him for making her leave early, but Melbourne had pushed his patience to the limit. Not even the delightful Lady Marian could entice him to stay at the ball a minute longer.

"John," Rob said when he found his valet just outside the front doors. Most people didn't bring their valets to events, let alone call them by their first names. Society would likely hate the idea if they knew, and some probably did, but Rob always felt better when he knew young John was nearby. Besides, they had been through far too much together to bother with niceties and rules. It was just another reason for people to avoid Rob as he threw tradition to the wind. "Fetch the carriage while I round up Miss Loxley. We have work to do."

Melbourne had set his eyes on two ladies that night, and Rob was not about to sit back and do nothing about it.

CHAPTER *Three*

MARIAN COULD NOT STOP THINKING about Lord Portstone. It was rather horrid, his flabby face popping up in her mind every few minutes, but she couldn't very well think about him without picturing him, though she wished she could. And she wanted to think about him—at least, about the fact that he had been robbed only a week after she'd worked in the tavern. She had a good guess at who the mysterious thief was, and she had several extra coins in her reticule to prove it.

Robin was, most assuredly, a thief. That much was clear. But whether he had been the one to steal from Lord Portstone was less clear, as much as she wanted to believe her guess was right. In Marian's opinion, Portstone certainly had the sort of face that could be compared to a fish, and his turning out his entire household was a fair enough reason for a thief like Robin to choose to steal from him. Not that she knew anything about Robin, really. She had spoken to him only briefly, and she hadn't actually said much. He had done all the talking and the smiling and the charming and . . .

Marian shook her head to clear her mind of the thief, trying to focus on her embroidery since Mother was also in the room and would become concerned if Marian finished the afternoon with nothing but a few measly stitches to show for it. The Marchioness of Waverly, Lady Eliza Russell, was not necessarily strict, but she certainly knew how to make a girl feel guilty when she got that look of disappointment in her eyes.

"Pretty lass like you," Robin had said.

Marian sighed at the memory. At the ball last night, she had had more than enough gentlemen commenting on her beauty, and the more often she heard it, the less she believed it. Her *accounts* were beautiful, more likely, and the fact that whoever secured her hand secured her fortune. No one at that ball had cared about who she was as a person, and though she tried not to let that bother her, she could not help it. Was that all she was destined to be? A lump sum dressed up in fancy gowns and honey-colored curls? Every single one of them had—

Marian paused in her sewing again. Not *every* man had been focused solely on her beauty or her money. Two men hadn't breathed a word about her looks. One had been a handsome young man keen to dance with her but who had been called away before introductions were made, and the second . . .

"What do you know of the Earl of Huntingdon?" she asked.

The marchioness looked up from her embroidery in surprise, as if she had forgotten her daughter was in the room with her. That happened often, and Marian had always wondered how her mother managed to shut out everything happening around her and focus on one thing so completely. Marian seemed to notice everything, from the tick of the clock to the carts and carriages constantly rolling past the house.

Mother frowned a little. "The Earl of Huntingdon?" she asked, musing over the subject. "Have you met the earl, my darling?"

She would have known that if she hadn't spent the evening discussing the latest gossip with Lady Calloway, who lived nearby. Resisting the urge to sigh again, Marian pushed the conversation onward. Mother had been attentive once upon a time, but she seemed to have been caught up in the pretense of Society and forgotten what it meant to be a real person, one who should take an active role in her daughter's life.

"I met him at the ball last night," Marian said. "What do you know about him?" Surely Mother spent enough time with the gossips to have some sort of information to share.

Setting her needlework aside, the marchioness sorted through her thoughts before she spoke, as she always did when discussing a new topic. Marian certainly hadn't gotten her quick wit from her mother. "I believe he is a young man," she said slowly. "Twenty-six or twenty-seven. His father was the second son, a lieutenant in the navy, and died at sea. The lieutenant's brother, the late earl, did not have children, so young Robert Loxley inherited when the earl died some years ago."

That was particularly useful information, and Marian was surprised. Usually such questions gained her answers of a more superficial nature, like—

"He is quite the eternal bachelor," Mother continued and picked up her sewing again, as if she'd forgotten she was even speaking to anyone. "Never seems to take interest in anyone, no matter how persistent the ladies are. Spends as much time in the country as he can, and most people suspect he attends events only because of his sister."

He had a sister? Perhaps that was why he was so forward-thinking when it came to a woman expressing her opinions. Marian had had to hold her tongue so often when speaking to gentlemen of high Society that she hadn't had the faintest idea how to act around a man who apparently enjoyed hearing what she had to say.

"Did you like him, my darling?" Mother asked, though she started humming a moment later, lost to her own world again.

Marian wouldn't have had an answer anyway. There had been something strangely familiar about the young earl, though she hadn't been able to figure out what it was, and it had unnerved her enough that she had forgotten to check her thoughts before they'd left her tongue. True, he had rescued her from the gossips, but she had also gotten the feeling he was mocking her when they danced. Lord Huntingdon was a mystery, and Marian did not need another mystery.

What she needed was nightfall to come so she could seek out the thief and find out if he had stolen from Lord Portstone because of what the odious man had done to his servants. If that was the case, and she suspected it was, she absolutely wanted to help with the next target. Thievery was a far cry from any of the plans she had come up with on her own, but from what she had overheard at the tavern, Robin planned to share the spoils of his escapades. If that money was going to the poor, she wanted to help. People like Lord Portstone did not deserve their wealth and power if they were going to hurt those beneath them. Nor did people like Lord Melbourne, who had been robbed just last night and was generally known for his unwanted attention to single ladies, particularly young ones. Marian hoped Robin was the type to rally for the sake of the less fortunate, and if anyone could give her an insider's look into the lower classes, it was a thief who had gotten into the habit of stealing from the rich to benefit the poor. He was exactly the sort of man she was eager to know.

"Remind me why I agreed to this," Will muttered as they approached the Bow and Crown again a few nights later.

Marian had a near skip in her step as they got closer. Sneaking around like this was strangely invigorating. "You agreed because I am your favorite cousin and needed your help," she said and touched a kiss to his cheek.

"You are my only cousin," he grumbled back. "But have you really thought this through? Mrs. Tuttle is not going to let you back in after you walked out on her."

"Then, you go in," Marian replied, lifting one eyebrow. "I can wait outside."

"On your own?"

"I will be s—"

"Safe. Yes, you said that the last time, and look what happened. You ended up in the lap of a *thief*. I don't trust him, and you most certainly shouldn't."

So he *had* seen that? And worse, he knew what Robin was. Marian winced, fearing Will would use that reasoning to keep her from talking to Robin. If she couldn't have this conversation, she would have to find some other way to help the poor, and she had no idea where to start.

To her relief, Will sighed. "Mrs. Tuttle is not happy with me for recommending someone so flighty. She might not even let *me* in."

Marian did feel bad about that part. The Bow and Crown had been Will's favorite tavern since it was where many of his fellow soldiers spent their evenings. Because he had recommended her for the job, her little experiment had likely ostracized him from the one place that felt like home to him. "You could always start going to White's," she suggested and playfully nudged his arm.

Will laughed out loud. "I am not about to set foot in there with all the dandies and self-important cads," he said. "Now, are you going to explain to me why you need so desperately to talk to this man? I cannot like the idea of you—"

"It is nothing like you're thinking," she assured him, though a bit of heat spotted her cheeks as she thought about Robin's overwhelming appeal. Maybe it was a little bit like Will thought. "This man might be able to help me change the world," she said. "I just want to talk to him. You can watch from a respectable distance and see that nothing goes wrong."

"And now I am just a chaperone," Will mumbled, but he grudgingly made his way forward anyway and stepped into the tavern to retrieve Robin for her.

A chill seemed to settle over Marian now that she was alone. It was not overly late, but the streets were far emptier than she was used to. A lady on her own, even a servant like she appeared to be, was an easy target for anyone up to no good, and she was far too small to fight off a man if the need arose, though Will had told her a few things to keep in mind. Still, she would rather be out in the quiet than inside that noisy tavern, where she would be dodging advances from drunks. At least out here she could think.

What was taking Will so long? Had he gotten in trouble with Mrs. Tuttle? Was Robin even inside? If the thief was not in the tavern, Marian had absolutely no idea where to find him, and she would be left wondering for the rest of her tedious little life. She doubted Will would be willing to check the pub every night for her, and she could not ask around about a thief. Especially not if she wanted to keep his activities a secret.

The door to the tavern opened at last, bringing with it the noises of laughter and shouts, and Marian slunk a little closer to the wall, just in case. But it was Will who stepped out onto the pavement and approached her. To her dismay, he was alone, and she tried not to look too disappointed, in case Will read too much from her expression. He seemed to do that a lot, and she had gotten into trouble with him more than once without saying a single word.

"You did not find him, then?" she asked quietly.

Will frowned and looked behind him. "What? No, he was right behind—"

"Ah, if it isn't Miss Clumsy," a soft voice just behind Marian said.

She jumped high enough that Will caught her by the arm to steady her. "Sir!" She gasped and pressed a hand to her heart. "Where did you—"

"It's not every day a stranger comes up to you and says you've got yourself a woman wanting you to come outside," Robin said, and his smirk was the only visible part of his face beneath the shadow his hat created. "I wanted to see what all the fuss was about before I decided if I wanted to talk."

He must have gone out the back door and snuck around in the darkness. Marian wanted to be annoyed, but that grin of his was just as breathtaking as it had been the first night she saw it. "And?" she said. Had he decided she was worth his time?

"And I am quite intrigued," he replied. "For a girl who lasted less than a night in her new job, you're a headstrong lass, aren't you? Mrs. Tuttle would skin you alive if she saw you."

That is why I am out here instead of in there, Marian thought to herself. But she frowned because something about this thief was strangely familiar. More so than anything had been the last time she saw him. She certainly had not spent enough time around the lower classes of Town in the past, so where would she have seen him before?

Will cleared his throat, pulling Marian's attention away from Robin's somewhat dirty face. "Is this satisfactory?" he asked with a grunt. He evidently still did not approve of the meeting, despite how easily she had persuaded him to do what she wanted.

Marian put a hand on his arm and smiled to tell him she would be all right. She hoped. "Thank you, Will. I will need only a moment."

Scowling at Robin, Will slowly made his way several feet back so the two of them could talk in private, though he was not willing to go much farther than that.

Now that they were relatively alone, though, Marian suddenly had no idea what to say to the thief. Could she really just ask him outright if he was the man who had robbed Lord Portstone? He would likely deny it. But she still had the coins he had given her, and he hardly looked the sort to have excess money to just give away freely. So did she even need to ask?

Yes, she did. She wanted to know *why* he had done it. She wanted to know if he had been behind the other robberies that month as well, like that of Lord Melbourne. There had likely been others before that. What sort of man put himself in danger on a crusade to steal from the rich?

"You are quite the chatterbox, aren't you, Miss Clumsy?" Robin asked, folding his arms.

"My name is Mary," she replied, giving no surname.

"And you already know my name, so there's introductions out of the way. What is it you wanted to say to me, Miss Mary?"

It was an easy enough question he had asked, but the answer stuck fast in her throat. Accusing a man—even a lower-class one—of being a thief was far from proper, and Marian's governess had been quite the stickler for doing what was proper. Marian had already broken a multitude of rules just by being out on the street at night dressed as a servant and talking to a man the likes of Robin the thief. So was it really all that bad to break another?

Robin was clearly getting impatient, so Marian said the only thing that seemed to come through: "I am not sure I should . . ."

He huffed a sigh. "What you *should* do is entirely in your own hands," he said. "You can act however you'd like, and it's not my place to dictate a woman's actions."

Marian's stomach twisted inside her because not twenty-four hours ago she had heard a different man say almost the exact same thing. A man around the same height as this thief, with the same broad shoulders and charming smile. Could it possibly . . . ? Clearing her throat, she decided to test her theory. "So you are not about to tell me to smile?" she asked as sweetly as she could.

The grin dropped from his face immediately. "Are you . . . ?"

Marian felt a thrill of excitement. Could it be she wasn't the only one like her? "You are not . . . ?"

"Lady Marian," he whispered and pulled his hat from his head to slap it against his thigh nervously. "I see now why you looked so familiar."

Robin was most definitely the Earl of Huntingdon, though without the fancy clothes and intricate cravat, he looked quite different than he had at the ball several days ago. But his green eyes were the same bright color, and Marian would have recognized that smile of his if she had only opened her mind to the possibility before.

"I do not understand, my lord," she whispered.

The earl stuffed his hat back onto his head and ducked his face as a couple of men exited the tavern, singing loudly as they passed, and then he took Marian by the arm. His hold was firm but gentle. "You *cannot* tell anyone what you know," he hissed.

That much was obvious. "My secret is just as dangerous as yours, my lord."

"Do not call me that. Not out here." He glanced over at Will, then quickly released her when he caught sight of Will's glare. "We . . ." He took a deep breath. "Perhaps we should talk."

Marian wanted nothing more. "But we cannot talk here," she pointed out as another man left the Bow and Crown in a drunken haze.

Watching Will avoid the drunkard, Robin thought for a moment, then said, "Tomorrow. I will take you for a drive."

"A drive?"

"As our better halves," he clarified. "I do believe the earl owes Lady Marian a call after that dance the other day." Then he bowed and slipped off into the darkness.

Will quickly returned to her side, a question in his eyes, but Marian was not entirely sure what she could say to answer his unspoken inquiry. She could not very well tell her cousin what she had just learned, since the key to her secret remaining undiscovered outside of Will and her maid was keeping the earl's secret in turn. If she told her cousin, there was nothing to stop Lord Huntingdon from telling any of his own acquaintances about her. She just hoped tomorrow would bring answers because all she had gotten from her excursion tonight was a lot more questions.

"We should get back," she said and slipped her arm into Will's. "Thank you."

He likely found no satisfaction in that response, but to his credit, he did not push the issue. Will was her dearest friend, and she knew he understood that if she wanted to confide in him, she would. Perhaps someday they could laugh about it all, but not yet.

Now Marian's life had just reached a level of excitement and intrigue she never could have anticipated.

And she was absolutely thrilled.

CHAPTER *Four*

ROB HAD NOT TAKEN A lady out to the park in almost four years. It was a topic of sadness for his mother and sister, who were both convinced he needed the diversion of courting someone since he worked too hard for their liking, but for Rob, it meant he had less to worry about. For the same reason he avoided balls and dinner parties when he could, Rob never went out with a lady because he simply did not have the time. He was already living two lives—that of the earl and that of the thief—and adding a third persona to the mix would complicate things beyond what he was capable of handling well.

But this particular excursion was unavoidable. He had not slept at all the night before and had simply lain awake in his bed, imagining the sort of gossip that would race through the upper class like wildfire as soon as Lady Marian spilled his secret. True, she had a secret of her own, but dressing as a maid a couple of times was far different from stealing from his peers. He had over a year of severe misdeeds riding on his anonymity, and Lady Marian could cost him his life with a single sentence slipped to the papers.

He had skimmed the morning paper and, to his surprise, had found nothing of his double life, and his valet had had nothing negative to report from the servants' talk of the morning. Perhaps, though only time would tell, Lady Marian was willing to keep his secret as long as he kept hers.

That had been an unexpected addition to the night's events, most assuredly. That first night he had met her, when she had tripped into him, he had suspected she was not entirely who she pretended to be. She had had an air of nobility about her even then, but he had simply assumed she had been forced into working by unfortunate circumstances; it happened more often than he liked. And when that gentleman friend of hers had sought him out, Rob had been undeniably intrigued. He had thought maybe she had wanted to speak to him because she already knew his secret, but her surprise had been just as obvious as his must have been. So there was another reason for driving her to the park. He would have to uncover her motives today.

But that meant he had to actually go up to her door.

There was nothing for it. Rob had sat in his conveyance outside the Marquess of Waverly's home for far too long already, and people were going to start noticing. The two of them together would cause talk enough, but he could not have people thinking he was nervous to approach the Lady Marian. True, her father outranked him, so he had good reason to be a little nervous, but the Earl of Huntingdon was the epitome of confidence. Everyone knew that.

For the first time in a long time, that part was proving difficult to play.

Taking a deep breath, Rob forced himself to hop down from his phaeton and knock on the door before he talked himself out of the drive altogether. He had mused on the idea of simply ignoring the encounter, but the young Lady Marian had proved at the ball—and at the tavern as well—that she had a solid head on her shoulders and could not be ignored. Rob simply had to grit his teeth and get things over with so he could carry on with his solitary life.

Giving his card to the butler and requesting an audience with Marian's father, Rob forced himself to stand tall and still. It was not easy, when all he wanted to do was wring his hat between his hands until it was a lumpy mess. How was it he could go a full year playing his double life without incident, and all it took was an eighteen-year-old girl to completely unravel him?

"Lord Huntingdon, what a pleasant surprise."

The Marquess of Waverly was a rather boring man, in Rob's opinion, but he was considerably more tolerable than most of the other peers he had to interact with. He may not treat all men as equals, but at least he interacted with them cordially. That was more than Rob could say for most of the upper ten thousand.

As the marquess approached, he added, "For what can I credit this welcome visit? I am just on my way out, I'm afraid, but I was surprised to hear it was you at my door."

Rob bowed his acknowledgment. "Actually, Lord Waverly, I was hoping for your permission to take Lady Marian for a jaunt around the park this morning," he said, still tempted to twist his hat until he would be forced to buy a new one. He had never liked this hat anyway, and he much preferred the one he wore to the tavern to hide his face.

The marquess's thick eyebrows rose high on his head, but he was intelligent enough to hide his shock a second later. "Yes, yes, I do remember you danced with her some nights ago. Caused quite a stir, according to my wife. It seems no one knew you were much inclined to dance."

Rob clenched his jaw, cursing the gossips. Not that they were wrong about him . . . but Marian did not deserve to be talked about, no matter whom she danced with. "Generally, no," he said. "Dancing is not my favorite pastime. But your lovely daughter was worth the exception. If I could—"

"Yes, of course," Waverly said and ushered the butler to fetch his daughter. "I daresay you will find her an agreeable companion, even if she speaks her mind far too often. My daughter has a fast tongue."

Rob's hat would most certainly have to be replaced now, and he did his best to repair the damage his fingers had just done to it as his anger spiked. "I rather liked her tongue," he muttered under his breath, though he knew saying such a thing out loud would draw more attention from the lady's father than he was willing to face. That was not the sort of compliment a man would readily accept for his daughter, particularly when it set her apart from the rest of Society.

Thankfully, Lady Marian arrived at the staircase not a moment too soon, so Rob did not have to endure any more unconscious insults from the lady's father.

"Lord Huntingdon," she said, a little breathless after her hurry down the stairs.

"Lady Marian," he replied and matched her curtsy with a bow.

She looked just as beautiful as she had at the ball, but now that he was truly getting a good look at her, he had to wonder how he hadn't realized she and Mary Clumsy were the same person. The barmaid had had the same self-assured gleam in her eyes that only the truly elevated could manage without trying, and the lady held her fingers in tight fists to hide the energy she had exhibited while serving drinks. In fact, Rob was rather put out that he had been so easily deceived. He was usually rather observant. Planning his attack on Lord Portstone must have distracted him more than he'd realized.

Holding out his arm to the young lady, he met her gaze and asked, "Shall we?"

"Indeed." She placed a delicate hand on his arm, all proper and poised.

Technically speaking, he should have allowed place for a chaperone, but he had chosen his phaeton because it would fit only the two of them, and this particular conversation required the utmost discretion. He could have brought his valet, John, and he assumed Lady Marian's maid was likely in on her secret since she had to have gotten her servants' clothes from somewhere, but things would be easier if their secrets were shared with as few as possible. At least there would be plenty of people at the park on such a warm morning, even if a layer of clouds covered the sun, so no one could fault him too much for taking the girl out alone. She was, after all, quite the diamond already, and the Season had only recently begun.

But how was he supposed to begin a conversation like this? They had already reached the park before either one of them said anything, and he could almost not bring himself to even look at her. Perhaps the whole night had been a dream, and the moment he opened his mouth he would ruin everything by spilling a secret that had not been discovered in the first place. But as he glanced at Lady Marian, he found her waiting with a raised eyebrow and a touch of impatience in her tapping fingers.

Even without saying a word, the young woman managed to tell him there was more to her than he had first thought. That fiery personality of hers did much to her credit.

There was nothing for it; he just had to jump right in.

"What gave me away?" he said at last.

Lady Marian's lips quirked up. "You speak the same way as a lord as you do a thief, my lord."

Rob bristled a bit at that. "I have worked hard to mask my accent, my lady," he argued.

"That is not what I meant," she said. "You told a serving girl she could speak her mind."

"It is true, is it not?" He had always thought so.

She spoke with a sigh in her words. "I wish it were so, my lord."

Well, her *my lording* was going to have to stop. "At this point," he said, "you have seen me at my worst, Lady Marian. You might as well call me Rob when we are alone." It was not a common name, but he had never thought of himself as Robert. Particularly when he had been named after his grandfather, who had refused to acknowledge his "unsuitable" daughter-in-law and her children after his younger son chose a wife outside of what was considered proper.

Lady Marian's cheeks blossomed with pink, which made her rather prettier than before, and Rob couldn't help but chuckle at her propriety after the things she'd done at the tavern. It spoke volumes of her youth and innocence, and he was tempted to see just how far he could push the line with her. At what point did the lady beat out the maid?

"I will call you by your name if you call me by mine," she said quite confidently as she sat tall and met his gaze without wavering.

"A solid compromise. Marian," he tested. It was not much different from calling her *Lady* Marian, but it certainly felt more intimate without her title getting in the way. Rob had never been fond of titles, and he was pleased to see she was quick to forego hers.

As they rode through the park, he could not help but notice the many looks they were receiving. A good number of them, like from Misters Tilby and Weston, were probably more for Lady Marian, who was new to Society and therefore of interest to everyone, but he could not help but think many of those glances were reserved solely for him. For a man who had spent a good deal of energy avoiding these common social practices to be out on a drive with a marquess's daughter, alone no less, was bound to cause a stir.

He had to distract himself before he gave up the endeavor entirely. They still had an important conversation to have. Clearing the air and setting boundaries of trust was the whole point of this drive, not reveling in the fact that he was with the most desired companion of the morning. "I assume you had a question for me last night that did not involve my real identity," he said.

Lady Marian lifted her fan, though they were riding fast enough that she did not need it. It was likely more of an unconsciously nervous gesture, as if she knew as well as he did how little equipped either of them were to deal with this particular conversation. She kept remarkably cool under pressure, though she could not fully hide her nerves. "I . . . well, I came to ask you about . . ."

Goodness, she was more anxious than he would have thought. Rob quickly searched through the many questions he thought she might want to ask, trying to find one that would be improper enough to turn her face so red. It would have to involve him being a thief, not anything to do with his nobility. Something she could not have asked the first night they met. "You wanted to know if I was the one who robbed Lord Portstone?" he guessed.

She breathed a sigh of relief. "Indeed," she said.

He could laugh about his exploits at the tavern without issue, but admitting something like that to a lady of peerage was frightening to think about. If he was wrong about her and she shared his secret to practically anyone within her circle of acquaintances, he could be ruined by teatime. He desperately hoped he could trust this girl and her wayward tongue. "I was." He tensed, waiting for her reaction.

To his surprise, she hardly changed her expression, still a bit wary as she watched him with her hazel eyes glowing gold in the sunlight. "Why?" she asked.

Well, that was an odd question. He would have thought the answer was obvious after the things she had said in the ballroom the other night. "Because he dismissed nearly his entire household simply out of suspicion," he said with a shrug. "That many people suddenly out of a job with no recommendation? I was not about to stand for it."

Without warning, Marian took his arm in her hands and sat just a little closer to him as they drove. "Good," she said and gave him a smile that made his heart skip a beat and endeared her to him a little more than before. "I am glad to hear it."

So far so good, Rob thought to himself, but the conversation was far from over. As were the stares of the many people out enjoying the sunshine. The longer they drove through the park, the more attention they were gathering, and he was almost certain the gig behind them was the same one they had passed not ten minutes ago. Someone seemed to have found an interest in Rob's day-to-day business now that it involved someone else worth noticing.

That would make it much harder to hide in plain sight.

"I wonder," he said but paused as he considered the question rolling around in his head. But now Lady Marian was looking at him and waiting, so he grabbed hold of that thought and checked to make sure it would not cause him any problems. It seemed harmless enough. "Tell me, Marian. This is your first foray into the jungles; what do you think of Society?"

It was one thing to dislike those who treated others poorly, but not all the *ton* were awful human beings. Some of them were simply too wealthy to know what to do with all they had, and their lives were little more than a spectacle for the rest of the world. Rob had seen his fair share of both plus those outliers, like Marian, who sometimes puzzled him, but he was curious to know how a young woman with her ideals saw the world.

"I think there is a lot to learn about it," she said after a moment's thought.

Rob laughed a little. "What a diplomatic answer," he said. "But it says nothing of your thoughts. If you had to sum up your experience thus far, if someone forced you to cast judgment on your own kind, what would you say?"

She lifted an eyebrow as she watched him, though he reluctantly kept his eyes on the path in front of them and couldn't concentrate on her expression as well as he would have liked. "If I answer this question," she said, "will you answer mine?"

"You have another question?"

"I have several."

That tongue of hers was going to get her into trouble, and Rob enjoyed it immensely. She certainly was not afraid to speak her mind. Unable to keep back his curiosity, he nodded. "I will do my best to give pleasing answers, my lady."

"I think the upper ten thousand do not realize how fortunate they are and would do better to pay attention to the world around them instead of only to themselves and each other. They should not care so much about what others think of them."

Rob would have laughed out loud if he was not acutely aware that the entire park would take notice of it, and the irony of that was not lost on him. He cared a great deal about the attention of his peers, but not for the reasons Marian spoke of. What he should have said then was something of his admiration for her willingness to hold to such an unpopular opinion—first at the ball and now here, Lady Marian Russell was proving herself to be a breath of fresh air—but instead he said, "That is quite the opinion for someone your age."

She ignored his comment and jumped right into her first question. "Why does everyone call you the Elusive Earl?"

"Because I am an earl and an elusive one," Rob replied with a smirk. It was such a Robin thing to say, though, that he instinctively ducked his head when they passed Lord Bradley so he would not be recognized. He should have acknowledged the man with a nod, if nothing else, and he chided himself for forgetting his place. No matter how delightful she was, Lady Marian was proving to be rather distracting.

She was not about to accept his response, though, and she had a rather impressive glare for a young lady fresh to the *ton*. "I answered your question," she reminded him.

That she had, and Rob was glad of it. She had proven it was possible for the wealthy to have a heart as well as a pocketbook, something Rob had doubted his whole life. She deserved an honest answer from him. That did not, however, mean he had to give his answer seriously.

"I am elusive," he said, "because I have not found anyone worth my attention. At least, I hadn't until now," he added and leaned close enough to her to bring spots of red onto her cheeks.

The girl may have spent several hours working in a London pub, but that did not mean she wasn't affected by a charming smile. Now was as good a time as any to push that line of propriety and see if she pushed back. Once he truly understood her character, he would better know how worried he needed to be about her revealing his secret.

"So," he said when Marian did not respond, "did I answer to your satisfaction?" He leaned even closer than before so their shoulders touched. To his delight, she turned an even brighter red and fixed her eyes on the path ahead.

"Indeed," she said, her voice thin.

She was making it far too easy to keep her unsettled, and Rob had to fight the urge to laugh. "What else do you have a burning desire to know?" he asked.

She glanced at him, and her embarrassment was gone, replaced by a flicker of defiance in those hazel eyes of hers. "I hardly think I would go as far as that," she said sharply. "You cannot fault me for being curious about a man like you."

"Is that why you agreed to come on this drive with me?"

"I agreed because I, too, hold a dangerous secret, my lord, and I need to know I can trust you with it."

Rob guided the horse off to the side and pulled it to a stop so he could look at her directly. No more teasing and testing; this was important for the both of them. "You think I would expose you when doing so would risk my own secret coming out in the open?" he asked.

Marian lifted her chin in a show of confidence, but there was too much fear in her eyes for him to believe it. "You have far less to lose, my lord," she said.

That was probably true. Assuming anyone actually believed it if they heard what he did during his nights, Rob would likely lose only a reputation that had been based on lies to begin with. An earl would hardly be convicted as a thief when there was no definite proof, and he took great care never to leave any evidence of his involvement. Lady Marian, however, was a woman and therefore ill-equipped to salvage her status if accused of roaming the streets at night. She would never have an offer of marriage or hold any credibility with her peers again. Her fortune would keep her alive, but a girl like her needed more than money. She needed a future.

Bowing his head slightly, Rob thought through his words carefully so she could not possibly misunderstand them. "I give you my word as a gentleman and, more importantly, as a champion for the less fortunate: I will not speak a word of your life, lady or maid or otherwise. Your choices are your own, and I have no right to judge. You have nothing to fear from me."

When Marian spoke, she put her hand on his arm. She likely meant the gesture to add sincerity, but it simply brought her closer to Rob, well within reach for him to do something that might truly shock her. He held himself back, however, and listened to what she had to say.

"Thank you, Rob," she said. "I feel as if I can breathe again. And I promise I will not speak a word of your identity to anyone. I would not risk the benefit you provide to the poor."

Now that that was out of the way . . . "So . . ." Rob shifted so close to the girl that his nose brushed hers. She froze in horror, and he grinned. "What else did you want to know?"

Scowling, she shoved him away and faced forward again, stiff as a rod. "You are insufferable," she said through her teeth.

She was absolutely right, but Rob was having far too much fun to stop. He had had little opportunity as an earl to entertain himself like this. "You make it too easy," he replied. "You should not allow yourself to be so unsettled, Marian."

"You are mistaken, my lord. I am not unsettled in the least."

The quiver in her voice did little to convince him of that. If he could so easily make her uncomfortable, how easy would it be for someone else to pry her secrets loose? "Let me give you a bit of advice, from one pretender to another," he said and flicked the reins to continue their drive. "If you are going to keep secrets, you need to learn to stand your ground and not be surprised by what people might say. You have your opinions, I know, but you cannot let others frighten them away like you did at the ball. If you let the world see only what you want them to see, you'll be safe."

She glanced at him. "Lie, you mean?"

She put it so bluntly, and Rob could not help but smile again. She had a good heart, but she had no idea what she was getting herself into. "People like me lie because we have to," he said with a shrug. "To protect those who do not get a choice. It is a dangerous game, but someone has to play it."

"And what made you that player?" she asked.

As simple as that question was, it made Rob hesitate. His whole life had led him to this point, but he wasn't sure he could tell his whole history to someone he had only just met. He believed she would keep his secret about being a thief, but could he trust her to protect the rest of him? There was a lot more to Rob Loxley than the thief or the earl.

But not telling her would only lead her to make assumptions, and he needed to know which details Marian knew about him. It would be better to give her a portion of the truth and hope it satisfied her.

Speaking about his past, however, was not something he did easily, and he took a deep breath as he pulled the safest details from his history to present. *Be careful, Rob*, he told himself. It had been a long time since he'd trusted anyone outside of his family or John, and trusting this girl was quite the risk. But it was one he knew he had to take.

"We were as poor as church mice when my father died," Lord Huntingdon said, his eyes focused on the crowded path ahead but distant all the same.

Marian could tell what he was saying was important—she had not yet seen him quite this serious—so she listened carefully as he continued. "I took what jobs I could to help feed my mother and sister, but I was only eight, so we could barely afford our rent let alone anything beyond."

"How did you become the earl?" she asked him. She already knew the answer, thanks to her mother's gossip, but she was curious to know what answer he would give. From her limited acquaintance with him, she already knew the man was more secretive than most.

He scoffed. "I was fortunate enough to never have any paternal cousins," he said. "So when my uncle died, I was next in line, no matter how much he hated the idea. It was either me or some distant relation living somewhere abroad. When his solicitor discovered us in Nottinghamshire and gave me a chance to give my mother and sister a better life, I stepped into the role and elevated my rank tenfold overnight."

His father had been in the navy, but Marian's mother had said nothing about the rest of the family. How had the earl spent his time before it was taken up by the duties of a peer? "And before you were the earl?" she asked.

"I was a sheep farmer." He chuckled. "Now I own the lands I used to work."

The man was fascinating, and Marian was confident few people knew much about him. Even her mother had not had anything else to tell her when she had asked at breakfast this morning, which meant the gossip mill had very little to present. That explained the nickname he had been given. Somehow the Elusive Earl had managed to spend eight years among the upper class without them knowing every little detail about him. She wished she could have the same luxury. But with the mother she had, there was very little chance of that. Lady Waverly wanted all of Society to know how perfect her precious daughter was.

"So why did you become a . . ." She could hardly bring herself to say the word out loud. Not when there were so many people around them.

He smirked, the same smile he had used at the tavern as Robin. It was even more attractive in broad daylight than it had been beneath the shadow of his hat. "A thief?" he finished for her. When she nodded, he shrugged. "Because I lived in the squalor of the poor, so I have seen firsthand the corruption of the nobility. There is only so much I can do in the House of Lords without other peers thinking the way I do, and stealing from the worst of the best was a more direct solution to the problem I could see all around me. Like I said at the tavern, a redistribution of wealth."

"You are taking quite a risk," Marian said in awe. "If anyone discovered you—"

"That is precisely why we needed to have this conversation, Marian."

She had not been sure what to expect from this drive, but Marian was enjoying herself more and more as the morning went on. Even with his ridiculous teasing. She had hardly been able to sleep the night before because she was so worried she would wake the next morning to find her parents wise to her nighttime excursions and determined to hole her away in their country estate until she could act like a proper young lady should. Instead, life had continued as normal, and now she was riding around the park with the Earl of Huntingdon . . . and having to endure more stares than she was accustomed to weathering.

She had known her first Season would gain her a bit of attention. She was the daughter of a marquess, after all, and that was not something to laugh at. But clearly it was unusual for people to see the Earl of Huntingdon out and about, and she was not sure how he managed to ignore all the pointed glances and hidden whispers when she could hardly pay attention to anything else.

Flicking the reins to urge the horses faster and maneuver expertly around a particularly slow gig in front of them, the earl—Rob, she reminded herself—waited until they had put some distance between them and the people behind them before he spoke again. "Care to explain what you were doing working in a tavern?"

Marian knew he wasn't threatening her, but his question was one she had been dreading ever since she'd first concocted the idea with Will. Although she had hoped it would never happen, she knew someone would eventually find out about her adventure and question her motives. "I've been treated as delicate my entire life, my lord," she said. When he raised an eyebrow at her, she sighed. "Rob. As a lady of rank, I am considered unfit for anything beyond embroidery and music and dancing, and I know there's so much more I could do with my life."

"You mean like hunting and fencing?"

She scowled at him, which only made him laugh. He was incorrigible. "I've seen the way people treat their servants," she said. "And yes, I've spent most of my life in luxury, but that is why I wanted to get out there and experience a different side of life. I can't know how to help people if I don't know the lives they live. I want to fix things. Change the world."

"Well," he replied, "it's unfortunate there isn't much you can do as a lady of rank. Your good intentions will likely remain only that."

She had really been starting to like this man, but all good feelings suddenly disappeared. Did he really think she could do nothing? "That is why I was so excited to find you," she said, scowling again. "You can teach me how to do what you do."

He laughed. And it wasn't just a short laugh of surprise. He was genuinely amused. What happened to his sentiments that a lady could do whatever she pleased? "You can't do what I do," he said, his laughter glittering in his eyes.

Pulling away from his arm, she fought the urge to hit him. He would probably only laugh at that too. "You're dismissing me just like that?" she asked.

He glanced at her, then pulled the phaeton off to the side of the path again so he could turn to fully face her. "Like I said, you have good intentions. But you just admitted it yourself; there's nothing you can do."

That was *not* what she had said, and he knew it.

"Besides," he said, "what I do is dangerous. You would get yourself caught or killed in minutes."

Did he really think so little of her? Though she knew arguing would get her nowhere, Marian was bubbling with anger. She'd been entirely wrong, and this man was just as odious as the rest of them. So when she looked ahead, tears stinging her eyes, and recognized Will walking the path in front of them, she called out his name almost desperately.

Will obviously sensed her distress, but he kept his questions to himself as he approached the phaeton and eyed the earl with suspicion. Did he recognize the man she'd sent him to find last night? Marian didn't think so. But that didn't mean Will wasn't slipping into his protective mode as he often did.

"Lord Huntingdon," Marian said, and her voice trembled a bit. *How irritating.* "This is my cousin, Mr. William Russell. Will, this is Lord Robert Loxley, the Earl of Huntingdon."

Will bowed, and the earl lowered his head, each of them eyeing the other rather coldly. "It's a pleasure," Will said.

"It's all mine," the earl replied.

And Marian made a decision. It wouldn't be wise, going out with one man and returning with another, but she didn't particularly care. Rising to her feet, she waited until Will outstretched his hand and helped her down, as she knew he would, and then she looked back up at the earl. "Thank you for a pleasant drive," she said with a clipped curtsy, then took Will's arm and steered him away before she had to listen to whatever the earl might say.

As soon as they were a decent distance away, Will glanced behind him. Had the earl carried on his way yet, or was he watching her? "Is everything well, Marian?" he asked.

Marian was still fighting to hold back tears. The earl had dismissed her so easily. She'd been sure he would at least listen to her. He was probably right about it being dangerous, but he didn't have to laugh at her. She wished she could tell Will everything, but she had promised to keep Rob's secret. *Rob.* The irony of that name would have made her laugh if she weren't so angry with the man. "Nothing is wrong," she said, though her quick pace contradicted that.

"When did you meet the Earl of Huntingdon?" Will asked.

At the tavern that first night. "We danced together a few nights ago."

Will twisted again to look behind them, but he didn't look as long as he had before, which probably meant the earl had driven off. "And he asked you to the park?"

"Is it so surprising that a man would want to spend time with me?" Marian said, and her voice broke a bit. She took a deep breath, willing herself not to cry. The earl thought she was just as delicate as everyone else did, and she was determined to prove him wrong.

Pulling her closer, Will put his hand over hers where it rested on his arm. "That is not what I meant, and you know it. Huntingdon never makes social calls."

How much did Will know about the earl? Perhaps he had gained different information than her mother since he would have spent time in places like Tattersall's, where the men had their own gossip mills. "Do you know much about him?" she asked, pleased to hear that her voice stayed steady this time.

"No one knows much," Will replied. "Somehow he's both a mystery and a paragon. Every man wants to be him, but no one knows who he is."

Every man wanted to be a superior misogynist? They'd certainly managed that.

"Do you want me to take you home?" Will asked.

"Yes, please," Marian whispered. She wished it weren't a faux pas to pull him into an embrace in the middle of the park. She had always wanted a brother, but she was pretty sure no brother could have been kinder and more protective than Will. She had been blessed with her family, and she was starting to fear she would never find anyone to compare with them. The man who could compete with Will certainly wasn't Rob the earl.

As she walked arm in arm with Will, Marian knew that if the earl wouldn't teach her the ways of thievery, perhaps she would just have to teach herself and prove to him that he wasn't any better than she was. She just had to come up with a plan for how she could do it. She would have to start small, of course, as she didn't know what she was doing, but surely she could figure out how to steal something, even if it would be of little consequence to begin with. Something like a bit of lace or a pair of gloves.

And luckily for her, she had the perfect unwitting accomplice right at her side. "Do you have plans this afternoon?" she asked cheerfully.

Will glanced at her and shrugged, though he seemed confused by her sudden change of mood. "Well, I was hoping to—"

"Good. Instead of taking me home, I need you to take me shopping."

He spluttered, caught completely off guard by her statement. "You need me to what?"

Marian did her very best to maintain her innocent expression and not give away her true intent. If Will knew she wanted to try stealing something, he would march her right back home and refuse to help her. She didn't much like deceiving her cousin, but this was innocent enough that she wouldn't change her mind. It was important.

"If I go back home now," she said, "Mother will just drag me around as she makes social calls, and I can only stand to sit in drawing rooms and chat about the weather for so long before I start to lose my mind."

"Why can you not go shopping with your mother instead?" Will asked. The pain in his expression was far more acute than Marian would have expected, though she had no idea why shopping would be such a horrid pastime. True, he had no use for ribbons or lace, but surely he made purchases now and then. He had started to dress more like his station demanded and less like a soldier on leave.

Marian tried to be sympathetic, though she wasn't sure how well she could manage that. Appealing to his softer side was easier than explaining why taking her mother along would not in the least help her accomplish her new goal. "I know you are not fond of the busier parts of Town, but I have hardly spent any time with you since we got here for the Season."

Will groaned. He would not be able to say no to something like that, as much as he might want to. "You are a pain, Marian Russell. You know that?"

Grinning, Marian held tighter to his arm to show her gratitude. "I know I am," she said, "but you love me despite it."

"Sometimes I think I love you because I have to," he mumbled. Marian knew he didn't mean it. "Just promise me you won't take hours. I do have things I need to accomplish today as well, believe it or not."

When they arrived at Marian's favorite haberdashery, the shop was far more packed with people than she would have expected for such a fine morning. Ladies were everywhere, giggling together and whispering about colors and dresses and holding ribbons up to match each other's eyes. Marian would not have guessed a shop such as this could be the place to be, but it seemed half of Town was crammed inside.

That was going to be a problem if she really planned to steal something. Surely someone would see her. But she couldn't very well turn around and find a different place to try, not with Will on her arm with the expectation that she had come here to buy some ribbon.

"I am going to look at the white ribbons," Marian said and slipped away from him, even though he tried to protest and keep her nearby. She wasn't sure why he was so clingy suddenly until she glanced back at him and saw four ladies surrounding him. The poor man's face had turned a deep shade of scarlet, and he seemed to have lost his tongue as they battered him with questions and comments.

For his sake, Marian would have to do this quickly.

She did not know where to start, however, and her anger with Robin returned just as strong as it had been at the park. How could he so easily dismiss her? She had not been entirely useless at the tavern—he must have seen that— so why was he so convinced she could not become a thief given some time and practice?

"I have not seen you around much, Mr. Russell," a young woman said loudly, her voice carrying over the buzz of conversation around the shop.

Marian glanced back at Will again and snorted a laugh when she realized he had been backed into a corner by even more ladies than before. Now that he was heir to a marquessate, her cousin was a rather desirable companion. Unfortunately for the ladies hoping to get in his good favor, Will was also terribly shy, and he seemed to be searching for the best escape.

Marian would just take a ribbon, hide it in her skirts, and grab Will so he would not hate her forever for dragging him into this.

"Lady Marian, how lovely to see you!"

Marian jumped as Miss Bennett appeared at her side and took hold of her arm. She had met the young lady at the very start of the Season, but Marian had done her best to avoid her. Miss Bennett could talk for hours without taking breath, and she would make this whole stealing endeavor impossible if Marian let her get started.

"Oh, I did not see you there, Miss Bennett. If you will excuse—"

"Is that your cousin, Mr. Russell, over there?" Miss Bennett grabbed Marian's shoulder and lifted herself up onto her toes to better see the poor man. "I have hardly seen him around Town since we met at Vauxhall last month."

Marian fingered a length of pink ribbon that would look absolutely stunning if she added it to her cream-colored morning dress. But Miss Bennett was still holding on to her, so how was she supposed to take the thing without being noticed? She would definitely not be able to convince Will to accompany her another time to try again. What would Robin do in this situation?

"My cousin is a busy man," she said and moved on to another ribbon so she would appear as if she were simply browsing.

Miss Bennett gripped her shoulder even more tightly than before, though her eyes were on Will. "Any man worth as much as he will be should most certainly keep himself busy," she said with a little frown. "But I wonder why he does not talk to any of the ladies."

Probably because he thinks they are all vapid and vain, Marian thought. "Perhaps he has not found a lady worth talking to," she said instead, since that sounded far kinder. "Have you tried speaking to him yet? I am sure he remembers you."

Poor Will was most certainly going to hate Marian because Miss Bennett's eyes went wide as she apparently realized she had not attempted a conversation and therefore had a chance to impress the thus-far-quiet heir. "Good afternoon to you, Lady Marian," she breathed, then disappeared into the crowd.

Marian wrapped her fingers around the delightful pink ribbon and bunched it up in her fist, and after making a quick glance around the room to confirm everyone was either focused on their own ribbons or on Will, she tucked it away into her bodice and went back to browsing. Though her heart pounded in her chest, she could not help but inwardly cheer because she had made the first step to becoming like Robin. It was a small step, of course, but it was a step in the right direction. She could never be a thief if she did not keep calm when working.

Now that she had her ribbon, though, it was time to rescue Will. She quickly perused the rest of the wall of ribbons, then hurried past the many ladies crowding the space until she reached Will's side. "I am satisfied," she said and took hold of his arm, much to the annoyance of Miss Bennett and her fast-flying tongue. She likely had not even begun what she'd wanted to say to the someday-to-be-marquess.

Will recoiled at first at Marian's touch, but when he realized it was her, he relaxed a bit. But then he saw her empty hands and frowned. "Did you not get your ribbon?" he asked in alarm, likely fearing he had endured all that unwanted attention for nothing.

Marian shook her head. "I already have what I need," she said and gently tugged on his arm to get him moving. It was not easy to get to the door with so many ladies still hoping for a chance to speak to Will, but the cousins eventually made it out onto the street where Marian could breathe again.

"I am sorry," she said immediately. "I thought I needed ribbon, but I realized I had already gotten it last week. Perhaps I should let you go back to your business and do my shopping another time after all." She was tempted to try taking something from another shop, but she feared she would not have the fortitude for another misdeed so soon after the first. The ribbon already weighed on her chest like it knew it had been wrongfully taken. The owner of the shop likely would not even notice it was gone, but . . . "Give me one moment," she said and darted back into the store before Will could question her.

The ladies inside had gone back to their gossiping and ribboning, so Marian managed to pull the ribbon from her bodice and make her way up to the counter without notice. "I would like to buy this," she told the shopkeeper quickly, then counted out the coins from her reticule. "Thank you." And when she returned to Will's side on the street so he could walk her home, she muttered something about how she'd changed her mind and then went silent, deciding it was best to pretend nothing out of the ordinary had happened.

What was important was the fact that she had gotten outside with the stolen ribbon without getting caught. If she stole from people like Robin did, people who deserved it, guilt would not send her back to rectify the deed. Now that she knew she had the strength to do it, it was time to consider her first real target. Robin thought she could not be a thief? She was determined to prove him wrong.

CHAPTER *Five*

JOHN HAD TRIED VERY HARD to keep Rob from going out tonight, and Rob was starting to understand why. It had taken him more than five minutes to pick the lock to the servants' entrance of Mr. Pitt's house, which was nothing short of ridiculous. He was being sloppy, and that was going to get him into trouble if he didn't pull himself together.

Finally gaining access to the merchant's house, Rob found himself a hiding place behind an open door where he could pause and get his thoughts in order. He really had to focus if he was going to get in and out without being seen, and this was likely his only chance to hit Mr. Pitt where it hurt most. The man had been growing more fearful by the day; according to Alana this afternoon, his wife had beaten one of their maids that morning and seemed to think that would make them a target for the mysterious thief of London.

"Clever man," Rob muttered. As soon as his sister had absently mentioned the maid's treatment by the wealthy trader, Rob had quickly gone through his research and made his plans to break in. Half a day wouldn't have been enough time for Pitt to transfer his latest payment to the bank for safekeeping, so tonight was the ideal time to strike.

But Lady Marian Russell was making focusing rather difficult.

Growling to himself, Rob tried yet again to forget the expression on her face when she had left his phaeton yesterday. He had not intended to insult her, but clearly, he had done wrong by her when he'd told her it was too dangerous for her to become a thief. But it was true! The moment she tried to follow in his footsteps was the moment she got herself into a world of trouble, and he knew there was little chance she could learn. It had taken him more than a year of practicing before he'd felt confident enough to actually go out and steal from someone, and he had a feeling Marian did not have that kind of patience. She was likely to get herself killed, and that would be on his head.

First things first. He had to stop thinking about the lady and concentrate on the task at hand. He had been inside this house only once, and it had been rented by someone else at the time. There was no telling what changes Pitt might have made, so he would have to be careful. He could only guess where he would find the money, and he had limited time before one of the servants wandering the house happened upon him.

"Focus, Rob," he whispered, then pressed forward with one finger against the wall next to him. From the floor plan he had mapped out over a year ago, Pitt's study was most likely on the second floor and to the left. The town house was, thankfully, a smaller one, so he had fewer places to search, and he started to count down time in his head. He would give himself twenty minutes before he moved on and gave up.

He had not expected Marian to give up so easily. When she had gotten down from the phaeton and walked away with her cousin, Rob had realized his mistake. He had spent nearly the whole night at the Bow and Crown just in case she came to find him again and beg him to teach her how to be a thief. He thought she would have been of stronger stuff than she was, and his disappointment had led to a particularly odious afternoon after that morning in the park. If he had just taken the time to explain himself better . . .

She hadn't exactly let him though. Her offense was her own fault and a testament to her age. She was far too young and inexperienced to get herself mixed up in something like this.

Finding the room he hoped was the study, Rob slipped inside soundlessly and took stock of his surroundings. The window to this room faced the street, but the night was cloudy, so he could see very little. He would have to feel his way, which took precious time he probably did not have. *Think, Rob*, he told himself and imagined most of the studies he had set foot in among the *ton*. He laid them out side by side in his mind, comparing their floor plans and considering the habits of their owners. If this were the average of all studies, particularly those among merchants, the desk would most likely be close to the window in order to provide natural light and save some money on oil. Merchants pinched pennies wherever they could. Slowly making his way to the right, Rob followed the wall until his knee bumped ever so gently against an object in front of him. A quick search with his fingers revealed a desk, but the drawers were locked.

Cursing under his breath, he crouched down and started picking the lock, knowing his twenty minutes were quickly dwindling. The house was quiet around him, but he had met quiet servants before. His own servants, in fact, had taken to being almost silent as they moved about the house. Rob had complained more than once of them keeping him up during the wee hours of the morning when he allowed himself to sleep, and they had promptly removed the issue.

He wondered if Marian had quiet servants too. She would have to, with her little late-night excursions, if she and whoever helped her wanted to go undetected.

The lock clicked open, and Rob took a moment to breathe and bring himself back to task once again. Why was it so blasted difficult to stop thinking about the woman? "Please be money," he whispered and reached into the drawer to find a stack of papers. He would never know what they were without some light to read them, but he could not just light a candle to check. He wasn't sure what to do at this point. Should he leave them and keep searching the rest of the desk, or should he take what he could get and hope luck was on his side?

This was exactly why he did not want Marian risking her reputation and her life just to prove she could. There were too many variables in this profession; it was not an exact science. She would get herself hurt, and—

"Who are you?"

Rob froze as the room filled with the smallest bit of light from a candle behind him. Cursing, he pulled his hat a little lower over his face and turned just enough to catch sight of a footman or kitchen assistant staring at him. He was a young fellow, not quite a man, nor a boy, and that presented a problem. Either the lad was intelligent enough to shout for help before Rob could get away, or he was equally smart enough to take a bribe.

Rob prayed for the latter to be true. Reaching into the pocket of his overcoat, he pulled out a small bag of coins and presented it to the lad on his outstretched palm. "I would appreciate it if you did not tell anyone I was here," he said softly.

"You stealin' from the master?" the boy asked.

Rob winced at his volume, just a touch too loud for his taste. Someone would likely hear him and come investigate. He looked about the same age as the maid Pitt's wife had beaten, though, and Rob hoped for the same solidarity among servants as he had seen elsewhere. "I am here to help Kitty Price," he said slowly. "Do you know Kitty?"

"The maid?" Frowning, the lad glanced behind him and took a step deeper into the room. "How're you goin' to help her?"

Rob held the bag of coins a bit closer. "I am going to give the Pitts what they deserve," he said and bit his tongue. If the lad was loyal to Pitt, that one sentence would spell Rob's doom and make this whole endeavor a lot harder than it needed to be. "Do you know where he keeps his bank notes?" he asked when the boy didn't react.

"You mean those there in your hand?"

He could have laughed, but that would surely turn fate out of his favor. "Tell no one you saw me," he said and moved quickly, stuffing the coins into the lad's hand, then slipping out of the room, using the little light from the candle to guide him back the way he'd come. There was still a chance the lad would change his mind and sound the alarm, so Rob was not about to stick around and find himself in more trouble than he would like.

By the time he got back to Huntingdon Manor and slipped through the back door, his heart was pounding wildly as he made his way up to his chamber. For once he regretted giving John the night off, since he would very much like a good strong drink to calm himself down but did not have the energy to go downstairs and find one. Not for the first time, he wished he would remember to keep a bottle in his dressing room for emergencies like this.

That had been too close. He'd been lucky with the lad, but that would not always be the case. One of these days he was going to get caught by someone less easily persuaded, and if he did not figure out how to stop thinking about distractions like the beautiful Marian Russell, his ultimate demise would come sooner rather than later.

Rob lumbered into the breakfast room late the next morning with a pounding headache, wishing he could have slept until noon. Mother did not seem to notice, thankfully, as she was reading the paper, but Alana gave him a look that told him he probably appeared as awful as he felt. John was a good valet, but he could not work miracles.

"Did you not sleep last night, Robin?" his sister asked, quirking an eyebrow up.

Rob could not keep from smiling at the childhood nickname. His sister and mother had never stopped using the moniker, even after he'd taken up the mantle of nobility, and he loved them for it. It gave him a chance to feel normal when he was at home since he did not get that anywhere else. No, outside of the protective walls of Huntingdon Manor, he always had a part to play.

He kissed the top of his sister's head as he made his way around the table, and then he gave his mother's shoulder a squeeze. "I just have a lot on my mind."

"You mustn't listen to the gossip, Robin," his mother said.

"I haven't a clue what you are talking about, Mother," Rob said, although he had his suspicions that people were still talking about his little jaunt through the park with Lady Marian. He settled into his chair with some coffee, not feeling particularly hungry this morning. Not now that he was thinking about Marian again. The precocious young woman set him on edge, and he did not like it.

"Have you gone out with Lady Marian again?" Alana asked. She sipped at her cup of chocolate but leveled him with a look of feigned innocence as she watched him from across the table. If that spark in her eyes was any indication, she had noticed his attentions at the ball and likely thought him affected by the Lady Marian. He most certainly was not, no matter what his sister thought she saw.

Rob scowled at her. "Of course not," he said. In fact, he rather hoped he never had to interact with her again, no matter how intriguing she had been at first. Based on last night's near miss, Lady Marian would only lead to trouble.

"She has a very good family," Mother said, and though her attention was still on the paper, amusement hung in her eyes. For a woman who had spent most of her life in poverty, she had taken to high Society incredibly well and talked about good families as if she had been doing so her whole life. Rob both loved and hated how easily she had adjusted over the last eight years. He had found no such ease.

"I am sure she does," Rob said through his teeth.

Then his mother spouted a little "Oh!" and flattened out the paper on the table. "There were more robberies last night!"

Rob shook his thoughts clear because he was pretty sure he had heard her wrong. "Robberies?" he asked. *As in plural?* He leaned a little closer to try to read for himself. "Who?"

"Looks like a merchant called Mr. Pitt," his mother said, frowning down at the paper as she read. "And Mr. Howard Tilby."

Tilby? Rob sat back in his chair, his thoughts running wild. Why would anyone go after the likes of Mr. Tilby? He had a decent rank, to be sure, but he was not a particularly wealthy man. And, as far as Rob knew, he certainly wasn't the sort to wrong his employees or cheat his peers. He was far too shy for that. And who would have robbed him? Surely not John, who only ever went out when Rob did. And Tilby was hardly the sort of target a thief would choose when there were higher bounties within the same neighborhood. Besides, thievery had generally gone down since Rob had started his little crusade and put the Quality on their guards. It was too dangerous a profession now that he had made a name for himself, so to speak. So who would . . . ?

Without thinking, Rob smashed his fist onto the table, making his mother and sister jump. *Lady Marian* would. Of course she would. What was she thinking, going out and stealing from a man like Tilby? She could have ruined her entire life if she'd been caught. "My apologies," he said with a cough and forced himself to relax. "I just . . . all these robberies make me fear for your safety."

Alana reached across the table to pat his hand. "Only a fool would try to steal from you, Robin," she said.

Despite his frustration with Marian, Rob smiled again at the name. "I pray you are right," he said, still distracted by the news about Tilby. So much for forgetting about Marian and moving on with his life. He would have to talk some sense into her now, and he had a feeling that would not be a happy conversation. "What is on the calendar tonight?" he asked, hoping the evening's entertainment would bring him somewhere he could speak with her. The sooner he steered her clear of her path of destruction, the better.

When no one responded to his question, he looked up in confusion. Both women were staring at him as if he had said something nonsensical. "What?"

Sharing a glance with their mother, Alana frowned and said, "You never want to go out."

That was true, but this was important. "But *you* want to go out," he argued.

"It is only the theater," Alana said. "Mother and I can—"

"I'll go with you," he said and rose, leaving little room for argument. Yes, they could easily go to the theater without him, but he was on a mission, and not even their gaping stares would stop him from going. Even if he would hate the whole ordeal.

Going to the theater was a horrible, terrible, awful idea, and Rob cursed himself for forgetting the spectacle his appearance would cause as soon as he set foot in the building. Based on the stares and whispers as he followed the ladies to their box, it had apparently been years since he'd last attended, though he honestly could not say when that had been exactly. Perhaps it really was years ago. First a jaunt in the park with a lady and now a trip to Drury Lane; he truly was starting to feed the gossip mill to the extreme.

It was all Marian's fault, Rob reminded himself. Without her little venture into the tavern, none of this would have happened, and he could have continued his life in peace.

Pinching the bridge of his nose, Rob willed himself to ignore the hundreds of faces pointed up at him as he entered the box with his family and took his seat. He asked himself if this excursion was worth the rumors that would start spreading and was tempted to turn around and head back home. He could find another way to speak to Marian. But when he opened his eyes, he saw her sitting with her parents almost directly across from him, and he knew he would not sleep soundly until he had stopped her from stealing again. She was so young. So innocent. And when she met his eyes across the theater, there was still that fire in her eyes that told him she would not give up so easily.

Rob settled back in his seat, trying to disappear into the shadows before too many people caught sight of his undoubtedly nervous expression. The looming conversation he would have with Lady Marian would be a difficult one indeed, and he was eager to get it over with. Once he had the young woman under control and staying away from thievery, things could get back to normal.

Blissful, uncomplicated normal.

The first half of the play was the longest Rob had ever sat through, and he had to resort to tearing the program into shreds to keep from pacing the box and counting down the minutes. It was not a very good play, and most of the crowd was not paying attention anyway. They were too busy throwing surreptitious glances up to him and filling the entire space with their whispers.

"You're not very subtle!" he wanted to shout into the crowd, but he figured that would not help his cause. No, he would just have to endure it and hope the gossip died down before too long. As long as he stopped acting out of the ordinary, he could weather this particular storm for a few days.

By the time the intermission rolled around, however, he was about ready to give up on the whole endeavor. He could already see several people rising from their seats with their eyes right on him, and he knew he was very soon to be accosted by the more forward women of the crush. If he did not make it out of his own box and over to Marian's, the whole evening would simply be a waste of time.

"I will return shortly," he said to Alana and his mother, then slipped out of the box, doing his best to keep from running, though he very much wanted to.

By some miracle, he arrived at the marquess's box without having to speak to anyone, though perhaps that was simply because of the speed he had taken to get there. He greeted Lord Waverly and his wife as warmly as he could manage, but he really had focus only for their daughter. Lady Marian either had terrible hearing, or she was pretending he did not exist, and Rob honestly could not say which he preferred.

"If you don't mind," he said to the marquess, then took the liberty of approaching Marian. "Are you enjoying the production, my lady?" he asked and grimaced when he heard how cold he sounded. He would have to do better than that if he wanted her to listen to him. Otherwise, she would find some insult in his words and storm off.

Most of the theater had now turned their attention to the Waverlys' box, which was not going to make things any easier, but fortunately, Marian recognized the need for civility. She rose to her feet and matched his slight bow with the smallest of curtsies. "Lord Huntingdon. What a pleasure to see you." Everything about her expression said otherwise.

Rob clasped his hands behind his back to hide his clenched fists, and he mustered up a smile. "It is fortunate to find you here tonight, my lady," he said.

For a girl of eighteen, she managed a steely glare quite easily. "And where else would I be, my lord?"

He half-wondered if she spoke to everyone like that or if she reserved that bite just for him. Had he really insulted her so badly at the park? "That depends," he said, and though she had not offered an invitation, he sat, forcing her to do the same. "I'll admit I am rather curious about your evening endeavors." *How to put it delicately?* "Howard Tilby was an interesting choice."

Fire flashed in her eyes, and Marian seemed to use every bit of strength she had to avoid unleashing it on him. She had spirit; he would give her that. "Is that what you would call him?" she said.

"There are better ways of doing good, my lady."

"There are better ways of causing a scene, my lord."

Rob suddenly felt like laughing, which was an odd sensation. She really thought he had come to make a scene? He wanted the exact opposite. And the longer he sat here in this box and kept the marquess and his wife standing at the back pretending they were perfectly content to socialize in the corridor, the more people would start to talk. Oh, how he hated when people talked.

Leaning closer to Marian, he decided his best course of action was to be direct. "Robbing from people like Tilby makes you little more than a petty thief, Marian," he whispered.

Her eyes went wide. "Robbing from Tilby?"

"I told you how dangerous it was, and you went ahead and—"

"You think *I* stole from him?"

Rob blinked. "Well, yes. Who else—"

Marian leapt to her feet, her hands in fists at her sides and her expression flashing with fury. "You could not have delivered a deeper insult, sir, and I must ask you to leave this box immediately. There is nothing else you could possibly have come here to say."

This was not at all what he had anticipated for the evening, and he really had no idea what to do at this point. He had planned his speech so thoroughly throughout the day, but he had not planned to learn that he was wrong. And while there was the slight chance she was putting up an act to defend herself, Rob had a feeling those sudden tears glistening in her eyes were real. Lud, how was he so good at making a fool of himself whenever he spoke to the lady but could quite literally sweep her off her feet when she was a simple barmaid?

"Lady Marian," he said, glued to his seat as he fumbled for something to say. Blast it all, he should have stood when she did, and he forced himself up before all of London remembered his poorer upbringing. He had bungled this whole thing, and he had no idea how to fix it.

Realizing he was not planning to leave as she had insisted, Marian huffed and left the box herself.

Cursing, Rob chased after her before he was painted as an utter buffoon who had insulted the daughter of a marquess. "Lady Marian!" he called, passing a baffled Lord Waverly and praying this evening did not stick in the man's memory. The last thing he needed was a marquess thinking he was a cad.

Heavens, the girl was fast, and she deftly slipped between the crowds on her way to the door. Rob could not manage quite as easily, especially when the other theater guests realized who was pushing past them.

"Good evening, my lord."

"Lord Huntingdon, we were so excited to see you and your darling sister here tonight."

"My lord, do you plan to attend the Middletons' ball next week?"

Rob ignored them all and focused solely on the girl who could lead to his utter ruin.

Finally, he caught up to her just before the doors and slid to a stop in front of her, somewhat breathless but determined to keep her from leaving. "Lady Marian," he said and bowed low, hoping she would take it as a gesture of apology. "I am truly sorry for accusing you of—"

"Of being like you?" she finished for him.

Rob was not prone to embarrassment, but heat crept up his neck. He deserved that. "Please keep your voice down," he begged, though she had not said anything incriminating. Yet.

"Or what?" she asked. "You'll tell me again how incapable I am? I assure you, Lord Huntingdon, you have done plenty in that regard."

He had not been cut down so swiftly since his first Season as earl when he'd realized Society cared very much about the way a man presented himself. No title or fortune could replace good breeding, and Rob had quickly adapted before his family suffered for his ignorance. "Please," he said. "I should not have assumed you were the one who went after Tilby."

Narrowing her eyes, Marian cocked her head ever so slightly. "And you weren't?" she asked.

He shook his head, rather offended she would think so little of him. "Of course not. Tilby is a good man."

"But Mr. Pitt," she finished with a nod. "I heard what happened with his maid."

Taking a deep breath to steady his racing heart, Rob fought for a way to keep the conversation going in a better direction. Perhaps Marian had not stolen from anyone yet, but that did not mean she would not try another day. With the way she stood her ground against him, he was starting to wonder if she could potentially be up to the task after all. "Marian," he said and let out his breath all at once. This was probably a mistake, but it was simply another to add to his growing list of misdoings over the last few days.

"Lady Marian, are you well?"

Rob was so on edge that his first instinct was to turn to the man who approached and land him a facer, but he fought the urge, if only barely. Then he wished he had not resisted when he recognized Mr. Jason Taylor, a man with as horrid a reputation as his fortune was vast. "Taylor," he said by way of greeting and barely managed a nod.

"Lord Huntingdon," Taylor said in return, but his eyes were focused entirely on Marian. "My lady, would you allow me to accompany you back to your box? A beauty such as yourself should not be left so unattended."

Rob had never liked Taylor, particularly because of the way he spoke, as if his words were sent from heaven itself to overpower any lady privileged to hear him.

Marian turned rather pale and had to search for her voice for a moment. "No, thank you, Mr. . . ."

Rob bristled. They had not even been introduced, and yet Taylor was making advances in front of an entire theater crowd? Blast it all, did the man have no shame at all? Rob knew the answer to that question already, and he stepped forward, attempting to stand between Marian and the bounder. "My lady," he said slowly and offered his arm.

"It would not do to cut a man of my fortune, Lady Marian," Taylor said and put his hand on her arm. "If you'll grant a dance to the likes of that worthless fool Tilby but not allow a man of my caliber to accompany you, you will end up a penniless bit of muslin."

It was all Rob could do not to call the man out right there. "Watch your tongue, Taylor," he growled. "You heard the lady. She does not require your assistance."

Taylor's eyes swept over Rob, finding something amusing about him. They had not interacted much after Rob had become earl since Taylor was not part of the upper ten thousand. Neither had they known each other in school like most gentlemen, as Rob had been educated at home by his impoverished parents. Despite Rob's high rank, Taylor had always seen himself as superior strictly because he had been born to polite Society and Rob to hardship.

"I do not believe she requires yours either, Huntingdon," he said with a chuckle. He turned back to Marian and brushed a thumb across her cheek. She recoiled, but he pretended not to notice. "Do not fret, Lady Marian. I have won many a lady's heart, and you will be part of my collection eventually. Until next time," he said and slunk away through the watching crowd.

Rob was clenching his jaw so hard he thought his teeth might crack, and when he looked at Marian to make sure she had endured the encounter, he found her trembling. But it was not a tremble of fear. No, unless he was mistaken, she was angry. And when she looked at him and met his eye, he was fairly certain she was thinking the exact same thing he was.

"Meet me outside your house at midnight," Rob muttered to her. "It seems we have work to do."

CHAPTER *Six*

MARIAN COULD NOT HOLD STILL. She was both excited and terrified, and she felt like her whole body sparked with light, like the flickering flame in the fireplace she had left behind to venture out to a corner of Park Street and wait for Lord Huntingdon to arrive. She was incredibly grateful Millie had found a pair of trousers to fit her, as the night was cool and the trousers kept her legs warmer than a servant's skirt would have, but she still shivered as she hid in some foliage that grew beside her house. Perhaps it was as much from anticipation as it was from the chill of the night.

She still could not believe the earl had let her come along. After his big show of telling her off for being a thief—which she technically was not—he had been the one to initiate this adventure. She hadn't even said a word, though she had been thinking the same thing as him after that unpleasant encounter with Mr. Taylor: if anyone deserved to be robbed, it was that incorrigible rake. And now she was here, dressed as a boy and crouched in some bushes after midnight.

But where was the earl? Marian did not want to think it, but maybe he had set her up for failure. Maybe he had never intended to let her steal from Mr. Taylor, and he had only told her to meet him so he could do his work unhindered. After the things he had said to her at the park, was it so outlandish to wonder? She had already been waiting ten minutes at least, and Robin the thief did not seem the sort to be late.

"But what do I know about the man?" she whispered to herself.

"Clearly not much," a soft voice replied behind her.

Marian barely stifled a scream as she twisted in her hiding place and fell backward, searching the darkness for the owner of the voice. Robin stood in a small patch of moonlight, resting a shoulder against the wall of the house and looking for all the world like a man without a care. How long had he been standing there? How had she not noticed him arrive?

"You presume I was speaking about you?" she said, fighting to sound as if she had not been scared out of her wits. She thought she managed it, but it would have sounded stronger if she wasn't sprawled in the dirt. Catching his every wince as she snapped twigs and breathed words of pain as she crawled from the bushes and got to her feet, she pretended she was just as silent as him, if only to keep from dying of embarrassment. She was better than this, and she knew it, but Robin had caught her off guard and made her nervous.

He frowned as she brushed the dirt from her clothes, then looked her over. "Interesting attire," he said with a tip of his hat. "Come."

The walk to Mr. Taylor's house was shorter than she'd expected, though perhaps that was because Marian was so excited to be involved. Though she had hoped for this, she hadn't thought the earl would actually let her join him. When they arrived at Taylor's town house, Marian did her very best not to get overwhelmed by the thrill of what they were about to do.

She needed some kind of distraction to keep herself from getting overexcited. "I thought the clothes would help," she said as if she needed to justify her decision to herself as much as to Robin. No matter how warm, the clothing was entirely uncomfortable and unfamiliar, and she now thought maybe she could have been quieter in her own skirts. She had spent her life in them, after all.

Robin coughed and pulled his hat a little lower over his eyes. "No, it was a good idea. The hair might give you away though." Without asking permission, he took hold of the plait that hung between her shoulder blades and lifted her cap from her head so he could tuck her hair up inside it. "The goal tonight is not to get caught, but it will be safer for you if no one knows your true sex."

Marian could hardly believe how casual he was about touching her and had been from the very beginning. He may have been a thief, but he was also a peer of the realm. Surely he knew how many rules of polite Society he disregarded every time they were together. Then again, she was standing in men's clothing, alone with a man in the middle of the night. Perhaps she should allow him some liberties, unless she wanted to start condemning her own actions too.

Removing his coat like that was not helping things, however.

"So how do we get in?" she asked, coughing to hide a slight strain in her voice as the earl rested his hat and jacket on the nearest bush and rolled his shirtsleeves up to his elbows. "Through the back door?" she guessed. Goodness, the man was stronger than he looked when fully clothed, and she had a hard time looking away when she could see his shoulder muscles shift beneath his shirt with every little movement. She had seen stablehands back home with that level of strength, but never had she seen it among the upper classes. It made Lord Huntingdon seem more human, in a way. It made him real.

He chuckled and looked up at the house next to him. "If I know anything about the despicable Jason Taylor," he said, "I know he is intelligent enough to keep guards at his doors. Especially in times like these. Pardon me." He ran straight for the wall and jumped, seeming to run straight upward until his fingers clasped hold of the lowest windowsill. The muscles in his arms straining, he pulled himself up and tucked the toe of one boot on top of a protruding bit of stone to act as leverage. Holding himself with one arm, he used the other hand to unlatch the window and pull it open, and he seemed to weigh nothing as he effortlessly pulled himself into the dark room.

As much as Marian enjoyed watching his performance—as in far more than she would ever admit to anyone—she stood below the window and silently grumbled about how stupid she was. The earl would know she could not replicate a maneuver like that, and he had used the window instead of the door to prove she was incapable of being a thief like him.

What was she to do now? She could wait for him to come back out with his treasure and make it clear to him that he could not get rid of her so easily. There was no telling how long he would take, however, and she did not like the idea of waiting so long on her own. She could go back home and admit defeat. Or . . . A pit formed in Marian's throat. There really was no *or*.

"Come on, then," a voice said above her, and she looked up in surprise. Lord Huntingdon leaned out the window, his eyes on the street and his arm stretched out toward her.

She did not waste a moment on questioning him and took several steps back so she could get a running start since he was much too high for her to reach without jumping. She had never done anything like this in her life, and a bit of doubt churned in her stomach as the reality of what she was about to do hit her. She was going to climb through a window of a house belonging to someone nowhere near related to her. He was not even a casual acquaintance. This was a perfect stranger, and if someone caught her . . .

The earl looked down at her, his frown speaking his impatience, and Marian ran. She kicked off the wall and jumped up, and her hand barely reached high enough to clasp around his. As his fingers wrapped around her wrist, she scraped her feet across the stones in the wall, trying to find a foothold, but it felt like she was simply going to slip and fall and break both her ankles when she landed, and she would have to explain to her mother and anyone else she met that some strange accident had befallen her in her bedchamber while she slept.

"Will you stop moving around?" he grunted.

Marian froze and looked up, realizing that he held her quite steady. She was small, but she wasn't *that* small, and he lifted her up to the window with ease. Even after she had gotten that good look at his arms, his strength surprised her. He was still a man of the *ton*, after all. Once she got a knee up onto the sill, she thought he might let go, but he kept pulling, disrupting the little balance she had managed to find. He could release her now and let her climb the rest of the way on her own, but that did not seem to be his intention. "I am—" Her leg slipped, and as her foot caught on the sill, she tumbled inside the room and right into the earl, knocking him to the ground and landing on top of him.

He barely even grunted, though Marian had not been able to keep from letting out a slight cry of pain when her foot twisted as she fell.

From the little she could see of him in the moonlight streaming in through the window, he was doing his best not to completely lose his temper as he looked up at her, his face just a few inches from hers as she lay on his chest. Goodness, in a position like this, it certainly did not feel as though she could think of him as the earl anymore. An earl did not allow himself to be knocked to the ground, nor did he clench his jaw and silently wait for the girl on top of him to scramble away and let him loose. No, this was simply Robin, a man who was likely regretting his decision to bring her along.

In the strangest way, she missed the playfulness he had shown her when they were on their drive through the park. She had disliked his teasing advances, but she far preferred it to feeling like she had no skills to offer in this particular situation.

"Sorry," she whispered when she was back on her feet. "I will get better at that; I promise."

His response was almost too quiet to hear, but it sounded very much like, "I'll not hold my breath."

Good idea. Marian took several deep breaths, holding them in her lungs until her heart started to slow to a normal rhythm again. She was being ridiculous, and unless she pulled herself together and focused, she would never be able to prove to Robin that she could do this sort of thing. And if she couldn't do that, what else could she possibly do to fix the broken world around her?

Nothing, she thought. "So what now?" she asked, the thought of getting caught keeping her from having any real volume. "Should we light a candle to see where we are going?"

Robin chuckled and glanced around what looked to be a library, though he couldn't possibly see into the dark corners. "You have a lot to learn, little thief," he said and slowly made his way to the door, pressing his ear to the wood.

Marian both loved and hated the moniker, but a shiver of delight ran through her and told her she definitely preferred it over Miss Clumsy. It seemed Robin was opening up to the idea of her becoming like him, and she knew she would have to work hard to keep him from changing his mind. It would not be easy, but she would do it.

"By the way," Robin muttered, still listening at the door, "does that cousin of yours know you're here?"

The shiver at her spine turned a little colder. Why would that matter? "No," she said. Perhaps she should have said yes, just in case the earl was not as good a man as he presented himself to be. As it was, he could turn on her any second, and no one would be able to rescue her until it was too late. Spotting a penknife on the desk near the door, she slipped out of Robin's view and grabbed it, just in case. It was small, but it would be more useful than nothing.

"Now," Robin said and slid his fingers around the handle of the door. Apparently, his question truly was one of curiosity. "The important thing to remember is we have limited time once we step out of this room. The closer we get to Taylor's bedchamber, the more likely we will encounter a servant."

"His bedchamber?"

Robin threw a smirk in her direction. "Taylor collects trinkets as trophies," he said, and his voice dipped low and cold. "He likes to keep them close."

"And you know this how?" Another shiver ran through her, and she gripped the knife a little tighter.

"Because he showed them to me. People like Jason Taylor need to feel important, and they are willing to divulge all sorts of secrets to people like me if they think it will make them look superior. You could not imagine the things I have seen, Marian."

He said that so easily, as if the dark secrets of the wealthy were common-place things. But as curious as Marian was about the things he had learned over the years, she could not bring herself to ask about them. Perhaps living in ignorance was better than forming deeper relationships with the people around her. She did wonder, however, if Robin had any of those dark secrets. If he had anyone he shared them with in order to feel important.

"You should not use my name," she whispered as a chill settled over her. She hated to admit it, but she was starting to think coming here was a bad idea. Robin had been right when he said it was dangerous.

He smirked again. "What should I call you, then?"

She had absolutely no idea, and she thought through the names of all the male servants back at home as she tucked her hair a little more securely beneath her cap. Any of them would do, really. Except, if she used one of their names and someone heard Robin say it, there was a chance—however small—suspicion would fall on them, and it would be all her fault. She needed a name that was not commonly used. Maybe even a name that wasn't real. She tucked some more hair beneath her cap, then paused.

"What about Tuck?" she asked.

Robin raised an eyebrow, and then he made a face and pressed his ear to the door again. "It doesn't matter what I call you. We need to get moving."

Marian huffed, a little annoyed by his dismissal of her idea, but then he gently pulled the door open just enough for them to slip through, and all thoughts of her new little name fled her mind as she realized what was about to happen. Standing in an empty library was one thing, but wandering the rest of the house was another.

"Keep silent," Robin whispered, then pressed forward.

Marian was sure the whole household could hear her heart beating, and she willed it to quiet down as she followed the thief down the corridor, her hand on the wall just like his. The tiniest bit of light was coming through the windows on either end of the town house, but it was hardly enough to guide their way. Using the wall was quite ingenious, she thought, and then she bumped into Robin when he stopped suddenly.

"Taylor," he whispered, the word barely audible. He had stopped just in front of a door at the back of the house, where a faint snoring reached Marian's ears.

Her heart seemed to stop beating altogether as she realized how close they were to the man. She held her breath, waiting for what felt like an eternity before Robin reached for the door and ever so gently pushed it open.

The room was bathed in a soft red glow from the dying fire in the hearth, just enough for Marian to see what lay inside. It was a smaller chamber than she would have expected, without a dressing room or any other chamber connected to it. The large bed took up most of the space, and a desk and dresser took up the rest of it. Fear gripped her heart as she realized how near Taylor actually was, though he seemed deep asleep.

She did her best not to look at him, bare-chested as he was beneath his covers.

Robin pointed to the dresser, upon which glittered several pieces of jewelry that most definitely did not belong to the man who slept nearby. Flitting to that side of the room, he raked his eyes over the collection and seemed to grow more agitated the more he saw. He touched a finger to a space that seemed oddly empty, as if something had sat there recently and had not been replaced by a new item yet.

"Blast it," he breathed, glaring at the empty space as if he knew exactly what belonged there. "The cad must have put it on display downstairs like he said he would." He added a few more under-the-breath curses for good measure, then put his hand on Marian's shoulder. "Go back to the library and wait for me there," he said. "Under no circumstances are you to be anywhere near this room alone. Do you understand?" He didn't even bother to wait for her response. "I'll be back shortly." And before she could protest about being told what to do, he was gone.

There was wisdom in his words, though Marian was loath to admit it. In the few seconds after Robin left, the room seemed to grow even darker and left her chilled to the bone as Taylor continued to lightly snore. Maybe waiting in the library was a good idea after all.

But she was right there! The jewelry was only a couple of feet away, and she could grab it quickly, before Robin came back. What was the point of wasting time?

Fingers trembling, Marian picked up a bracelet and slid it into the pocket of her coat. She glanced at Taylor to make sure he was still asleep. She took a necklace next, moving slowly so as not to make a noise with the chain as she slid it in with the bracelet. Every piece made her more nervous, and she could not help but pray Robin returned soon. She didn't know what she was doing. Her pockets were full. If something went wrong . . .

With her eyes on Taylor, she reached for the final piece of jewelry, a gaudy ring set with an emerald, but she overshot and bumped a comb that rested on the edge of the dresser. It slipped out of her reach and thudded to the floor.

Taylor grunted and his snoring stopped. Marian froze where she stood, her arm still outstretched across the dresser and her heart pounding so loudly that she was sure it would wake the man far more easily than the comb. She stood there for what felt like hours until finally the rake's snoring resumed as he slipped back to sleep.

Knowing she likely would not be so fortunate a second time, Marian decided she had better do as Robin had said and return to the library to wait for him. Turning quickly, she darted into the corridor and closed the door behind her as quietly as she could, and then she took a step down the corridor and froze again.

A young girl stood in her way, a candle in her hand and her eyes wide and frightened. She looked about ready to scream.

Marian searched the corridor for any sign of Robin, but the house was painfully silent around her, and she knew she had to act fast if she wanted to avoid disaster. Moving slowly, she crouched down so she was at eye level with the girl who could not have been older than ten. "Hello," she whispered gently.

The girl swallowed, the candle shaking in her hand.

"What is your name?"

"L-Louisa."

"And you work for Mr. Taylor, Louisa?"

Louisa took a stumbling step back as her eyes flashed to Taylor's closed door. Her fear was almost tangible, and Marian wondered if it was because of her or because of Taylor. The candlelight wasn't all that bright, but it was enough for Marian to see the sorry state of the girl's ragged clothes on her thin frame. Had she only just started to work in the household, or was this just how life was for her?

Taking in a slow breath, Marian held up the ring she had snatched from the dresser on her way out. "This is for you," she whispered. "You can use it to buy yourself some extra food."

The girl whimpered just a little, looking at Taylor's bedchamber door again as if afraid her master would come tromping out and discover her. And then she reached out and grabbed the ring from Marian's fingers before retreating back to a safe distance.

Marian smiled. "I want you to sell that as soon as you can," she told Louisa. "If anyone asks questions, you can say your grandmother gave it to you."

Louisa nodded, clutching the ring to her chest, and then she turned to dart down the stairs. Only, she stopped dead at the top and backed away, and Marian's heart leapt into her throat until she recognized Robin in the candlelight. Her relief, however, disappeared as soon as she saw the look on his face. He looked positively livid.

"Rob," she said, ready to defend her actions and keep the girl safe.

But he put a finger to his lips, silencing her, and crouched down so he was at eye level with the trembling child. "I cannot let you keep that," he said.

Marian wanted to scream. So he was allowed to steal from rich people, but only he could keep the spoils?

Louisa still held the ring tightly in her fingers, and she shook so hard that Marian was afraid the candle would fall from her hand and clatter to the floor. The child had likely never owned anything in her life, and she obviously had not been treated well to look so terrified.

Robin held out his hand, palm up. "Please," he said.

And to Marian's surprise—and fury—the girl handed over the ring and seemed to deflate until she was nothing but a tiny wisp of a thing. Her little moment of hope had been shattered, just because a big bully of a man had decided she was not worthy to hold such a treasure, however small.

"Mr. Taylor will be watching all of you when he finds out his treasure is gone," Robin said and slipped the ring into his jacket pocket. But then he reached into another pocket and pulled out several coins that he set in Louisa's hand. As he closed her fingers over the little fortune he had just given her, a smile lit up his face. "Just be sure you don't spend it all at once," he said. "Only buy little things. Stockings. A loaf of bread. Maybe a pair of shoes. Do you understand?"

Louisa nodded, and Robin smiled wider.

"If you ever need a place to go," he told her, "go to Huntingdon Manor. The lord there will help you."

Louisa nodded, then scurried away as if afraid Robin might change his mind and take back the money as well as the ring.

And Marian stared at him, trying to understand how he kept surprising her at every turn.

"We should go," he said, rising to his full height and taking her by the elbow to pull her up too. "We have been here too long already. I'll grab the—"

"I already got it all," Marian said, grabbing his arm before he returned to Taylor's chamber. She felt his muscles stiffen beneath her fingers as he realized what she had done.

His eyes went wide as he stared at her. "You did what? I told you to—"

"I know." There was little point in standing around arguing about it.

"Marian."

"Are we going to get out of here or let ourselves get caught by another mistreated servant?" she asked and gritted her teeth. "I thought you said we've been here too long." Was he really so put out by a disobeyed order? She would most certainly argue her case if it came to a confrontation.

But Robin snarled a little and led the way back to the library, and Marian breathed a sigh of relief. Arguing with him seemed more daunting a task than anything so far. There were more important things to worry about anyway. As Robin slipped out through the library window and landed gracefully on the ground below, Marian glanced back toward the dark corridor where Louisa had disappeared. How could she just leave that poor girl behind? What if she got into trouble?

"She will be all right," Robin said, and Marian looked down at him. How could he possibly know her thoughts? He smiled, the gesture just as soft for Marian as it had been for the child. For how infuriating he could be, the man was far too handsome for his own good. "I'll catch you," he added and held his arms out.

Well, that was just humiliating, and Marian shook her head, even if she knew it was foolish. If Robin could climb so easily out a window, so could she. The problem was maneuvering herself through the window when there was nowhere to put her feet once she got out there. She sat on the sill and twisted around so one foot dangled below her and she was looking into the room. If she could just find that same stone Robin had used to get himself up, perhaps she could—

A light suddenly appeared on the other side of the door, and Marian squeaked in alarm as she lost her grip on the windowsill and fell backward. For a moment there was nothing but air around her, and then she landed hard and found her face just a few inches from Robin's as he held her securely against his chest. He seemed about to laugh as he caught her gaze. This was nearly as close as he had gotten at the park, and he evidently enjoyed the intimacy far more than Marian did. She was wrong earlier; she did not like this playful side of him one bit.

"Put me down," she ordered.

"Of course, my lady." But he didn't move, his strong arms tight around her as he bent his head closer to hers.

Marian knew she should fight to free herself, but she was frozen in place. The look in his eyes seemed to speak volumes but in a language she did not understand. "What are you doing?" she whispered.

The corner of his mouth twitched. "I am thinking I might kiss you," he said.

With those words, Marian lost all defiance and thought she might faint. Robin was joking—she knew he was, with the way his eyes danced with amusement—but that did not make his nearness any less real. She could have lifted her head just an inch and touched her lips to his. For all the bravery she liked to think she had, the idea of actually kissing the man was utterly terrifying.

Her fear must have shown on her face, because his smile softened, and he set her back on her feet with a small apology that surprised her to no end. Maybe he was not as incorrigible as she thought. "Come," he said as he grabbed his hat and coat, "we should run," and he took hold of her hand, pulling her from the bushes and out onto the street.

And while she knew the importance of getting as far from Mr. Taylor's house as possible, Marian was having a hard time keeping up with Robin as he guided their mad dash through the dark streets of London. He was so tall that his long stride was nearly double hers, and she was unaccustomed to more than a brisk walk at most. Before long, she could hardly breathe and was sure she would stumble and fall flat on her face, Robin dragging her behind him without noticing. Finally, when she thought she could go no farther, he stopped at the edge of Hyde Park and pulled her into a dark bunch of trees.

"Rest for a spell," he said and stalked the length of the little grove, probably to make sure they were alone and hadn't been followed.

Marian grasped the nearest tree and did everything in her power not to collapse to the ground. The shoes she wore had started to pinch, her braid had slipped from her cap, and she felt altogether a wild mess as her heart beat in her chest as if it wanted to escape. And though she took several long, calming breaths, her heart did not seem to want to stop racing, and she was quickly realizing it was not just from their run.

She was positively buzzing with energy as the impact of what she had just done hit her square in the face. "I just robbed someone," she gasped.

Robin glanced at her from his lookout point and chuckled. "That you did. It is an exhilarating feeling, isn't it?"

Saying it out loud didn't make it feel any more real, so she plunged her hand into one of her pockets and found herself with a handful of jewels that most certainly were not hers. "I climbed through a window," she said, "and sneaked into a man's bedchamber, and I took his things. Right out from under his nose."

Snorting a laugh, Robin approached her and looked down at her little treasure trove. "It's not enough to hurt him financially, of course," he told her, "but it will most certainly cut his pride to the core. Well done, even if you didn't listen to me when I told you not to do it."

Marian scoffed. Why was he so bothered by what she had done? Taylor hadn't woken, and she was perfectly safe. "Where did you disappear to?" she asked as frustration bubbled up inside her. Robin was the actual thief, after all, and he should have been doing what she had done. "What was so important downstairs that you had to risk everything by separating?"

"Something far more valuable than you probably realize." Reaching into his pocket, he pulled out the most magnificent diamond necklace Marian had ever seen. Eight of the transparent jewels lined the setting, and a large pendant sat in the middle. She couldn't quite see the crest engraved on the pendant, not when it was this dark, but something told her it was important. "Rule number one of thievery: always go for the most important item first, as you have no idea how much time you will have. This is the Montgomery crest," Robin said.

Marian's head snapped up. "This belonged to the Duchess of Montgomery?" she asked in alarm. "But how did . . ." She swallowed when Robin gave her a pointed look. Her Grace was known throughout the *ton* as a woman most chaste and virtuous. She was generous to all and spent most of her time improving the lives of the poor, and everyone knew she was entirely devoted to her husband. Or perhaps not as devoted as she wanted everyone to believe.

"Her Grace is a good woman," Robin said, frowning down at the necklace, "but I believe Taylor somehow tricked her into giving him the necklace or obtained it by other means. His having it makes it seem as if she is among his conquests and gives him a good deal of notoriety among his friends. If I had known he would truly keep this in his drawing room, I would have gone in there long before now to save her from the embarrassment and shame."

Marian felt a chill run through her, and she hugged herself around the middle after stowing the jewelry she'd taken back in her pocket. She was not ignorant of the infidelity that often ran rampant among the Quality, but seeing firsthand its effects and consequences made all of it feel more real. She had never been more grateful that her parents seemed perfectly content to have each other.

"So what now?" she whispered, feeling the weight of so many indiscretions in her pockets. "What do we do with all of this?" She was not about to keep it and wear any of it herself. They might not have had identifying traits like the necklace Robin held, but she could imagine many a young lady recognizing her missing accessory, and that would only create suspicion about Marian's relation to Jason Taylor.

Smiling gently, Robin held out his hand. "I have a man who can redistribute the wealth," he said, and his fingers curled around the objects when Marian placed them on his palm. "These could feed a whole street for a month, maybe more. Come." Taking her hand again, he led her back out into the night at a much more manageable pace.

When they finally reached her family's house, Marian felt her exhaustion settle on her, heavy and thick, as her excitement dwindled. Now that the whole thing was over and she was back home, she feared it would all fade into a dream. She had not excelled at it, like she had hoped, but neither had she failed. She had calmed down Louisa before the girl got her caught, but she had almost gotten her into a lot of trouble by giving her the wrong thing.

Robin seemed to be thinking the same thing, frowning down at her as they approached the back door. "You have a lot to learn," he said, shaking his head. "But . . ." Apparently whatever he had to say was not easy, because he grimaced. "But not bad for your first run."

Marian grinned. "Was that a compliment?" she asked, surprised by how good it felt to have the man praise her. She would have preferred to care little about his good opinion, but instead she craved it. *How infuriating.*

Chuckling, he leaned against the doorframe beside her and looked down at his fingers as if he found something fascinating beneath his nails. "Don't go getting a big head," he said, "or you'll end up like me."

She hardly thought that was a bad thing. Despite his flaws, Lord Huntingdon was proving himself to be a man worth knowing. So far, no one else had managed that outside of her own family. But she said, "I certainly wouldn't want that. You are insufferable."

Robin's eyes flicked up to meet hers, and he slowly moved closer to where she stood. Would he never stop? "Insufferable?" he repeated. "Then, how is it you nearly kissed me outside Taylor's?"

"I did nothing of the sort." Marian tried to take a step back, but she had managed to trap herself against the wall. Very well. If she could not retreat, she would stand her ground. "Kindly keep your distance, sir. Will has been teaching me to fight, and I am not afraid to hit you."

"Has he now?" To her utter relief, he paused, though his grin only grew. "Are you afraid of a little kiss, Marian?" Truth be told, she was terrified, but she would never tell him that. "Because if you are going to be a thief," he continued, "you cannot let your fear dictate your decisions."

He was right, as always, and Marian scowled at him because he was far too intelligent for his own good. She could never get the upper hand with him. "You're telling me you fear nothing?" she asked.

"That is not what I said," he replied. "But I know how to get past my fears; can you say the same?"

All thoughts of trying to be brave left her as she considered his words. She had barely managed to steal Taylor's collection, and she had been lucky with Louisa. Could she really carry on without finding the same courage Robin seemed to possess? "How do you do it?" she said, frowning up at him. "How do you stop being afraid?"

He leaned closer again, but this time it was not with the teasing glint in his eyes. He was serious now, and his nearness seemed to emphasize his point as he said, "You have to remember *why* you are doing it. Who you are doing it for. This job is not about you or me or the people we take from. It's about the people we can help. Remember that, and you will make it through anything." He reached out and brushed a bit of hair from her face, pushing it behind her ear. Despite the night, his fingers were warm. He opened his mouth again, but whatever he was going to say got stuck in his throat, and he sighed before he took a step back and gave her some space again. "Good night, Tuck," he said. Then he grinned, stunning Marian with that dashing smile that a thief should never be able to manage, and he disappeared into the night.

CHAPTER *Seven*

ROB RECEIVED THE NOTE AT half past nine in the evening, and at first glance, he nearly threw it away, as he did most correspondence that came from Town. It was always invitations from ladies hoping to get him to spend time with their daughters, or fellow peers who wanted to be able to say they were among the few privileged to be a friend to the Elusive Earl of Huntingdon. There were wealthier and more prestigious men than him in London during the Season, but for some reason, Rob had become a highly sought-after target among high Society.

He usually tossed such correspondence straight into the fire without reading it. But tonight, he caught the name on the parchment and paused, smiling despite himself. The note, apparently, came from a Miss Clumsy.

"Marian," he muttered to himself and opened the note with interest. It was a good deal more intriguing than reading through the report his man of business had sent him. He had far too much work to do with the Huntingdon estate, but this missive grabbed his full attention.

There were only a few words written on the paper in an elegant hand, but they induced several different reactions at once.

> *I am going to be picking the lock at Huntingdon Manor at midnight tonight. Help me or don't.*

Rob read the note through three times before he was sure he had read it right, and annoyance was the first emotion to creep up. What did she think she was doing, wandering the streets so late at night? And if someone saw her trying to break into his house? She was going to get herself caught or worse. But then he smiled again, shaking his head as he began pacing the library, where he had sequestered himself for the evening. It had been less than twenty-four hours since their foray into Taylor's home, and Marian had clearly enjoyed her taste of wrongdoing.

Then worry filtered into Rob's gut as he realized what that meant. She was not going to let it go. He had hoped bringing her to Taylor's would convince her that it was too dangerous to do the things he did. That she would find a different way to help the poor, one more suitable to a lady of her status. But, of course, he had not been so fortunate, and Marian Russell was quickly proving to be a more determined woman than he had anticipated.

Scaring her off with his advances hadn't worked either, but he had a feeling he had known from the beginning that tactic would not actually work. Nearly kissing a lady to keep her away? What a foolish plan that had been. He could still feel the softness of her cheek where his fingers had brushed her skin. And it had not been fear in her eyes, though he had no clue what she had actually felt. He couldn't read Marian as well as he could read everyone else, and that drove him mad.

Glancing at his pocket watch, Rob quickly sorted through his options, lining them up one by one inside his head so he could examine them all with equal attention. He could send a return note telling her that she was to stay at home. But what if one of her parents intercepted it? He would be expected to make her an offer. That wouldn't do.

He could go to Lord Waverly's house in disguise and sneak into her chamber to warn her not to put herself in danger. But that would likely get him attacked, and he was not about to retaliate if Marian got it into her head that she should fight him. He had seen the penknife she'd grabbed from Taylor's library, and he could imagine the little knife would offer plenty of sting with Marian wielding it.

Rob groaned as he stopped his pacing. He would have to let her come. That opened up two other routes of action, neither of which he liked much. Either he could let her try to get through the lock on her own and spend her night frustrated, or he could teach her what to do. The first posed the risk of her getting caught. The second posed the risk of him further toying with the idea of Marian joining him and John as a thief.

Of the two, Rob preferred the latter, though it was not a particularly safe choice. At least, if he included her in his late-night adventures, he could keep an eye on her. She was likely too stubborn to give up easily on her own, and Rob would feel inordinately guilty if something happened to her through his inaction.

How had she managed to back him into a corner with no good escape? She was intelligent, and Rob liked her all the more for it.

By the time midnight rolled around, he was still pacing in the library and searching for the right choice. He was never so indecisive—quick thinking was a crucial skill for a thief—and his head had begun to hurt from the constant circles his thoughts pulled him through. But the time for deciding had passed, and Rob made a first choice, however small it was. He was going to make his way outside and watch her attempt to get through the lock. From there, he would hopefully have enough information to make a final decision and put the matter to bed so he could go to bed himself.

He took the front door, figuring Marian was intelligent enough to try to get through the back, where she was less likely to be seen, and he paused. A fog had come in, and he took a deep breath of the night air. Most people preferred clear skies; Rob liked the cover poor weather offered.

He didn't bother sneaking around; the fog was thick enough that if anyone did venture out in this weather so late, they would not be watching for ne'er-do-wells because they likely were themselves. He walked casually, his hands tucked behind his back, and was tempted to start whistling, just to see what Marian would do. He refrained, however, and he was infinitely glad he did when a soft curse reached his ears through the mist. Marian, it seemed, had a more colorful vocabulary than he would have guessed.

Peeking his head around the corner of the house nearest the back door, he fought a laugh when he found the trouser-clad young woman kneeling at the door with a couple of sticks stuffed into the lock. She would never get the door open that way, but he had to acknowledge her determination. She kept wiggling her two sticks around and muttering angry words under her breath until one twig snapped and made her jump.

"It seems I have caught myself a thief," Rob said.

Marian only just stifled her scream, though she could not prevent herself collapsing to the ground in her fright. "Rob!" she gasped when she caught sight of him leaning against the house.

He folded his arms and raised an eyebrow. "It is far too easy to startle you, Marian," he muttered. "If nothing else, you should have been expecting me. But what was your plan going to be if I did not show up?" He almost wished he had stayed inside to see for himself.

Marian likely blushed since she turned her head down to hide her face. "I had not thought it through that far," she admitted.

"And what made you think I would not get angry and try to have you arrested?"

She looked up again, and apparently realizing she was still sitting on the ground, she scrambled back to her feet. When her eyes met Rob's, however, she ducked her head again. "I thought, seeing as you brought me with you last night, you were on my side. I would not have let you take me if you weren't. Like I said yesterday, Will has been teaching me to fight."

Her cousin didn't look like he had fought anything in his life. From the little Rob had listened to gossip, he knew the man had been a soldier, but Mr. Russell's demeanor was nothing of the sort. He was far too quiet and gentle for a military life, so in a way, his unexpected inheritance must have been a blessing. But teaching Marian to fight? She needed someone who actually knew what he was doing.

"You'll never get a lock open that way," he said and nodded toward the stick still jutting from inside it. "You need something stronger." Reaching into a hidden pocket in his waistcoat, he pulled out the pair of lockpicks he had made for himself years ago and held them out to her. "Try these. Use one to hold the lever and the other to turn the bolt."

Marian stared at him as if he had just spoken gibberish.

"What?" he asked. "You thought you could wiggle things around until it opened? These are meant to mimic the key." Holding one in each hand, he demonstrated the motions she would need to do to open the lock. With his right hand, he lifted an imaginary lever up, then twisted the tool in his left hand. "Simple," he said and placed them in her hands.

She still looked bewildered, but at least she bent down and stuck both tools into the keyhole to make an attempt. Within a few seconds, though, she was back to wiggling them around like she had the sticks.

"No, like this." Rob grabbed hold of the picks but froze when his hands wrapped around Marian's. Her fingers were tiny. Warm. *Focus, Rob.* Her hands had been distracting enough last night as they ran, and he did not need to pay attention to them now. Clearing his throat, he released her hands, then demonstrated what he was trying to tell her. "I learned by feel," he said, and his voice came out a bit strained. *Ridiculous.* "I was only a child, so I didn't have anyone to walk me through it. I just had to practice until I managed to learn the trick." With only a moment of fiddling, the lock clicked, and Rob slowly pushed the door open and gave Marian a little smile before pulling it closed again.

She seemed torn between annoyance and awe, which was quite a fun place for Rob to be as he watched her. "You were only a child?" she asked.

He nodded. "Maybe eleven years old. The man my mother was working for paid her only half of what he agreed upon for her wages, and no amount of pleading on her part could sway him in our favor."

"So you took matters into your own hands," Marian guessed and smiled.

She was terrible at lock-picking and pretty much every other aspect of thievery, but she most certainly knew how to smile.

It took several long seconds of silence for Rob to realize he was staring at her, and he cleared his throat again and looked away before she read into his gaze. There was nothing more to this relationship than strictly business, after all.

Handing over the lockpicks again, Rob folded his arms and leaned against the wall. "You try," he said. "See if you can feel the mechanism inside the lock."

"But it is not locked now."

"I know. I just want you to feel what it should be like when it is open so you have a place to go."

Marian bent down to the level of the lock again and pushed the picks into the hole, and within two seconds her tongue slid out between her lips as she concentrated. Rob bit his lip before he laughed—he highly doubted she would appreciate being teased for that—and was grateful when she struck up conversation again and removed the distraction.

"Does your family know about what you do at night?" she asked.

"If they do," he replied, "they are being awfully supportive. But I have not told them, and I don't plan to unless I have to. It's better if I keep them far from the danger this double life puts me in. I think my mother would die of shock if she found out."

"If my mother ever found out I was wearing trousers and picking locks, she would probably lock me in my room and not let me leave unless I had a prospective husband come calling. Although, assuming this lesson goes according to plan, I could just free myself and not have to fret about it." Apparently satisfied with her probing, Marian straightened again and held out the lockpicks in her open palm. "I probably just need to practice on my own," she decided out loud.

Rob didn't move. He worried what he might do with his hands if he did. "So keep the tools," he said.

"Oh, I don't—"

"Keep them, Marian." He loved how easily she blushed, even though it was difficult to see in the darkness. At some point he would have to spend more time with her in daylight just so he could see the pink rise up in her cheeks.

"Well then." She hesitantly put the picks into her coat pocket, then glanced at the fog around them. "I suppose I should go back home," she said.

That was for the best. Rob needed to get some sleep since he had been out the night before. He still had appearances to keep up, as did Marian, not to mention a good deal of work he had been neglecting as an earl. "I should probably teach you how to fight," he said, then grimaced because that was a terrible idea.

But Marian perked up. "But I told you Will is already teaching me," she said, though she was far too eager for her argument to have any strength in it.

A young lady who wanted to know how to fight? She was certainly one of a kind. And if she already knew the basics, Rob would do better to let her go back home. "Let's go inside where it's warmer," he said, then clenched his hands into fists. He really was making a mess of this whole thing. "You need a proper teacher."

As he expected, Marian followed him straightaway and stayed right on his heels until they reached the little ballroom inside Huntingdon Manor. "You think you are better than a soldier?" she asked.

Rob laughed. "That soldier has the temperament of a sleepy kitten," he said as he closed the doors behind him. The room was smaller than most ballrooms, but it provided enough space for them to work without bumping into things and waking someone up. Both their reputations hung on not being discovered. It was a touch too dark, though, and the room felt even smaller when he could not see her well.

He could certainly feel her presence, which was unnerving.

Finding flint and steel in a drawer, he lit a few candles and placed them around the room. *Better.*

"Now," he said and turned to the lady, who was nearly bouncing on the balls of her feet because she was so excited. "What has that cousin of yours taught you so far?"

She grinned. "He taught me to know my enemy's weak points," she said. "So most men are easy."

Rob made a mental note to keep his guard up whenever he was around her. "Do you know how to throw a punch?"

She scoffed. "Of course."

Well, that was something he simply had to see. "Show me," he said, trying not to sound too eager.

For some reason, that request caught her off guard, and she cocked her head to the side. "You want me to hit you?" she asked, a hint of alarm in her words.

Rob chuckled. "Hit my hand," he said and held his palm out to her. "I just want to see if the kitten soldier knows what he's doing."

Though she frowned, as if she had lost all her confidence, Marian took a deep breath, then nodded. "I do not want to hurt you," she warned.

Rob just smirked.

With the fierceness of a child playing war games, she balled up her fist and slammed it into Rob's hand. "Well?" she asked immediately.

He had to bite his lip before he burst out laughing and woke the whole house. "Well," he said, "my sister was stronger than that when she was ten. You will have to do better than that if you ever hope to defend yourself."

"You think I will have the need?" To her credit, the question was more out of curiosity than of fear.

Rob shrugged and held his hand out again. "It is better to be prepared for the worst and hope you never have to face it," he said. "Try again, but this time use more of your shoulder. You have a whole arm; use it."

Marian's second punch had more force than the first, but the difference was marginal. When she caught sight of Rob's frown, she matched it. "Will told me I was getting better," she said.

"Then, I would hate to know how you were when you started. Put some power into it, Marian."

She tried.

"Pretend you're fending off an attacker and put everything you've got into it."

"You are not helping," she growled, but her hit had more strength in it this time. Her anger helped, but she couldn't rely on that.

Rob needed to see what she was doing wrong. She was small, but not so small that she could not do better. There had to be something he was missing. Something holding her back. "Come closer to the light," he instructed, leading her along with him so they were closer to the candles. He held up his hand once more. "I want to better watch what you're doing."

Marian gritted her teeth and curled her fingers as tightly as she could. "You know," she muttered, "I do not know what me doing this over and over will prove if you do not do some actual teaching."

"Just hit me, Marian."

"Happily."

Rob watched as she went through the movement, slowing it down in his head as she shoved her fist into his palm again and hardly knocked his hand back. She pulled her arm back a little too far to begin with, maybe, but it gave her room to move forward, so that wasn't it. She probably had little muscle in her arms after living a life of leisure, but Alana had not had strength either when he'd taught her, and she had managed a better punch than this. Maybe it was Marian's feet, which remained motionless on the floor. She did not have full movement of her body when she hit, and that limited her to only a portion of her strength. Yes, that was it.

"Think of your arm as an extension of the rest of your body," Rob said and put one hand on her elbow, the other on her shoulder. "When you move, you need to think not just of what your arm is doing but the rest of you as well." He gently pulled her arm forward, at the same time nudging the heel of her right foot to twist out at the same time. "Your strength comes from here," he said and moved one hand to her waist, "and here."

Then he froze.

This was not his sister he was instructing. This was a near stranger, one whose family outranked his and who had more to lose than he did by standing there in that ballroom in the dark. And though he knew he should distance himself and return to a hands-off approach, he remained rooted to the spot with his palm pressed against her waist and his other hand on her shoulder.

Marian turned her head to look up at him, and in the dim light it was hard to judge what her expression meant. Did she want him to leave? To stay? To run upstairs and pretend the night had never happened?

He was leaning toward that third option.

"So how do I wield this hidden strength of mine?" she asked.

It may have been his imagination, but he was pretty sure she leaned closer. They were only a few inches apart, and Rob had apparently forgotten how to breathe. It was not like he hadn't been close to her like this before. He had teased her plenty of times and nearly kissed her more than once. But something had changed, and his whole body felt on fire as he held her.

He was wrong. Her strength was in her hazel eyes, a mixture of brown and green. She could command armies with those eyes.

"You twist," he said after what felt like an eternity of simply gazing at her. His voice came out rough, and he cleared his throat and forced himself to step back and break the contact. He was acting ridiculous, and there was nothing different about this situation than any other. "Move your whole body and pivot your foot just before punching."

"Like this?"

Rob barely got his hand up in time, and when Marian's fist collided with his palm with a definitive force that left his fingers tingling, he grinned. "Exactly like that," he said. "Maybe we'll make you a decent thief yet, Tuck."

She laughed, and the sound sparked an even stronger heat inside Rob's chest. "That is a ridiculous name," she said. "I am sure I could come up with something better."

Rob did not doubt it, but he had already assigned the name to her in his head. Even if she thought up a different moniker, he would have a hard time thinking of her as anything else. Except maybe Marian . . . That name fit her so well that he hardly wanted her to have a nickname to begin with.

"I suppose anything is better than Miss Clumsy," she added, then ducked her head as if to hide an embarrassed blush again. She sounded almost miserable, as if that nickname alone was enough to keep her from becoming the compassionate thief she clearly wanted to be.

If Rob had known what this woman was really like, he never would have given her such a name back at the Bow and Crown. "You are not clumsy," he said, though it was a downright lie. "You just need to practice." That sounded better, at least. He wanted her to smile though. To return to that confidence she so often had in herself. It had been in full force tonight, and he had killed it by inadvertently reminding her he had called her clumsy. "You certainly have the potential to be a fabulous pugilist," he decided on. Then he made a show of shaking out the pain in his hand, even though it was a long while after the tingling had disappeared.

She snorted a little laugh, and that blessed smile spread across her lips as she looked back up at him. "I do not," she said, "but thank you. I suppose I should let you go to bed now. I have stolen enough of your time."

That was for the best. "You don't have to leave," Rob said, then grimaced again. How was it his mouth was so intent on ignoring his head? He needed to take control over himself before he said something truly stupid. "But you should probably get your rest," he added. "You were out late last night as well."

Exhaustion seemed to suddenly weigh her down, as if she had not even realized she could be tired until he pointed it out. She still smiled, though, which was nice. She didn't take his comment as a dismissal but as genuine concern. At the very least, he was getting better at avoiding accidental insults.

"You are right," she said and let out a heavy sigh. "I cannot practice fighting if I do not get any sleep." There was a bit of a twinkle in her eyes, and Rob laughed as he led the way to the back door again.

When he stepped outside with her, Rob saw the confusion in her eyes before she even opened her mouth. "I'll walk you home," he explained.

"You don't have to—"

"Marian. It was bad enough that I let you come on your own. You can't expect me to sit idly by while you wander the streets of London alone."

Though she looked ready to argue, Marian was intelligent enough to know when her battle was a losing one. "Very well," she said, almost on a sigh. "Though, you're the one who said I have the makings of a pugilist." She took his arm, and Rob did his best to ignore the thrill her touch gave him.

"Even fighters get attacked in the middle of the night," he replied. "Let me make sure you return safely, Marian. For my own sanity."

They were both quiet the whole walk back to her home, but Rob didn't mind the silence. He was used to it, even if he wasn't used to sharing it with someone as beautiful as Marian Russell.

When they reached the servants' door, which must have been left unlocked for her, Rob reluctantly released her arm and took a step back. "Don't stay up too late fiddling with your lock," he said.

She surprised him by throwing her arms around his shoulders. The embrace was brief, but it left him stunned. "Thank you," she said again. "I know you haven't any good reasons to be helping me, so I am immeasurably grateful. I can do this, Rob. I know I can."

He had no doubt she could, and as he watched her disappear into the house, he decided Marian could do just about anything she wished.

CHAPTER *Eight*

"Confound it all." Rob had just read the same line in the *Times* four times and had not understood a word of it. He tossed the paper aside before he drove himself mad. Not for the first time, he was glad he had earned himself a quiet corner of White's without ever being bothered by the many gentlemen who hoped to be called his friend simply for the sake of befriending an earl, particularly an antisocial one. He had refused enough people over the years that they had stopped trying, and that meant he could glare at the table and not worry about needing to explain himself. Somehow, his inability to focus was only getting worse, and he had a feeling that was not going to change anytime soon.

Not now that he had started planning robberies with Marian in mind.

It was ridiculous, including her in his mission. She was unskilled and untrained, and she was far too small to pull herself up through windows and jump walls when making a quick getaway. She could barely crawl through a bush without waking the whole neighborhood, for heaven's sake, and yet . . .

Rob glanced at the paper again and smiled when he caught sight of the announcement that Jason Taylor had been robbed. Taylor had refused to give a detailed sum of his losses, but he had clearly wanted to make it known that he had, in fact, been stolen from. And Rob had not seen him once in the two days since, which was an odd sort of thing. Taylor liked to make his presence known, as he was not titled and had no other way to gain recognition than garnering it himself and with his money. There was nothing quite so satisfying as knowing Rob—and subsequently Marian—had managed to drive the cad into hiding for a while.

Marian had done that. He had been doing a grand job of ignoring it, for the most part, but Rob still could not believe she had had the bravery to stay in Taylor's *bedchamber*, of all places, simply to cut the man down a few pegs. He did not approve of her choice in the least, but she had a courage in her he hadn't seen in anyone before. Add to that her precociousness when she'd tried to break into his own house, and Marian was turning out to be far more than he could have expected.

He also thought about her far more than he should.

"May I sit, my lord?"

Rob had never been uncivil, but he considered it when a timid voice spoke that question. Perhaps the *ton* had not learned to avoid him after all. But when he looked up, the man standing warily nearby caught him by surprise, so he found himself nodding his assent. It was the sleepy-kitten soldier, Marian's cousin.

The whole of the club behind Russell stared in wide-eyed amazement as the young man took a seat. Rob considered pretending he was thrilled to have the company to put them in an absolute uproar, but he doubted he could make it look fully genuine. This may have been Marian's cousin, but that didn't mean Rob had to like him. He had met soldiers before, and few of them had given him any reason to be impressed.

"Mr. Russell, yes?" he said.

Russell nodded, though he seemed a bit too distracted by something to have any idea what whispers had started up behind him. He rolled his hat in his hands and kept his eyes on the floor. "Yes, my lord. I am, ah, Lady Marian's cousin."

"Indeed. What can I do for you, sir?"

Scoffing, he gave Rob something close to a scowl. "I wish you wouldn't call me that, my lord," he muttered.

Rob fought against a smile. So the soldier was not fond of his new impending rank, was he? This was the man who was set to inherit the marquessate of Waverly and all the accompanying titles when Marian's father passed. Anyone else in his position would have insisted on receiving whatever esteem he was due, even if he had no honorary title to claim until he inherited. Interestingly, it seemed where Marian was all fire and indignancy, young Russell was humility and reticence. How did the pair get along as well as they did?

"You will not be able to run from your title forever," Rob said, raising one eyebrow.

A bit of defiance flitted in the man's eyes. "Perhaps not," he said, "but until then . . ." He took a deep breath. "I, er, I hoped I could talk with you this morning, if you are not otherwise engaged, my lord. But I see you are reading the paper, so perhaps I should—"

"You want to talk?" Rob reclined in his chair a bit, hoping the casual manner in which he sat would put the poor man at ease. He was intrigued by this fumbling conversation, to say the least, and it was a welcome distraction from his near-constant thoughts of Marian. "What about?"

"Nothing in particular." Russell shrugged.

Rob did not believe that for a moment, and he sighed. "You want to talk about Lady Marian," he guessed. *So much for avoiding her . . .*

Russell's head snapped up, his face red up to the tips of his ears. He was a rather young man, maybe twenty-two or twenty-three, but if he truly had been in the military, surely he would not be this skittish. "Lady Marian?" he stammered and gripped his hat a little tighter. "I, well, it is not really my place to . . ."

Pity was not something Rob was unused to feeling, but he generally reserved it for the poor and depraved. The fact that he felt it now for a peer-to-be made him wonder what kind of life young Russell had had before now and what kind of man that life had turned him into. Rob had seen the way he acted with Marian and had gotten quite the glare when they'd taken their drive in the park, which would have surprised him more if he had not predicted already how protective the young man was of his cousin.

"You want to know what my intentions are with your cousin," he guessed again.

Russell nodded, apparently accepting his sudden inability to find his voice. Perhaps taciturnity was a common state for the man.

Unfortunately, Rob did not have an answer. At least, not one he could give here. If Marian had spoken true the other night, Mr. Russell did not know about her adventure inside Jason Taylor's house, so most likely he was wondering if Rob intended to court the lady. Maybe if she didn't drive him absolutely crazy, Rob might have considered it, but . . .

Marriage was not high on his list of future accomplishments. In fact, he was not sure it was on the list at all.

"What exactly is your concern?" he asked instead of answering the question. Even mentioning the topic inside this particular club could lead to far more gossip than Rob needed.

Mr. Russell was back to strangling his hat, and Rob fought back a chuckle. The nervous habit was one he knew all too well. "I love my cousin as dearly as if she were my sister," the man said quietly. But then he looked up, and there was a bit of steel in his gaze. Surprising. "And Marian would make a good match for anyone. But I plan to see to it that her husband is her equal if I can."

Rob sat up a bit straighter. That was quite the statement. An earl was not *that* much lower than a marquess, so there was likely another motive behind Russell's words. "Meaning?" he pressed.

Mr. Russell swallowed but spoke more strongly than before. "Meaning the man who wins her hand has to add to the world, not just exist in it."

Biting back a smile, Rob looked the man over and found a plan forming in his head, almost on its own. *Perhaps there is more to William Russell than meets the eye*, he thought. "I am hosting a dinner party tonight," he said loudly, even though he had not planned to do anything of the sort. Alana would be thrilled, assuming anyone actually showed up on such short notice. "I would like you to come. I think you and I could do a lot for each other."

Rob rose to his feet and bowed quickly to Russell, who sat too stunned to react, and he could not stop himself from smiling as he passed a couple dozen men who were realizing they had never once been invited to a dinner party by the Earl of Huntingdon, and yet a nobody who was only to be wealthy by circumstance had garnered an invitation within minutes of knowing him.

The gossip column would explode tomorrow, but Rob didn't much care. He wanted to know exactly the sort of man William Russell was because he had a feeling the man would prove to be an invaluable ally in his war against the rich.

"You have been acting strangely all week, Robin Loxley, and I want to know why." Alana had been following him around the house for the last half hour, doing everything she could to get a straight answer out of him. She had apparently forgotten that he was just as stubborn as she was, if not more so. "You hate dinner parties, and you have never once let us host one here because then you cannot escape."

"Why should I want to escape?" Rob asked and looked into the drawing room, which was cleaner and brighter than he'd ever seen it. The servants seemed just as excited as Alana had been when he announced his intentions, and it warmed his heart to see them all so happy. Maybe he should have given them more to do over the years, but he had thought a light workload was the best thing for them. From what he had seen this afternoon, they far better liked being productive and appreciated. "It looks wonderful, Mrs. Keller," he told the housekeeper, who blushed at his words. "Truly."

Alana latched on to his arm like she had when they were children. She was a good seven years younger than him, so he had always let her hang from his arm as if he were a tree branch she could swing from, since living on farmland hadn't provided many actual trees. She was far too tall to do it now, but that didn't stop her from making the familiar action. "Robin," she whined.

Rob laughed and kissed her cheek. "Maybe I have finally seen the error of my ways," he said.

"Do not tease me. You hate social gatherings."

"But you do not," he replied, though he was not fond of the fact that he was having this same argument with her again. Could she not just let him throw expectation to the wind without questioning every move he made? "Think of this as practice for your future life as mistress of a household," he said.

That got her to release him and stand openmouthed as he made his way down to the kitchens. He was in a better mood than he had been in for a long time, and it seemed to be uprooting his sister's conceptions of him. He did not mind, especially when she was as excited as she was for the evening's events. He was just as eager, though he did feel a bit sorry about what would unfold later in the evening. It would not be a perfect night, but he hoped it would go well enough for the both of them, despite their very different plans.

Alana wanted to host a perfect dinner party. Rob wanted to see what Will Russell did under pressure.

"John!" Rob called his valet's name as he entered the kitchen and found the boy almost smiling as he talked with one of the maids. At the sound of his name, however, John started and turned quite red as the girl scurried away. Rob raised an eyebrow, but he decided he had best not say anything about it. John so rarely showed an interest in anything. "Is everything set for tonight?" he asked.

John nodded, though still apparently embarrassed, as it took him a moment to compose himself and say, "I moved the locket to the drawing room like you said, and it'll be easy to nab, sure enough."

"Good lad." Heavens, with everything that had happened with Marian and now this, Rob couldn't remember ever smiling so much. He should have laid more schemes long before now. "I will cause a distraction after dinner, but you have to be sure no one sees you. That is very important."

John puffed out his chest, making himself look rather sure of his abilities. On the rare occasions he showed any emotion, it was often overblown and humorous. "Ain't no better thief than me. You know that, Rob."

Rob did know that. The only reason he had taken the boy into his employ was *because* he'd been stealing. That day felt like ages ago, though it had been only four years, and Rob could hardly believe little John was already sixteen and growing by the day. He had hired the lad to get him off the streets, never suspecting he would come to consider him a dear friend. He highly doubted anyone else was as close to their servant as Rob had become to his.

Except maybe Marian and her maid, he thought with a wry smile.

"Guests should be coming soon," he said, forcing himself to forget the young woman, at least as much as he could forget her. The difficulty of the thing had really started to irk him. "Be ready, John."

"Aye, I will."

Rob made it back up to the entrance hall just as a knock sounded with the arrival of the first attendee. As Mr. Hoskins, the butler, went to open the door, Rob slid to a halt just behind Alana and his mother, choosing to let them be the primary hosts of the evening. He hardly knew how to host a social event anyway, and the Loxley ladies were both determined to prove they had the skills he lacked. He really should have allowed them more opportunity over the years.

Beaming with pleasure, both women greeted their guests with enthusiasm as they arrived. Though most of them bowed to Rob and attempted conversation, he deftly steered their attention back to his family and kept his focus on the door. He really only cared about one of the invitees, and the whole night depended on whether young William Russell was brave enough to attend.

A few of Alana's friends arrived first with their mothers—the elder paid more attention to Rob and his mother while the younger were content to talk to Alana—and were soon after followed by the few gentlemen he could stand to spend any length of time with. He did his best to be friendly since technically he was the one who had sent out the invitations, but Rob grew increasingly anxious as he followed his sister and mother into the drawing room, until Mr. Russell finally arrived just a few minutes before dinner was supposed to begin.

"I am so sorry for being late, my lord," Russell said, bowing low when he reached the earl. "I don't have any good excuses, unfortunately." He glanced around the drawing room, apparently searching for someone, and he seemed to dim when he didn't find them.

"I believe Lord Waverly and his family had a prior engagement," Rob said, guessing at the object of his search. In other words, Rob hadn't invited them. He had to focus tonight, after all, and play his part well if he wanted this to work. That would be impossible if Marian were nearby. "Have you met my sister, Miss Loxley? Alana, this is my friend Mr. William Russell."

Alana was all gracious smiles; Russell was entirely in awe and barely managed a proper bow as his eyes took in Rob's sister. "My lady," he said, his voice timid.

"Mr. Russell," she returned, a spark of amusement in her eyes that said she had probably caught Russell's anxiety as easily as Rob had. "I do not believe I have ever met a friend of my brother's. You must be something special."

Rob worried the man wouldn't ever find his tongue again, but he wasn't sure how he could help the situation. Not when Alana was as charming as she was beautiful. No man was safe when she smiled like that. Thankfully, Mr. Eldridge caught his attention, so he did not have to stand by awkwardly and silently watch the pair of them carry on.

"Is this a new addition to your decor, Huntingdon?" Eldridge asked. He pointed to the mantel, where John had dutifully displayed on a small pillow the locket that would be at the crux of the evening's entertainment.

Smiling, Rob approached the man and looked every bit as casual as he could manage. "Indeed," he said. "It has been in the family for seven generations now, and I found it tucked away in some odd corner of the country house, gathering dust." That was not exactly true. The locket was old, but it had come from his mother's side and wasn't worth a penny outside of pure sentimental value. His mother had been kind enough to lend it to him, even if she did not know the reason he would want to display such a trinket.

"It is truly quite beautiful," Eldridge muttered and touched the chain of it with his finger. "Is it valuable?"

Rob kept his expression aloof. Eldridge was unknowingly laying the scene quite spectacularly. The whole room was paying attention now, exactly as he wanted them to. "It is worth quite a lot to my family," he said and shot a casual glance at Mr. Russell. The young man seemed as interested as anyone, but no more so.

Just then, Hoskins stepped into the room and cleared his throat before announcing dinner and pulling the crowd's attention away from the locket.

Dinner passed without incident. Mother was quiet at the other end of the table, as always, and Mr. Norrington, who had been acquainted with the family for some time, was plenty loud to make up for her reticence. Rob had never much liked the man because he tended to think himself more important than he was, but the man had been a helpful resource when Rob first became an earl, so he grudgingly kept up the relationship. Alana and her friends shared little looks and giggles, and the gentlemen among them seemed thrilled to have the honor of being near them. Rob spent most of dinner watching Mr. Russell, who ate just enough to be polite but didn't seem to have much of an appetite.

"Is it true that there have been more robberies of late?" a Miss Young asked, directing the question to Rob and catching him by surprise. Generally, people didn't talk to him unless he spoke first, and he was nearly on the other end of the table from Miss Young. But judging by the pinkness in Alana's cheeks, she had been the one to suggest Miss Young's bold move. His sister confirmed it when she could not fully hide the mischievous smile that played at her lips.

Rob smiled a bit. Even if Alana was trying to catch him off guard and see if he stumbled in forced interaction, he liked being considered an authority on actual news such as this rather than simple gossip. "There have been several these last few months," he said, "but I believe that can be attributed to the fact that most of high Society is in Town for the Season. Simple correlation."

His robberies *had* been somewhat prolific as late, though, what with Frank Melbourne's comment about Marian at the ball last week and Mrs. Pitt and Mr. Taylor proving themselves particularly horrible. He liked to keep his thefts to one or two a month when he could, just to keep up the threat but not risk exposing himself.

"Should we all be afraid of being next?" Miss Young continued.

Every eye turned to Rob, and he shrugged a shoulder. "I suppose. There does not seem to be much of a pattern, however, so it is difficult to guess where the thief might strike next."

"You think it is one man, then?" It was Mr. Russell who asked this question, though he seemed just as surprised as anyone that he had pushed himself into the conversation, and his eyes dropped down to his plate.

"I think there is someone out there who thinks he is better than the lot of us and wants to play judge and jury," Rob said. "He is likely a fool. But however imbecilic he may be, I do not think he is foolish enough to set his target too high. The likes of us, Mr. Russell—an earl and an heir to a marquessate, if you will—are far too lofty for him to risk his life unless his motivation is strong enough to raise the stakes higher than they are now."

"So you think you are above a thief who obviously has the upper hand," Russell surmised, and it seemed he did not like the taste of those words in his mouth as he frowned across the table. Clearly, he was not impressed by Rob's feigned confidence. In fact, he rather seemed to abhor it. There was still that second thief out there, the one who had gone after Howard Tilby. Could it possibly be young Mr. Russell?

Rob was probably pushing things too far, but this was more fun than he'd had in a long time. "Am I not above him?" he asked and lifted his wineglass into the air, almost in a toast.

Alana and his mother were giving him strange looks, probably wondering why he was suddenly so high in the instep, but the rest of the gathering looked on with something akin to awe. Rob knew he had been a bit of an enigma ever since his entrance into Society when he was eighteen, and he had managed to turn himself into a successful and wealthy earl without the lifetime of education most of the nobility received. It was the confidence that sold the part, he was sure, but he had never been cocky. He was pushing the line between protecting his secret night life and becoming the sort of person he loathed.

Coughing a bit, Rob signaled to the servants to begin clearing the last of the meal. "Shall we?" he said and gestured for the men to join him while the ladies went to the drawing room. He would make conversation for as long as formality required, but he was far too eager for the rest of the evening to unfold for him to remain with the men for long. Besides, Mr. Russell didn't talk to a soul; the poor man could endure only so much humiliation in one evening, and the night had just begun. Better to move on with things.

Just as it was supposed to be, the locket was still prominently in place when he and the other gentlemen returned from their port. After asking if Mr. Norrington had seen the locket, to make sure others had seen it still sitting there, Rob took to his stage on the other end of the room, determined to command the attention of all his guests. To his delight, Russell lingered at the back—very close to the locket, in fact. He was a tad *too* close, but Rob had faith in John's ability to slip in and out of the room undetected.

Clearing his throat loudly, he waited for conversation to die down and then offered the party a look of deep thought. "You know," he said, sounding as much like a puffed-up dandy as he could without actually looking like one, "I think we might owe this thief our gratitude."

Alana was the first to express the confusion many of the others wore on their expressions. "And why is that, Brother?"

Rob winked at her. "Because he has given some of us quite the distinction," he explained. John poked his head through one of the doors, so Rob spoke just a little louder as he continued. "I have been thinking all night," he said, "and I do believe I was wrong when I said the thief has no pattern."

"What pattern might he have, my lord?" Mr. Norrington asked.

"He goes after those of polite Society who are wealthy enough to take notice of but not so much that he risks—"

"You said this at dinner," Alana said, looking at him as if she had never seen anything more ridiculous. She was not as easily fooled as her guests, so Rob would have to be careful.

"Did I?" he asked.

Murmurs confirmed as much, and Rob had to admit he was impressed. So they were cleverer than he thought. "Yes, well, there must be something to the theory," he continued. "Take Mr. Norrington, for example. Has he been robbed?"

Norrington puffed out his chest. "I most certainly have not."

"And, Miss Young, I do believe your pin money has been safe so far."

She giggled, turning a bit pink. "It has, my lord."

Rob's mother was giving him a strange look from her seat by the window, and she seemed to know he was up to something. At least she looked more amused than concerned, and he hoped she did not mess things up by pointing out his insincerity. He had never been very good at lying to his mother, and she watched him, waiting to see what he did next.

"And then there is me," Rob said, standing a little taller and waving his arm toward the mantel. "I have a priceless artifact of tradition clearly on display, and the thief hasn't given a thought to—" He stopped and widened his eyes, though he was as much tempted to laugh as he was to look as horrified as he needed to. This whole thing was ridiculous.

But Alana gasped when she turned to match Rob's gaze, and her shock rippled through the rest of the guests as they came to the same realization: the locket was gone.

"Stolen," Rob whispered and let his stance waver as if he had lost his strength. "It was there when we came into the room. I saw it right there." Then he shifted into righteous anger as he took in the white faces of his guests. "One of you stole it!"

Cries of outrage replied to his accusation, followed immediately by the most ridiculous excuses Rob had ever heard:

"I can hardly stand with this rheumatism; I couldn't possibly."

"I was standing right next to you, my lord. You saw me."

"Why would I want a dirty old locket like that?"

"Perhaps there is a spirit haunting your house, my lord."

Then the excuses shifted into blame:

"It must have been Miss Kendrick. She was standing behind me, where I couldn't see."

"I watched Mr. Eldridge do it. I saw him!"

"It was the ghost, my lord."

There were far too many people in the world who believed in such nonsense as ghosts, Rob decided, and he had to fight to keep his expression steady.

Mother did not seem the least bit concerned about her missing trinket; she must have seen John take it. Alana, on the other hand, knew the locket's worthlessness and seemed about ready to tell him he was acting like a fool for making a fuss about something he shouldn't. He had to maintain the balance between keeping his audience's attention and still acting within the usual mannerisms of the Elusive Earl. It was not an easy line to walk.

Taking a slow breath, Rob stood up straight and pointed a finger. At first, he must have looked like he was pointing to the empty pillow where the locket had rested, but as soon as the crowd parted, it became clear that he was pointing directly at Mr. Russell. "You," he said, his voice a mere whisper.

Russell turned a bit pale. "My lord?"

"You stole it, didn't you?"

Russell hadn't said a word since the missing locket's discovery, which was impressive on its own. The fact that he did not immediately shift the blame now was even more so. "You think I took your family heirloom?" he asked quietly.

Rob nodded and slowly crossed the room toward the young man as he spoke. "You were the last to leave the drawing room before dinner. You were the last to enter it again. You have been standing the closest, and never have I been robbed until this night, when I let you into my home as my friend and guest. What do you have to say for yourself?"

He first looked around the room, as if searching for an ally, but Mr. Russell stood tall as he returned Rob's gaze. "If you have proof, my lord, I will not argue against it."

Heavens, it was nearly impossible for Rob to keep his affected anger intact and not smile. Russell was proving himself to be even more than he had hoped for. "I do not need proof," he said. "Clearly you are not like the rest of the Quality."

Russell set his jaw tight. "Clearly," he agreed. "And I take no issue with that. If being Quality means I must treat my fellows with suspicion and ridicule, then I will sleep well tonight knowing I am not one of you. My peers deserve fair and respectful treatment, my lord, something I fear you know nothing about."

The room had gone positively silent as the whole gathering waited to see what the Elusive Earl would do with such an insult. Most seemed to be expecting him to pull out a pistol and shoot the man dead, while Alana was on the verge of tears. He would have to give her some sort of explanation later and profusely apologize with as many flowers as he could find, but he hoped she was not too upset by the events of the evening. Perhaps he would let her throw another dinner party to make up for it.

Despite the expectations of how he might respond to Russell's insult, Rob wanted to throw an arm around the man and declare them kindred spirits. But he could not very well do that with the spectacle he had just made of himself. Changing his mind too quickly would lead to suspicion and gossip, and the Elusive Earl was too well-known for his unchangeable nature.

Mr. Russell leaned close, and his next words were meant only for Rob. "I did not steal your little locket," he growled, "and I think you know I did not. If it was anyone here, it was probably Mr. Norrington, but I will not make a formal accusation against one of your guests because, unlike you, I operate within the bounds of evidence and proof. Consider what you wish to add to the world, my lord, because thus far, I am not impressed. Good night."

But Rob grabbed him by the arm, preventing him from leaving the room, and he leveled the young man with a look that was meant to express everything he could not say out loud. "This evening is over," he declared to the room in general. "Alana, if you could see our guests to the door."

She bit back what he guessed was an angry comment, intelligent enough to know that she would do well to save that drama for later. But no matter how angry she was with Rob, she put on a smile and led her friends to the door to say her goodbyes.

Everyone else, it seemed, was eager to get out from under lingering suspicion, and the room cleared quickly. Rob's mother was the last to go, pausing at the door and shooting Rob a look that said she hoped he knew what he was doing and would also demand explanation eventually. But she followed the rest of the gathering, leaving Rob alone with Mr. Russell, who was growing more furious by the second and tore his arm loose the first moment he could.

"John?" Rob said, keeping his eyes locked on Russell.

The valet appeared at his side almost instantaneously and handed him the locket.

Russell stared at the necklace, confused but quickly realizing the setup for what it was. His eyes went wide, and his face turned rather red as he began, "You—"

"John," Rob interrupted, "it seems we have a new target: Mr. Norrington. Fetch my clothes." John nodded and disappeared again, and Rob watched Mr. Russell carefully as he continued to unravel the events of the evening. "I hope you'll forgive me," he said gently. "There are few men in the world like you, William Russell, and I had to make sure you were truly one of the good ones."

John was back in a flash and began helping Rob switch from his tailored jacket and slippers to a ragged coat and boots that had seen too much mud over the last year.

Russell had lost his words again as he watched Rob transform himself from an earl to a thief, though it was the hat that caused the most recognition and sent his eyes going wide again. "You're the thief," he said, taking a step back in alarm. "The thief Marian spoke to at the tavern." His frowned deepened as more pieces fell into place. "She knows it's you, doesn't she?"

Rob grinned. "Your cousin is sometimes too intelligent for her own good. Out of curiosity, though I'm sure he deserves it, why would you accuse Mr. Norrington?" He badly hoped for a reason for tonight's impending visit that would be more justifiable than a simple dislike for the man.

"I overheard him at White's," Russell said. "He, ah, he was bragging to Mr. Hewitt about knocking a rival down a peg or two by cheating at cards several times."

"Ah, I hadn't thought of that." Rob made a mental note to play more cards with the men of the *ton*. If he had learned one thing living among the poor, it was how to spot a cheater. "Well, my good man, rest easy that I'll keep your reputation intact and nothing about tonight will reflect poorly on you."

"How?"

"Being an earl has its perks. For both of us. Good night, Mr. Russell, and thank you for allowing me my little test. You passed with flying colors." Rob was halfway to the door when he paused and looked back.

Russell still stood in the same place, his hands at his sides as he continued to process everything that had just been revealed to him. There was a high chance he would stay there all night, based on the expression on his face. Rob figured it would be doing him a disservice to just let him stand there. He was a good man, and his skills as a soldier could likely come in handy.

"Do you want to come?"

CHAPTER *Nine*

MARIAN HAD ALWAYS THOUGHT THAT once she was out in Society, life would get more interesting. Before her debut, she had watched her mother make social calls and attend events until late in the night and would stay up so she could see the brightness in her mother's eyes when she returned from her adventures.

Now that she was grown, however, Marian had come to realize she and her mother had very different ideas of what constituted an adventure.

Her mother *adored* sitting around talking the latest gossip and sipping tea. She delighted in embroidering a new pillow or listening to Mrs. So-and-so's daughter play a particularly difficult piece at the pianoforte. She could not be happier than when she spent hours shopping for the latest fashions and finding the perfect ribbon for her new bonnet.

And Marian hated all of it.

She had not always hated it. In fact, up until last year she had mimicked her mother to the last detail and thought she would make the most charming lady someday. She was wealthy and noble, and while it was true she did not have the same amiable and creative talents as her mother, she was certain she would make a good wife one day.

Then, after growing closer with her abigail, she had seen how the lower class lived, and so her barmaid scheme was hatched. She had thought she would be satisfied in her research and have a way to truly help the poor around her while still acting as a proper young lady should.

Then she met Robin Loxley, and all hopes of enjoying a quiet life of nobility had vanished.

"Lady Marian, you are quite out of sorts this morning."

Marian looked up and realized she had been staring down at her tea for several minutes, and the other young ladies she had met up with in the tearoom were watching her curiously. Apparently, none of them ever got lost in thought, waxing poetic about the twists and turns their lives had taken.

"Oh," she said and set down her cup. "I am tired; that is all." Tired of pretending she could ever be content to live the dainty lady life now that she had gotten a taste of something infinitely more exciting. She had not seen the earl since his little fighting lesson, and her fingers were itching to engage in another robbery. Goodness, if her mother could hear her thoughts now. She was dreaming about being a thief!

Miss Gordon, someone Marian had met only that afternoon, leaned a little nearer to her, as if she wanted to share a secret with her alone and not the others. "Did you hear the news, Lady Marian?" she whispered, though not quietly enough to keep it between the two of them. "There were *three* robberies last night!"

"Three? Who?" Marian squeaked a little in alarm. Robin had certainly been busy without her, and her heart sank. Why had he not taken her with him? He had said she did well with Mr. Taylor, and she'd thought that meant he would include her in future exploits. Apparently, she was wrong.

Miss Gordon leaned even closer but somehow spoke louder than before. "Your cousin, for one. Mr. Russell."

If Marian had not already set down her tea, she certainly would have spilled it. "What? Mr. Russell was robbed?"

Miss Gordon giggled. "No, he was the one who did the robbing. Didn't you know?"

Before Marian could respond to such a horrid accusation, another of the ladies spoke up and inserted herself into the "secret" conversation. "Stop spreading lies, Petunia Gordon," Miss Young said sternly. "Unlike you, I was at Lord Huntingdon's last night, and no one saw what happened. I heard the earl himself admitted at Lords this morning that he made a mistake."

Marian was completely baffled by the whole conversation now, and she held up a finger, hoping that would break the impending argument before it began. Thankfully, her rank was enough to keep the ladies' attention, and they waited for what she would say on the matter. "Lord Huntingdon was robbed, then?" she asked first. But what would that have to do with Will? More importantly, though, why would Robin steal from himself? Perhaps it was to alleviate any suspicion that might arise, but it sounded like the alleged robbery had happened when guests were there. He could not have done it on his own, could he?

Miss Young scoffed. "You know how men like that can be," she said as if she were an authority on the subject. "He overreacted, and I heard from

Mrs. Hustead, who heard it from Lady Carlisle, whose husband heard the earl telling several gentlemen outside Westminster that he found the locket in the fireplace this morning. It must have been knocked from its display during the evening."

Marian tried to make sense of it all, though she still had no idea how Will was a part of any of it. Had her cousin been there? At Huntingdon Manor? "Well, who else was robbed?" she decided to ask, hoping it would clarify things.

"Mr. Norrington," Miss Gordon said.

"Oh, he was at Lord Huntingdon's as well!" Miss Young exclaimed. "The thief must have known he would be away from home."

That was a subject of some fear, because the other three ladies in attendance joined in the conversation then, muttering behind their hands about how frightful it was that they could be robbed at any moment since they all spent a good deal of time away from their homes.

Marian, however, did not much care about their worries. She was more concerned about the fact that something significant had happened at Huntingdon Manor and she hadn't even been invited. "And the third?" she pressed.

Miss Gordon waved the question away and sipped at her tea. "Oh, the family of that unfortunate seamstress no one likes," she said, as if a poor family getting robbed was of little consequence.

"Which family?" Marian asked.

"I believe their name is Bernard or something German like that."

Marian felt as though she could not breathe, though she did her best to hide the sensation as the ladies turned their conversation to something far more interesting: men. Marian, however, could not think past the robberies. She *knew* the Bernhard family. In fact, she had visited Mrs. Bernhard only yesterday to inquire about a dress that had taken far longer than was promised. It was likely coincidence that they had been robbed so soon after she visited, but that did not make her feel much better.

If it had been Robin, she would have some stern words with the man about choosing targets who could actually afford to be robbed. If it had not been him, like with Mr. Tilby . . . "Excuse me," she said and rose to her feet. "I am feeling terribly faint, and I think I will return home for the rest of the afternoon."

It was not very polite of her to leave her acquaintances in the middle of tea, but she could not put up with the silliness of it anymore. Not until she figured out what had actually happened last night. But when she reached the street, she realized she was completely on her own, and in broad daylight, that would not do at all. She scanned the passersby quickly, hoping to see a friendly face who could escort her home, and she was about to lose hope when she spotted them.

Robin and Will were strolling together—together?—only a few buildings away. Marian took it as a sign from Providence that they could give her the answers she hoped for, and she gathered up her skirts, hurrying down the pavement until she was close enough to call Will's name.

He turned in alarm and held a hand out to steady her as she arrived. "Marian? Is something wrong? You're . . ." He looked around, searching for whichever companion he thought she might have, and when he realized she was on her own, he frowned. "What is wrong, Cousin?"

Robin kept his focus entirely on a passing carriage, swinging his walking stick lazily and smiling with contentment as if he hadn't a clue she was even there. Marian did not understand the Elusive Earl. Not one bit. And she scowled at him, hoping he would at least acknowledge her, before she returned her attention to her cousin.

"I am perfectly well," she told Will. "Actually, I was hoping to talk with you, if you would not mind walking me home."

"Do you have any objections, Loxley?" Will glanced at Robin, whose smile turned a little more mischievous than before, and then he nodded to Marian. "What is it you wanted to talk about?" Will said.

Though Marian took Will's outstretched arm, she had eyes for only the earl, who led the way toward Marian's home without a word and whistled to himself as if he were in the best of moods. When had he and Will become friends? Better yet, when had they even met? It had to have been in the last day or two, but they were acting as if they had known each other for years. Will never took a liking to someone so quickly.

Will nudged her arm, reminding her he had asked her a question.

"Oh," she said and felt her cheeks turn hot. She was not fully sure how to answer since she required Robin's attention more than her cousin's. "I just wondered if you heard about the robberies last night."

Robin paused but did not turn around. Will stopped too and pulled his eyebrows together. "Robberies?" he said, apparently bewildered. "But we robbed only one man."

At first, Marian did not know why anger shot through her limbs and propelled her to smack Will on the arm like she had often done when they were children. But as soon as he recoiled, she realized what he had said. *"We?"* she repeated. "Will, have you become a . . ." She leaned closer, though her whisper did not sound any less harsh in its lowered volume. *"A thief?"*

Ahead of them, Robin chuckled. "Says the woman who broke into Jason Taylor's house only a few nights ago," he said as he pretended to admire the stonework of the house they stood before.

Will's arm tightened around hers as he turned to her. "You robbed *Mr. Taylor?*"

Marian wasn't sure who she was angrier with: Robin for dragging Will into his nonsense or Will for keeping it a secret from her. "You robbed Mr. Norrington," she replied. "Or was it an innocent you ruined last night?"

Robin's walking stick suddenly passed between them and landed on Will's arm, cutting off Will's response and pulling their attention to the earl. "While I am surprised—and grateful—that the two of you have not confided in each other until now, I think perhaps we should take this conversation off the street." His words were calm, but his eyes were not, and he looked over them at what was likely a gathering crowd hoping to catch the latest bit of gossip before it circulated among the masses.

Heat rose up Marian's neck again, and she nodded as she took a calming breath. She would get angry with the two of them, most definitely, but she could wait until they no longer had an audience. "I would be happy to have you join my cousin and me for luncheon," she said to Robin, who bowed his acquiescence with a twinkle of entertainment in his eyes.

He looked all the more handsome when he was amused, and Marian very much disliked him for it. He had had the same look before he taught her to hit properly, and just thinking of that night—and how close they had been to each other—brought a nervous sensation to the pit of her stomach.

"Come, then," she said through her teeth and pulled Will toward her house, letting Robin bring up the rear. It was easier to concentrate when she could not see him.

Thankfully, Mr. Jones, the butler, told Marian that her parents had gone out, which meant their little luncheon meeting would not be invaded by people who should not hear what they would be saying. She was extra grateful that Will was there, even if she was angry with him; she couldn't very well enjoy a meal with Robin alone. She had somehow forgotten how handsome he was in daylight, when she could see every little detail of him. She had spent most of her time with him under the cover of darkness, when he wore that ridiculous hat of his.

Honestly, she thought to herself as they settled in their seats, *it's a wonder he has not been snatched up already*. The Earl of Huntingdon was handsome, charming, and overall rather cheerful, which was not a common trait among any men, let alone the wealthy ones. Marian couldn't fathom how he had gone so long without being eaten alive by the matrons of Society, especially without being so worn down that it showed on his face. He was a resilient man—she knew that already—but he kept surprising her.

"So now the both of you know my secret," Robin said as soon as they were completely alone in the room. "Unfortunately, that makes both your lives immeasurably more dangerous."

Marian scoffed a little, hoping to sound brave so he would not have more reason to think she couldn't go out with him again. There must have been a reason he did not take her along last night, and she refused to let him exclude her again. "I do not see why you think it is so dangerous outside of being caught by servants who are going to be on our side."

Will and Robin exchanged knowing glances, which was a strange feeling for Marian, who still did not know how long they had actually been acquainted. Given the way Will called him "Loxley" rather than "Lord Huntingdon," they must have been through quite a lot together. Will was nothing if not a follower of societal rules.

"Norrington had dogs," Will said, frowning.

"I've been shot at twice," Robin replied. "And there is no telling what would happen if you were caught and recognized for what you are, Lady Marian."

Now-familiar anger bubbled up inside Marian, and she glowered at the man who still had not figured out that a woman could be just as fierce as any man. "I hardly think that is reason to—"

"I will not tell you that you cannot come along, Marian," Robin said, and his eyes sparkled again. He was laughing at her! "I just want to make sure you fully understand the risks."

"You're going to let her come along?" Will asked in alarm. "Loxley, I don't think that is a good idea."

Marian had a few things she wished to say to her cousin, none of which she could repeat in polite Society, even if Robin was a thief. "I have done it successfully before," she reminded him through her teeth.

"Once," Will grumbled.

"And how many times have you gone out, Will?" she retorted.

"Perhaps save the family banter for when I am not here," Robin said with a smirk. "We have more important matters to discuss." When he was apparently sure both Russells were willing to keep their ill thoughts to themselves, he sat forward a little and focused primarily on Marian, who felt her face warming when he fixed that green gaze of his on her. "I have not seen the paper yet, so perhaps you could fill us in on who else was robbed."

"You, for starters," Marian replied, even though she knew very well Robin had already rectified that claim. "And the Bernhard family."

Robin sat up straight again, and his gaze hardened. "The dressmaker?"

The fact that a man like the Earl of Huntingdon knew of a seamstress deep in the heart of London gave Marian pause and made her wonder what other surprises he had up his sleeve, but she chose to pretend it was not strange for a man to have such information. "What do you know about her?" she asked, deciding *what* was better than *why* in this situation.

"Not much." Robin shrugged, deep in thought as he scratched his chin. "Alana prefers Mrs. Hudson for her gowns, but from your reaction to the news, I am guessing she is not well-off."

Marian nodded. "I went to her only yesterday, and though she seems to have plenty of work to keep her busy, her family is barely surviving. She is falling behind, and she would not say anything of her husband's affairs when I asked."

"They are probably in debt," Will said quietly. "I think I have seen Mr. Bernhard gambling more than once."

Something in what Will said brought a smile to Robin's face as he turned to him and raised an eyebrow. "You're a gambler, Russell?"

Marian could not see why that was important to the matter at hand, but Will responded without offense. "I was," he said. "Before I actually had anything to lose. There are better uses for my brother's fortune."

"Good. And if Mr. Bernhard has racked up considerable debt, it could explain why the family is struggling as they are. What it does not explain is—"

"Why someone would make them a target," Marian finished, if only to bring herself back into the conversation. She felt as if she had to contribute just as much as the other two if either of them was going to take her seriously. And when Robin raised an eyebrow at her, she ignored him and continued. "There must be some reason for it."

"There are all sorts of thieves out there, Marian," Robin reminded her. "I am not anything new."

"No," she agreed, "but no one reports a robbery to the paper unless they think it is of some importance. The Bernhards must have thought they were one of yours, or . . ." She frowned as another thought hit her. "Or they were not the ones who reported the theft," she whispered, still trying to sort through the new idea forming in her mind.

"Why would someone else report the theft?" Will asked.

"Because they wanted the attention," Robin replied, catching on. "You think it was the other thief who alerted the papers."

Marian nodded. "The Bernhards have nothing to gain by publicizing it. In fact, I would imagine something like this would only make Mr. Bernhard's creditors even more ruthless, knowing he has nothing to give now. They are more likely to call in his debts and get him sent to prison."

"So my admirer is trying to ride on my coattails to gain the same notoriety I've found," Robin said. Though he seemed bothered by the idea, he was intrigued as well, almost a smile in his thoughtful expression.

Will, on the other hand, shifted uneasily in his seat. "But he is not going after the scum of high Society," he said.

"He doesn't seem to have a pattern," Robin agreed. "At least, not yet."

Marian thought hard, but she could not make a connection between the two other attacks either. She had met Howard Tilby only once, at the ball last week, and despite being an utter bore, he had been kind enough and asked her to dance when her almost-partner disappeared. Thinking of that ball reminded her that she had met Rob the Earl for the first time that night as well, and he had made a much stronger impression than Tilby had.

Then there was Mrs. Bernhard, who was doing her best in a terrible situation and trying to care for her family in the shadow of her husband's poor choices. There was nothing unkind or despicable about her. Her husband, maybe, but it had been clear to Marian in her short visit that it was Mrs. Bernhard, not Mr. Bernhard, who ran their household.

"There has to be something linking the two together," she muttered and bit the nail of her thumb in frustration, though she knew she should have kicked the habit long ago. Proper young ladies did not bite their nails. *Nor do they steal from bachelors' bedchambers or fight in empty ballrooms*, she thought wryly.

Will rose to his feet, clearly thinking hard as well. "Perhaps I can go talk to Mr. Bernhard's creditors. I have been meaning to go talk with my man of business anyway, and he will be able to steer me in the right direction. I will see if perhaps Mr. Tilby is indebted as well."

"Capital idea," Robin muttered, though his focus was on the floor. "I'll send my valet into the streets to see what he can dig up."

"Your valet?" Marian asked in surprise.

The corner of Robin's mouth lifted in a half smile. "John spent most of his life on the street before I found him and gave him a respectable job, and he's likely to get more answers than we 'fancy folk,' as he likes to call us."

Will left the room with a bow and a determination Marian had not seen in him since she had told him he would never be able to climb the wall of the ruined abbey near her country home. He had scaled the wall in less than ten minutes and gloated about it the entire summer, though he admitted later that he would not have done it if she hadn't issued the challenge. Most of the time, he kept to himself and stayed in the shadows, but when he set his mind to something, he was a force to be reckoned with. Particularly if that task involved helping someone else. If anyone could get information from a creditor, it was Will.

Robin stood as well, and Marian suddenly realized she had offered up nothing to help. But what could she possibly do?

Robin must have caught something in her expression, because he chuckled and put a hand on her shoulder. In any other situation, the action might have seemed intimate, but Marian had been far closer to the man than this. This felt like a touch of camaraderie. "Chin up, Tuck," he said. "You are the brains behind this endeavor. I would have taken much longer to come to the conclusion that the thief might have made the announcement. Perhaps you could ask around about who might have alerted the papers to the theft. You have better access to the gossip mill than I do."

Marian was certain Robin was just as intelligent as she was, if not more so, but she appreciated the compliment nonetheless. She particularly enjoyed him calling her Tuck, even if the pseudonym was rather silly. It made her feel like she was a part of something bigger than herself. "I will see what I can do," she said and gave him what she hoped was a confident smile.

A sudden cough in the doorway made Marian jump, and Robin's hand slipped from her shoulder as she quickly stood and faced the butler.

To his credit, Jones hardly seemed to care about what he had just witnessed, though that did not mean he would not report to Lord Waverly later. "There is a Mr. Geoffrey Gisbourne here to see you, my lady."

Marian frowned. "Who?" She took the card Jones held out to her and stared at the name, trying to match it to a face. Had she met a Mr. Gisbourne? "Er, show him in, I suppose," she said, though the idea of someone calling on her without her having met him put her on edge. Was such a thing often done?

She had to wait only a moment for Jones to return and announce, "Mr. Gisbourne, my lady," then bow and step aside.

The man who entered the room was young, perhaps twenty-four or twenty-five and clearly a man of means, if his clothes were any indication, and though Marian was sure she did not know him, she thought he was at least a little familiar. She recognized his blond hair, the bright blue of his eyes, and the permanent smirk on his thin lips.

"Lady Marian," he said and bowed low, sweeping his hat wide. "I do apologize for being untoward like this, but I have been waiting much too long for an opportunity to present itself and thought I might speed chance along a bit."

"The ball last week," Marian realized out loud.

Mr. Gisbourne smiled pleasantly. "Indeed. We were just about to be introduced so I could ask you to dance when I was called away on business. And when I saw you leaving the dressmaker's yesterday, I knew I could wait no longer to become acquainted with a beauty such as yourself."

Robin cleared his throat, and for a second time, Marian jumped.

"Oh!" she said, realizing how many rules of etiquette she was breaking. "Do forgive me. Mr. Gisbourne, may I present Lord Huntingdon?"

The two men locked eyes, and though Robin's brow darkened, Mr. Gisbourne's smile grew. "It is indeed an honor to meet you, my lord," he said and bowed again. "I hope I am not interrupting."

Robin was clenching his jaw so tight that Marian thought he would never be able to open it again. "Not at all," he said after a pause that was much too long. "I was not aware Lady Marian had a social call, so it is I who am intruding."

Marian could not fathom why Robin would be so cold to a man he did not know, but she hoped Mr. Gisbourne did not notice. She rather liked this man, from the very little she knew about him; he was charming and cheerful. Still, she had not had a chance to prepare for his visit, so she felt very out of sorts and was not sure what to do. Call for some tea?

To her immense relief, Mr. Gisbourne bowed again and said, "I do believe I have interrupted, and I will take my leave of you until you are not already entertaining. I am very glad to have finally met you, Lady Marian." Flashing her a wide and warm smile, he slipped out of the room.

"Well, that was interesting," Robin muttered.

Interesting indeed. Marian had known she would have gentlemen calling now that she was out, but she never would have expected one of them to be quite so forward as to call on her without a prior introduction. Even more interesting, she found she liked that about him very much. In fact, she almost felt like giggling the longer she thought about it. Yes, she knew next to nothing about the man, but that simply meant she would get the chance to learn more.

"I should go talk to John before it is too late in the day," Robin said, and without a word of goodbye he strode from the room and disappeared, leaving Marian alone and confused.

Clearly, she knew nothing of men.

An hour later, a bouquet of the prettiest flowers Marian had ever seen arrived with a card from Mr. Gisbourne expressing again his delight at finally being introduced, and Marian put them in her dressing room so she could admire them and imagine what good things might come.

CHAPTER *Ten*

ROB USED TO THINK HE never could have gotten tired of wandering London at night, when most of the world slept and the streets settled into a misty haze of potential. Since the day he'd become the Earl of Huntingdon, it had been his favorite time of day. A time he could think. Reflect. Be himself. And he used to think he would live the rest of his life that way.

But he had never counted on bringing others into his little crusade, and somehow, that had dulled the sensation of hiding in the shadows like some supernatural specter.

John had come as an accident in the beginning, but he had proved useful in getting into small spaces and evading more prepared targets and their guards. The boy had become a dear friend, almost a brother, and Rob did not regret taking him in. He did, however, give him nights off, and Rob used those quiet nights to enjoy that time to himself.

But now young Will Russell was in the mix. Rob hadn't been sure what Russell would think about stealing since he seemed to be entirely honest and good. The man had a streak of daring in him and had risen to the challenge beautifully when they went after Mr. Norrington, however, and the kitten soldier had far more skill in fighting than Rob had expected. More importantly, he was quiet enough that Rob could pretend he was not there if he needed a moment to breathe and close his mind to the world around him.

Putting the two young men together, however . . .

"I can't feel my fingers, Rob. I swear I can't." John touched his hand to Rob's cheek to demonstrate.

"It is not nearly as cold as it was when I was stationed in Scotland," Russell muttered from Rob's other side. "Men nearly lost fingers to frostbite."

"That doesn't make mine any warmer, does it?" John shot back.

"You are such a child."

"You're not half as important as you seem to think you are."

"At least I haven't been complaining all night."

"Well, you—"

"Enough," Rob hissed and was tempted to smack their heads together and knock them both out cold. At least then he could get some peace and quiet. "I should hope the two of you would take things a little more seriously."

Truth be told, they weren't really doing anything. Without any useful leads on their mimic thief, they had decided to wander the city in the hopes of coming across him by chance. It was already nearly two in the morning, and Rob knew the odds were not in their favor. Until they had concrete evidence directing them to the thief, there was little point in them continuing on.

"We need a new strategy," Rob muttered.

"We need more information," Russell said.

"We need luck," John argued.

They were all right, and Rob pulled his collar a little tighter around his neck. John hadn't been lying; the night was cold. "This is inordinately frustrating," he said, more to himself than to his companions. He prided himself on being logical and methodical, always having multiple plans before he ventured out into a situation. Marian had been the first to mess up his careful approach to this life of his, and now it seemed he had lost all sense of strategy altogether.

Rob stepped inside a little grove of trees so he could try to come up with an actual plan before someone found them wandering the city after dark.

"How are we supposed to find someone we know nothing about?" Russell asked. It seemed he was feeling the cold as well now, since he hunkered down into a tight ball as he sat at the base of a tree. "What do you usually do in this situation, Loxley?"

Rob hated the answer. "I have never been in this situation."

"What about that Thrush fellow?" John said, his words muffled through the collar of his jacket, which he had pulled up over his mouth. "He was like this thief."

Frowning, Rob thought back on the man they had encountered six months previously. The situations were similar but not entirely identical. "Thrush was a common street thief," he explained to Russell. "He had a rather solid network of associates who roamed the city at night, and he caught wind of where I was going any time I set out after a new target. He generally got there before I did and cleaned them out."

"Sounds like he was doing you a favor," Russell said with a shrug. "What happened to him?"

Rob hated to think on it; he felt he was to blame for the consequences. He could not have helped the man, but it was because of Rob that Thrush had been inside Mrs. Delacroix's drawing room to begin with.

"He got caught," John said matter-of-factly. "Got cocky and hung around to greet us when we got there."

"But the authorities got there first," Rob said quietly. "Just ahead of us, actually. The target had heard Thrush and sent a footman to alert the constable."

"We were lucky," John said.

"Thrush was not," Rob replied. "We saw the commotion and kept ourselves hidden, but Thrush was taken to the gallows and hanged before I could try to rescue him." He sighed. "If we do not find this thief soon, I fear he may meet the same fate." And then there was always the chance Rob and his companions would run into trouble as well. He and Mr. Russell might be shown leniency, with their ranks, but John? He would be convicted without trial and likely lose his life.

Russell grimaced, biting his lip before he quietly asked, "Would it not be a good thing if our mimic was caught?"

"Not if he's doing this for the same reasons we are," Rob said, though that excuse had never sat well with him. He knew he was doing good for the poor, but he was still breaking the law. He walked a fine line, and sometimes he wondered if he had crossed that line too many times. "If he is in it for the money or the entertainment, then he needs to be stopped," he said. "If he is trying to be like us, we should still probably stop him, but maybe we can help him as well. We at least have to teach him the right targets before he hurts too many innocent people."

In a perfect world, Rob would find the thief and simply convince him to give up his goal, whatever it might be. But if his attempts with Marian were any indication, he was not as persuasive as he liked to think he was.

At any rate, they could not stand around all night and hope to accomplish anything. They would do better to get some rest. "We're done for the night," he said, reaching out a hand to help Russell back to his feet. "John, go straight to bed and get yourself warm. I won't need you tonight. And Russell, let me know what you learn when you meet with Mr. Bernhard's creditor tomorrow; that could be our best chance unless we find something new. Keep to the shadows, my friends, and make sure you're not seen. As always."

Both men nodded—John included a weird sort of salute he had adopted a few months back—and they dispersed, finally leaving Rob blissfully alone. He knew he should also go to bed, but he couldn't bring himself to go home just yet.

After a whole lot of long conversations with his mother and sister, during which he had falsely explained his reasoning for testing Russell's character like he had—making sure Will Russell was worth considering as a suitor for Alana if she was interested—Rob was ready for a bit of solitude. Alana had not been quick to forgive him for ruining her first dinner party, but he had promised to host at least three more before the end of the Season. That alone was enough to give him a headache. His mother had been a little more understanding, though that had not stopped her from warning him about forgetting who he was. She knew too much, it seemed. But he could not focus on that, or he might lose sight of the task at hand.

They had to find that thief before things went sour.

I should have brought Marian along tonight as well, he thought before he shook his head against the idea. Marian was already a dangerous variable to his carefully planned life, and she still had much to learn before she was ready to take to the streets regularly. He knew such a thing was inevitable, unless he somehow managed to convince her to give up on her dream of living a more fulfilling life, but he hoped to delay it as long as possible. Part of that was because she was terrible at it and had nearly ruined everything at Taylor's, but the other part . . .

Marian unnerved him. He did not know why, and he was not about to admit that he could have feelings for the woman, however small they might be. She was beautiful, to be sure, but so were a lot of ladies. He had plenty of lovely faces vying for his attention any time he went out in polite Society. And she was wealthy, but that mattered little to him. If he knew her as well as he liked to think, she would do whatever she could to use her wealth to its fullest in bettering the lives of those around her. There was just something about her that had him questioning everything when he was near her.

The other day, for example, he thought and grumbled a little as he began the trek back home now that John was out of sight. He had never met Mr. Gisbourne before, but at the first sign of attention toward Marian, Rob had felt his hackles rise, as if he were some dog defending his home. He had never given much thought to marrying—he rather planned to live a perpetual life of bachelorhood and leave his fortune to Alana and her future children if she had them—but the idea of someone pursuing Marian made his blood boil.

She was a headstrong, clumsy, quick-to-anger young woman who had hardly been in the world long enough to truly understand it, and she somehow managed to take every other word Rob said and spin it into some personal insult that left her glaring at him. And that bothered him more than it should.

Why should he care what she thought of him? Honestly, it would be better if she disliked him, because then they could keep this thieving arrangement strictly professional and he would not have to devote half his mind to wondering if she was cold or nervous or about to be in mortal danger. He certainly didn't worry about John or Will like that, and it was not simply because Marian was a woman. She had plenty of fire in her to be a worthy opponent to anyone who might try to cross her. She had proved that many times.

London had fallen beneath a sleepy fog as Rob finally reached his manor and slipped in through the hard-to-reach window he always left unlocked. Even if he chose to stay out and keep searching for the other thief, he could hardly see across the street anymore. No, it would be better if he went to bed and tried to get at least a few hours' sleep before returning to the life of the Elusive Earl. There was the Middletons' ball in the evening, and he had already promised Alana he would accompany her. Before that, there was plenty of work for him to do with securing the well-being of his tenants in Nottinghamshire, and his mother would likely want to talk to him for an hour or two, as it was never easy to spare time for her on top of everything else he did. He needed to sleep so he could even last through the day.

But once Rob had stepped into his dark bedchamber and dressed for bed, he didn't feel the least bit tired. His mind had strayed to imagining what it would be like to continue teaching Marian how to pick a lock or do more than a simple punch, neither of which he could do from a distance. He would have to get close to her again, and any excuses he might have had for avoiding such a thing were quickly fading away with every passing thought of her.

Sighing, he decided he was not likely to fall asleep anyway, not with her swimming around in his head like she was, so he might as well get started on his work now instead of wasting the time staring at the ceiling above his bed.

Two steps out into the corridor, however, Rob paused, sure that he had heard something. It could have been John seeing to his duties, but Rob knew the lad would listen to orders and was probably already asleep. Perhaps one of the other servants was checking on the fire in Alana's room, but a feeling in Rob's gut told him otherwise. Barefooted and in his nightclothes, he crept down the dark corridor and listened for any other sign that someone was where they shouldn't be.

There. A tinkle of metal or a string of pearls tapping against itself. He knew that sound well. Rob paused outside his mother's chamber and pressed himself against the wall, listening through the slightly ajar door. The smallest of lights glowed from within, like an oil lamp barely lit, and Rob knew it was not his mother rummaging through her own things. She could sleep through anything. No, this was someone who most definitely was not supposed to be there.

Keeping himself flat against the wall, Rob leaned just far enough to peek through the open door and take in the man who stood inside and stuffed jewelry into his pockets. *The thief.* Rob could almost not believe his eyes. After so many hours of searching, the wanted man was just a few feet away in his own home. And stealing from his mother, no less. Instinct pushed Rob forward, but he held himself back and simply watched the man as he worked. He needed information. He did *not* need to put his mother in danger by confronting the man without knowing what to expect. There were too many variables.

This was not a practiced thief, with the light and the noise, however small it was. Though the thief wore a mask across his face that kept his features hidden, and a hat atop his head, Rob could still see the golden color of his hair as he worked with ungraceful speed, and that alone was a decent clue. But there was something about him that confused Rob, though he wasn't sure what it was at first. It was something in the way he moved. Like he had been accustomed to living a certain way. If Rob had to wager on it, the thief was well-bred. Maybe even noble. He certainly was not lower class, and his boots alone were worth a pretty penny. But if the thief was wealthy, why would he take to stealing in the first place?

The answer to that question was worth far more than a few trinkets his mother would not miss. He could use this theft to his advantage.

If only he hadn't undressed when he returned home, he could pursue the man and figure out where he lived. It would take too much time to grab a coat and boots, but he could see which direction the thief went, if nothing else. Shuffling back down the corridor a bit, Rob hid himself in an alcove, then bumped his arm against the wall. It was not a loud sound, but it was enough that the noises from the thief immediately silenced and the man appeared in the corridor, nothing but his hand illuminated by the oil lamp he held. After a quick search of the empty passage, the thief darted in the opposite direction of Rob and disappeared onto the servants' staircase.

Rob moved quickly to the window, and sure enough, the thief appeared on the street, just a spot of light moving through the fog, until he vanished. Even the way he ran was Quality, and Rob stood at that window for a long while trying to understand how there could be another man like him. Surely there would not be that many men of means willing to risk it all to benefit others.

Then again, Rob thought as he made his way back to his bedchamber to think over what he had just seen, *there's no proof he is stealing to help the poor*. More likely the mimic thief was in it for the money and the fame.

And neither of those made Rob very comfortable.

CHAPTER *Eleven*

THERE WAS SOMETHING QUITE DELIGHTFUL about being on a drive with a man strictly for the sake of getting to know one another better. There was no underlying need for explanation, no secret to tiptoe around, no reason not to smile as the rest of the park took notice. Marian found herself enjoying the drive rather than waiting for an insult to fall or for endless teasing.

She had to credit that part to Mr. Gisbourne. While he had certainly pushed the boundary of propriety by calling on her without an introduction, he had made up for it with this drive, allowing a place for Millie to sit behind them as a chaperone. He did not want to make any more mistakes, he had told her, as he intended to keep in her good favor for as long as he could.

"So your father is a baronet?" Marian asked as they traversed sunny Hyde Park. Even the weather approved of the drive.

"Indeed." Mr. Gisbourne gave her a smile before returning his attention to directing the horses. "I know it does not measure up to your good name, but my father has done his best to give me a chance for a good life."

He may not have been of the peerage, but Marian found Mr. Gisbourne to be quite well-bred and as noble as any aristocrat she had met in her short life. She was not so knowledgeable of the lower ranks of the Realm to know how a man like Mr. Gisbourne might spend his time, and she was incredibly curious. Was he like her father, who went around Town discussing politics and looking after the people within the marquessate? Or was he like Will, who was trapped as he waited for his inheritance, left to while away the hours and find activities to occupy him?

"What do you generally do with your day, Mr. Gisbourne?" she asked.

Mr. Gisbourne seemed quite content as he drove and replied, "I try to make my life worthwhile where I can," he said. "There are a good many men of fortune who do nothing, and I would shudder to leave this world knowing I would hardly be remembered."

A thrill of delight ran through Marian, and she shifted ever so slightly closer to the man. After meeting many men of the Quality in London, she had feared people like Will were an anomaly, that those of privilege wasted their days simply because they could. That sort of life of leisure rested high among her nightmares. But Mr. Gisbourne, much to her pleasure, seemed to be of a different sort. The kind of man who might not see her desire to help the lower class as a bad thing.

"And what of you?" he said, turning his bright eyes to her. "What do you do with your days?"

Marian was feeling so good on this drive that her first instinct was to speak the truth, but she bit her tongue and thought for a moment. There was quite a difference between productivity and illegal activity. Breaking into houses with a single man in the dead of night and learning to throw punches were not the same as attending charity functions and feeding the poor. So despite wanting to say she was learning to pick locks so she could judge his reaction, Marian chose a different approach. "I try to learn as much as I can," she said.

"You are a bookworm, then?" Mr. Gisbourne asked.

Marian grinned. "I prefer more of a hands-on approach where I can, but yes. There is so much to learn about the world."

"Indeed. Have you learned anything fascinating lately?"

For nearly an hour, Marian chatted with Mr. Gisbourne about the most surprising topics, from economics to geography to mathematics. She fell short on nearly every subject compared to him—he was a lot more intelligent than she would have guessed—but he did not make her feel inferior even once. Instead, he shared with her the basics of what he knew and let her choose the next topic when the conversation lulled, even when her choice happened to be fabrics, a topic she knew a good deal about.

"You do have an eye for it," he told her and examined her current dress carefully, making her blush. "Some ladies cannot seem to find the right colors for themselves, but you do it beautifully."

Marian had never felt so flattered in her life, and she suddenly understood why young ladies enjoyed outings like this as much as they did. But were all men this good at paying compliments, or was it just Mr. Gisbourne? Based on her experiences so far, he had learned the art better than most.

"I do like to think I have some skills in life," she said and waited for him to take the bait.

He did it well. "From what I have learned of you so far, Lady Marian, you have more than a few. Any man should consider himself fortunate to know you."

Was it considered vain to hope he never stopped saying such things? She hoped not, though she told herself to be careful. Too many praises at once would likely lose their sweetness. She would do well to return the favor. "You drive splendidly," she said.

Mr. Gisbourne smoothly maneuvered around a couple who were walking. He did the job, but not as well as Robin had.

Marian frowned. Now, why did the earl have to go popping up in her head like that? She had managed to forget about the man for almost an entire morning, and now she could not seem to see anything but his smirk, even though she was trying to concentrate on Mr. Gisbourne's warm smile.

He did not seem to notice her annoyance, and he slowed the horses to a halt as he said, "I do believe you have a friend waving to you, my lady."

Marian looked ahead and recognized Miss Young. She would not necessarily call the pair of them friends—Miss Young had a tendency to laugh too often and flirt with any man she encountered—but she was probably the closest thing to a friend Marian had. Though she wished she could continue her conversation with Mr. Gisbourne uninterrupted, she thought it best not to be rude and returned the wave.

"Lady Marian," Miss Young greeted when she reached them. "I have been worried about you ever since you left yesterday."

Marian had all but forgotten her abrupt departure from tea the day before, but she smiled as she realized perhaps Miss Young thought of them as true friends. Marian had never really been worried over by anyone apart from her parents or Will. "Oh," she said, "you are kind to ask after me. I am much better. Do you know Mr. Gisbourne?"

The two of them exchanged bows, and then Miss Young reached up and took hold of Marian's hand. "I wanted to apologize for Miss Gordon accusing your cousin like that. She should not have been spreading rumors that were not true, especially when Lord Huntingdon admitted to his mistake about his being robbed."

"Huntingdon was robbed, was he?" Mr. Gisbourne asked.

Miss Young answered the question with a giggle. "No, he was not. He put on quite a display about it, but it turned out to be a misplaced locket, nothing more."

"Is that all?"

"Indeed, and it seems he has taken poor Mr. Russell under his wing to make up for the mistake."

That was likely just a cover so Robin and Will could discuss and plan their nighttime adventures—without Marian, apparently—but she was glad Will had a friend in Town, particularly one as highly ranked as Robin. Will had not had it easy, becoming an heir so suddenly, and Robin would be able to guide him through the rules of high Society.

"It seems he is a good man," she said thoughtfully.

"Or he is hoping to make a connection to Mr. Russell's family," Mr. Gisbourne muttered. "It is fortunate Lord Huntingdon has not been targeted by the notorious thief yet."

Miss Young seemed to take an eager interest in that topic, and she bounced a little, still holding Marian's hand. "This mysterious thief is quite the individual, do you not think so, Lady Marian? I am sure he is a handsome man."

He was. Marian forced herself not to grit her teeth in response to that comment. "What makes you say that?" she asked.

Miss Young clasped her hands with a look of delight. "A man who can steal from right under the noses of so many people must undoubtedly be handsome, as all rogues are."

Mr. Gisbourne harrumphed.

"What is your take on the thief?" Miss Young asked him. Marian was curious to know as well.

He sat back in his seat a little, adjusting his hat before he spoke. "I think the thief is far too confident," he said.

That was also true, but Marian was interested to hear why Mr. Gisbourne thought so. "Do explain," she said and gave him an encouraging smile. She did not like this grumpiness he had to him and wished for the cheerful man to return.

Thankfully, he warmed at the sight of her smile. "He has primarily been attacking the upper class, yes? Well, the more often he steals from the wealthy, the more careful they will get. He will get caught before long, and we will be rid of him."

"Oh, I do not think he will be caught," Miss Young said, touching a finger to her lips as she mused on the subject. "This has been going on for a year now, and only a few people have even seen him, though no one has gotten a good look at his face. It is almost as if he is a ghost."

Mr. Gisbourne chuckled. "He is certainly not a ghost. A ghost would not be able to touch things, after all."

It took Marian a moment too long to realize Mr. Gisbourne had not spoken in jest, and she stared at him in surprise. "Do you believe in spirits?" she asked, lifting one eyebrow.

Mr. Gisbourne returned her question with more vigor than before. "I do," he admitted, "but I have yet to see one. My aunt did, though, on multiple occasions. Swore up and down it was the ghost of a child who had drowned when she was a girl."

Marian was surprised that such an intelligent man would put stock in stories and legends. She had believed in ghosts as a child, but now that she was grown and understood more about the world, the idea of specters was almost laughable. And yet Mr. Gisbourne was perfectly serious as he sat there in the middle of Hyde Park and discussed ghosts as if they were the weather.

"Well, isn't this a lovely gathering?" a new voice, one Marian recognized without having to turn around, asked.

"Lord Huntingdon!" Miss Young said with clear pleasure, and she sank into a deep curtsy as Robin came into view, coming to a stop at her side.

"Miss Young," he said, "a pleasure, as always." He was perfectly civil today, though almost pompous, and he had yet to even acknowledge Marian or her companion. His full focus was on Miss Young, including that smirk of his.

Marian clenched her jaw tight as she watched them converse.

"We were just discussing the elusive thief of London," Miss Young said.

Robin's expression was bordering on mischievous, though Marian was pretty sure he was trying not to laugh. "The thief, you say? Has there been another attack of late?"

"There have been no attacks since Mr. Norrington and that dressmaker," Miss Young said sweetly. "At least, none that I know of, and I consider myself quite the expert on the news of the day."

"I am sure my sister would agree," Robin replied. "Most of her information seems to come from you, and Alana is always singing your praises." He finally lifted his eyes to where Marian sat. "Lady Marian," he greeted and bowed his head slightly.

Marian was tempted to hop down and show him that she had been practicing her punch, though she refrained. That was not a demonstration she would do well to make here in public. But Robin was grinning at her, daring her to release the annoyance building inside her, so she sat up straight and said, "Lord Huntingdon, are you well? It is strange to see you out and about among other people."

"Indeed," Miss Young said with wide eyes, as if she had not even considered the idea.

Robin's grin twisted until it was crooked. "Yes, well, the Elusive Earl does enjoy some sun now and then. I could hardly pass up a day like today, now, could I?"

Miss Young stepped forward before Marian could reply, putting her hand on Robin's arm as she said, "It seems you are not as elusive as you used to be, my lord. First the theater, then a dinner party, and now a jaunt in the park. You are becoming a regular man-about-town!"

"It seems that way," Robin replied, and he flashed the young woman a charming smile much like the one he had given Marian in the Bow and Crown. "I suppose I will have to do better if I am to keep my reputation."

Miss Young giggled, and the sound grated in Marian's ears. "I certainly hope not, my lord," the woman said and gave him what Marian assumed was her most coquettish smile in return.

"We should be on our way," Mr. Gisbourne said and offered a nod to Miss Young and the smallest of inclinations of his head to Robin, who did not appear insulted in the least by the lack of deference. In fact, he rather seemed to enjoy it.

Marian was more than happy to leave the two of them to their silly conversation, and she sat just a little closer to Mr. Gisbourne as he directed the horses onward. She did not understand Robin at all. Every time she met him, he seemed like a different person. Surely there had to be a version of him that was the real Robin, though she had no idea how she was supposed to discover it when he changed so often.

Thank goodness for men like Mr. Gisbourne, who were simply themselves and did not have any lurking secrets. She trusted that every word that came out of his mouth was the truth, and that was a powerful quality.

And yet, as they turned a corner, Marian glanced back at Robin and found him watching her in return despite Miss Young talking his ear off, and there was a look on his face that made her wonder what emotion was behind it. She might not have understood Robin Loxley, but she wanted to. And that was dangerous.

CHAPTER *Twelve*

"You seem distracted tonight, my darling."

Marian looked up from her hands, which she had apparently been staring at longer than she had realized. Both of her parents sat across from her in the carriage as it took them to the night's ball, and both seemed to have noticed how little attention she was paying to her surroundings. Putting on a smile, she quickly searched for a good excuse. "The Season is much more exciting than I realized," she said. "It is a lot to take in."

Lord and Lady Waverly exchanged knowing looks, which hopefully meant they knew firsthand the overwhelming nature of being out in Society for the first time. "Perhaps we should have waited until next year," Lady Waverly said thoughtfully.

"No!" Marian knew she spoke too quickly, but she couldn't stop herself. If she had been stuck at home again, she would have missed out on so much that was happening. "I mean, I simply need a few more days to adjust, and I will settle in to Society. I am truly enjoying myself."

"Good," her father said and reached across to pat her hand. "I have noticed you have been getting plenty of attention," he added. "Particularly from that Mr. Gisbourne." His smile shifted into one of mischief, a rare sight these days. When Marian was growing up, Lord Waverly had been a rather playful and attentive man, a side of him he did not get to show often as he'd taken on more responsibility after the death of Marian's grandfather ten years earlier. She particularly loved when his lighter nature had a chance to come through.

His comment, though, brought butterflies to her stomach. Mr. Gisbourne had left her after their drive that morning with the promise of seeing her at the ball tonight, and she was both wildly nervous and excited to see him again. There was something intriguing about the man, and the fact that he had asked her to call him by his nickname, Gis, just before he'd returned her home had brought a warmth to her chest that had not gone away over the course of the afternoon. Was she supposed to feel this way about someone she had only recently met?

"Do you like Mr. Gisbourne?" she asked. There was little point in entertaining the idea of a future with the man if her father did not approve.

"He is not as high as some men," Mother replied, though she returned her attention out the window as soon as she spoke. This, it seemed, was more lords' conversation than ladies', which was far from what Marian would have expected. With how dutiful her mother had been in turning her into a proper young lady, Marian would have thought she would take more of an active role in her daughter's pursuit of a husband. She hadn't always been like this, but over the last several years, Marian's mother had often left her feeling almost neglected. She left her alone far too often.

"Rank does not always mean acceptability," Father said. "Mr. Gisbourne seems a good sort of fellow, and his fortune is enough that he could care for you, if you were to consider him."

That was a relief, though it did not make Marian any less nervous to see Mr. Gisbourne. In fact, it rather made her anxiety worse since the obstacle of her father potentially disapproving was now gone. What was to stop her from letting the man truly court her?

"And what do you think of Lord Huntingdon?" Marian asked, though she hadn't realized the question was on her mind until it appeared at her lips.

Lord Waverly smiled. "There is a man of good rank," he said and patted his wife's knee, though she kept her gaze out the window. "I do not know much about him though. He mostly keeps to himself at Lords and speaks only when he is truly invested in a subject. But word around Town is he is as good a man as they come. Do you have an interest there as well, my dear?"

Marian hardly knew. Robin certainly never showered her with attention like Mr. Gisbourne did, unless she counted those little teasing moments when he got uncommonly close to her. "I suppose, maybe, if I knew him better," she said. She would not admit it out loud, but she doubted Robin had any interest in her anyway. He was far too busy saving the world one theft at a time, and until she had the time to practice her skills and get herself closer to his level, there was little reason for him to even look her way. As soon as they figured out who this second thief was and stopped him, Marian was sure Robin would no longer let her be a part of their little band.

Perhaps she would have to show him how valuable she could be. But how?

The carriage came to a stop outside Will's rented room, where he waited, and Marian scooted to the side to give her cousin space to sit beside her.

"Good evening, Uncle," Will said as he closed the door. "Aunt Eliza." He gave Marian's hand a squeeze, then settled in. "Thank you for the ride."

"Nonsense," Father said and waved the comment away. "You are a Russell, William, and my heir now that George is gone, God rest his soul."

"I do not see why you insist on renting a room when you could stay at Aspen House," Mother said. Now that Will was there, she had apparently decided she had had enough of her window-watching. How was it she could as easily pay attention to her nephew as she could ignore her own daughter? "You are always welcome, William, and I know Marian would enjoy your company now and then. We don't see you often enough."

"It's true," Marian said and slipped her arm through Will's so she could lean against his shoulder. She liked these warm moments with her family, particularly because her parents did not object to her closeness with her cousin. If they had disapproved of the way she treated Will like a dear brother, Marian might not have survived her childhood.

Will spoke quietly, flashing the briefest of smiles. "I like being closer to things in Town," he said. "I feel more a part of the city that way."

"You really should come by Aspen House more often though," Father replied. "You still have much to learn before you inherit."

"I will endeavor to be better," Will agreed.

"I hear you've become friends with the Earl of Huntingdon," Mother said. The news of their new friendship had traveled quickly if it had already reached Lady Waverly's inner circle.

Will swallowed, fighting to keep his expression neutral. When Marian gave his hand a reassuring squeeze, he took a deep breath, then said, "Yes, we have been spending time together of late. He is a good man, and he has much to teach me."

If Marian was not mistaken, Will had probably been spending *too much* time with Robin. He looked tired, dark circles beneath his eyes and his skin paler than usual. Had he stayed up the entire night looking for the other thief? She wished she could ask him, but that was not a discussion she wanted her parents to overhear.

"Ah, here we are," Lady Waverly said, and the carriage pulled up outside the Middletons' large home, ending the conversation.

Marian's anxious energy returned as she took Will's hand and stepped down to the street. It had been only a few hours since she last saw Mr. Gisbourne, but she was far more eager to see him again than she had realized. It was a strange sensation, one that left her trembling a bit in anticipation. She took Will's arm before he could get very far, and thankfully, he seemed to realize she needed support, because he pulled her a little closer.

The ball was an absolute crush, and Marian entered feeling overwhelmed and tempted to complain of a headache and go home. There were so many people, and even the thought of seeing Mr. Gisbourne fell short of convincing her she had the stamina to make it through the night. She had never been particularly adept at social graces in large gatherings, and her increasing nerves over her future life did not help anything. But then Marian caught sight of Robin standing with his sister, and he met her gaze and nodded.

Marian nodded back, and a bit of her stress eased away. If a man like Robin could be both earl and midnight thief, she could endure a ball.

Touching her elbow and asking her a silent question, Will nodded to Lord and Lady Waverly and led Marian into the crush. Together they crossed the crowded room until they reached Lord Huntingdon and greeted him with the appropriate bows.

"Marian," Will said, and his smile was warmer and brighter than it had been before. "This is Miss Loxley. Miss Loxley, this is my cousin, Lady Marian Russell."

Miss Loxley was beautiful but not much like the other ladies Marian was acquainted with. Unlike the porcelain dolls surrounding them in the crowd, she had clearly lived in the world and spent a good deal of time out of doors as a child. She held herself differently, and though she curtsied as well as anyone, there was still a bit of mischief in her brown eyes.

Marian liked her immensely. And, unless she was mistaken, so did Will. "Miss Loxley," she said and took the young woman by the hand. "I hope we can become dear friends."

A bit of pink spotted Miss Loxley's cheeks, but she returned Marian's hand squeeze with one of her own. "I would like that very much," she said. "Robin has mentioned you more than once over the last few days."

Marian glanced at Robin, who had suddenly become intent on grabbing himself a drink from a passing server, and wondered why he would have used a childhood nickname as his pseudonym while thieving. Surely someone could make the connection rather easily. She couldn't complain about his choice of name, however. It fit him well, and it was different enough that it set him apart from the rest of London. Just like the rest of him.

She returned her attention to Miss Loxley. "He's spoken of me?" she asked and laughed a little. "I cannot claim to know your brother well, but I hope he has said only good things."

Miss Loxley leaned a little closer and lowered her voice. "Truth be told," she said, "he hasn't said much, but it's a good deal more than he's said about any other lady since we were elevated. I was starting to worry no one would catch his interest."

Evidently Miss Loxley had not spoken quietly enough, because Robin cleared his throat and drained his entire glass as he continued to pretend he was not paying rapt attention to their secret conversation. Marian grinned, pleased to see the confident earl could be ruffled, but she knew her time for bonding with his sister was nearly at an end. She must give Will his chance to win the girl over if he so desired.

"Miss Loxley," she said brightly, "have you had the chance to dance with my cousin yet? He is wonderful at it."

Will turned a deep shade of scarlet, but Miss Loxley smiled, clearly delighted by the idea. "I have not had the pleasure," she said, her eyes fixed on Will.

Marian was tempted to kick Will in the shins, but she thought perhaps that was not the most subtle way to move things along. Instead, she nudged him with her elbow and prayed he didn't get too shy to ask the girl. Marian may have been uncomfortable in large gatherings, but Will was definitely worse.

To her relief, Will cleared his throat, then bowed a little. "It would be an honor," he said to Miss Loxley and held out his hand.

Marian turned to watch them arrive on the dance floor just as the orchestra struck up the next song, and she smiled. It would be a good match, though she wouldn't push Will if it was not what he wanted. He deserved to find someone who could make him happy.

"I haven't seen her like this before," Robin muttered at her side.

Marian looked up, surprised to see a bit of worry in the lines on his face. "Do you not approve of Will?"

He chuckled without any mirth behind it. "No, I very much approve of him," he replied. "That is exactly the problem. I don't know if I am ready to let go of my sister. Maybe I will never be ready."

As an only child, Marian didn't know what it felt like to have a sibling, though she thought Will was probably close. He had had his own brother growing up, but the two of them had never interacted much. Will had known he would inherit very little and had decided on a career in the military when he was only a boy, and George had spent his formative years learning the ins and outs of running an estate, mostly from Marian's father. He had always looked down on Will, saying if his brother could not bother to act like he had value, then he did not deserve a life of value. Marian could not imagine either of them caring about the happiness of the other, and she had seen similar sentiments among other siblings she had met over the years. With inheritances and titles disproportionately distributed, it was no wonder siblings often resented one another.

Miss Loxley, apparently, held no such animosity toward her brother, and Robin seemed infinitely willing to give her the best life he could manage.

"I believe I have myself an enemy," he said, breaking Marian out of her thoughts. He nodded across the ballroom, and it took only a quick glance for her to realize who he meant.

Jason Taylor had come out of hiding, and though his blond hair was not nearly as well-kept as it had been before and his clothing was a bit rumpled, he still stood with the bearing of someone with a good deal of self-importance. It was the glare in his eyes that must have prompted Robin's comment, seeing as it was pointed directly at the two of them.

Marian shuddered, wondering if somehow Taylor knew who had robbed him.

"I don't believe he is feeling any anger toward you," Robin said, and the fact that he sounded calm helped Marian feel less nervous. "I would guess our friend Taylor resents the fact that I am the one standing here talking to you, not him. I have prevented him from claiming you as a conquest."

Another shudder ran through Marian. She had never had anyone be jealous over her before, and she wasn't sure she liked it.

"By the way," Robin added. "Our mystery thief decided the Earl of Huntingdon was a good target last night."

Marian frowned. "But you are the Earl of Huntingdon."

"I am aware of that fact, yes."

"I haven't heard anything about that."

Laughing softly, he shook his head. "That is because I did not report it," he said. "I would rather the thief not get more publicity than he already has. And, thanks to my little stunt the other day and all the time I spent denying ever being robbed, no newspaper would acknowledge any other reports. He chose a poor time to try it and is likely just as angry as Mr. Taylor over there for being thwarted. In case you are concerned, he took my mother's least-favorite bracelet and a few other trinkets she was not sad to lose before I frightened him off."

"You didn't catch him?" Marian could have slapped the man for wasting such a promising opportunity. "We could have found out who he is and stopped all of this."

Robin pursed his lips, his eyes on the dancers. "I did not want to risk exposing myself," he said, as if that was reason enough to keep the poor of London in danger. "Besides, he is large enough that I might have failed in apprehending him and endangered my family. I was unprepared. I thought tonight I would lay a trap for him so I can be ready for him."

Marian felt her excitement growing at the thought, and she nearly started bouncing on her toes as she thought about catching the despicable soul who hurt innocent people. "What kind of—"

"Lady Marian?"

Marian jumped, not realizing how close she had gotten to Robin until he pulled away at the sound of another man's voice, and she was disappointed about being interrupted until she turned and saw Mr. Gisbourne just a few feet away. "Gis!" she said and slipped into a curtsy that helped hide the flush in her face.

The growl from Robin beside her made her pause. "Gis?"

Mr. Gisbourne grinned, as charming as ever, and offered his arm to Marian. "I do believe I have claimed this next dance. My apologies for taking her from you, Lord Huntingdon."

Marian could not have been sure, since Mr. Gisbourne was already leading her toward the center of the ballroom, but she thought Robin said something much like, "She isn't mine to take."

"I did not think it was possible," Mr. Gisbourne said, pulling Marian's attention back to him, "but you are more beautiful than you were this morning."

A familiar blush crept up Marian's neck, but it was colored by a twisting sensation in the pit of her stomach, and she had no idea why. Mr. Gisbourne had showered her with compliments from the beginning, and they had always brought a smile to her face.

Maybe it was the fact that she could almost feel Robin's gaze on her no matter where she was in the dance. She could not actually see him among the crowd, but she knew he was there, and that bothered her.

"You seem out of sorts, Lady Marian," Mr. Gisbourne said when the dance brought them together again. "Are you ill?"

"No," she said, sounding more breathless than she expected. "It's just . . ." What was it her mother had taught her to say when she wanted to hide something from men? Lady Waverly had said it with a barely restrained giggle and seemed to think deceiving men was as entertaining a pastime as gossiping. "This dance is more invigorating than I expected."

"Indeed," Mr. Gisbourne replied and sent her his usual charming smile.

When the dance ended none too soon, Mr. Gisbourne led Marian back to where her parents stood in deep discussion with some neighbors, but before they had even reached Lord and Lady Waverly, a young man Marian had never met stepped into their path.

"Gisbourne!" he said jovially and took hold of Gisbourne's hand. "It has been too long, my fellow." Without letting Gisbourne draw breath for a reply, his eyes shifted to Marian with eager interest. "Perhaps you might introduce me to your friend?"

"Certainly. Mr. Faraday," Gisbourne said, "allow me the pleasure of introducing you to Lady Marian Russell. My lady, this is Edward Faraday. He was one of my schoolmates at Harrow."

"Gis and I go back years," Mr. Faraday said, though the comment was rather unnecessary after Mr. Gisbourne's explanation. "And he has done well for himself, by the looks of things. It seems the entire room has fixed him as a point of envy when it comes to dance partners this evening."

The muscle of Mr. Gisbourne's arm tensed beneath Marian's gloved fingers, and she glanced up at him. His expression had not changed much, but there was a bit of a spark in his eyes that had not been there before. And when he drew her just the smallest bit closer to his side, a wave of pleasure ran through her despite her attempts to stay humble. Mr. Faraday had not even asked Marian to dance, and Mr. Gisbourne was already turning protective.

She had no idea how to flirt, but she wanted to ensure Mr. Gisbourne knew her desire to spend time with him. She would do her best. "I believe you have it backward, Mr. Faraday," she said with a gentle smile. "It is I who am envious of you; you have had much more time to grow close to Mr. Gisbourne than I, who have had the pleasure of his company for but a few days."

Mr. Gisbourne's barely suppressed grin warmed her to the core.

"Well, my lady," Mr. Faraday said, "perhaps I will need to dance with you so I can tell you all the man's secrets, and perhaps then you shan't be so inclined to hold to his arm." He offered his hand, which Marian took with interest. It seemed Mr. Gisbourne was rather well-liked by his friends.

Mr. Faraday was an average dancer who had to focus on the steps and did not actually speak to her during the set as he had suggested he would, though Marian did not mind. She was far too focused on Mr. Gisbourne, who had gathered several other acquaintances around him in her absence and was deep in friendly conversation.

And Robin seemed to have disappeared, which made her far more at ease than she had been before. The thief intrigued her, but more so, he unnerved her, and she could hardly pay attention to the dance steps if she was trying to ignore the way he got under her skin with every teasing smile. Every second she spent with the earl, she wondered if he would laugh at her or try to kiss her, and she found herself hoping he would at the very least give her a smile of pride every time he looked at her. Marian had never truly craved anyone's approval, and yet the idea of Robin thinking she was not good enough to be like him made her heart pound in her chest. So did his crooked smile, but that was unrelated.

Marian shook thoughts of Robin away, determined to keep her attention on her dance partner, even if he was rather dull. He was a friend to Mr. Gisbourne, and that made him her friend as well. There was nothing unnerving about Mr. Gisbourne, and though his smiles did not give her any great excitement like Robin's sometimes did, perhaps that was a good thing. She could remain rational with Mr. Gisbourne, and she did everything in her power to enjoy the rest of the dance with his friend because of it.

Returning Marian to Mr. Gisbourne's side, Mr. Faraday offered her a bow and his deepest wish to see her again.

"My lady." Mr. Gisbourne was quick to claim her company again, introducing her to two ladies and a man he had apparently not seen in years, though they all seemed eager to make his reacquaintance.

Not a single one of them was surprised or caught off guard by her rank when Mr. Gisbourne introduced Marian to them, and each of them expressed their utter delight at having met her. The more she heard it, though, the less she believed it. With each falsely delivered expression of friendship with Mr. Gisbourne, all of them followed by hungry looks directed at her, Marian suspected their inclination to befriend him again was simply because they recognized his connection to a marquess's daughter. He was an easy avenue to befriending *her*.

Mr. Gisbourne didn't seem to mind, though, and he all but grew taller as he stood there in their little circle, as if his being used as a means to advantageous connections was nothing less than the highest praise. He obviously enjoyed the attention.

Marian, on the other hand, wished she had a reputation like Robin's, one with which she was not expected to smile and feign politeness when really she abhorred making small talk with strangers. The Elusive Earl didn't even have to try to be left alone; all it took was a stern look and he sent his admirers scurrying away. Marian highly doubted she would ever be able to achieve that level of freedom, not when her entire life was laid out for public consumption. As a lady of privilege, she was expected to be the model of propriety and femininity, and all she wanted to do was slip into clothes that were not hers and try to better the world under the cover of night.

But until the world went to sleep, she was trapped as Lady Marian, subjected to fake smiles and ambitious fortune hunters hoping to make a well-bred friend of rank.

When Mr. Tilby interrupted to ask her to dance, Marian eagerly accepted, though the shadow that passed across Mr. Gisbourne's eyes left her feeling guilty for leaving his side. It was the second time she had been stolen from his side by Mr. Tilby since dancing with Mr. Tilby had prevented Marian from meeting Mr. Gisbourne at the last ball. But what was she to do? She could not very well spend the entire evening with Mr. Gisbourne, not unless she wanted all of Society thinking he intended to address her.

Marian's stomach flipped as the dance began. *Did* he intend to pursue her hand? That thought caught her so off guard that she nearly tripped into the woman next to her in the set, and she forced that thought away. There was no point in speculation until he made any sign in the affirmative or came right out and said it.

Forcing herself to keep her thoughts on what was right in front of her, Marian vowed to keep dancing until she cleared her head of ridiculous notions. Surely Mr. Gisbourne could not like her so much as to think he might make an address after only a couple of days of knowing her. Such a thing was preposterous! Simply girlish fantasy. Her first Season had only just begun, after all. Besides, she had far more important things to think about than marriage, and she would not let the likes of Mr. Gisbourne distract her from her goal to make England better.

From becoming a more permanent fixture in the world in which Robin Loxley made his home.

Don't be foolish, Marian Russell, she chided herself. Thinking about Robin was hardly better than thinking about Mr. Gisbourne. No, she had to force away thoughts of either of them and focus on Mr. Tilby, who was just as silent as the first time she had danced with him.

After many vigorous dances with various partners, all of whom made her quite forget about the nonsense that had filled her head as she did her best to be a pleasant dance partner, Marian found herself paired in the waltz with a Mr. Hewitt, a man of small fortune but large reputation. She had hoped to get a break and sit this particular dance out since the waltz was far more intimate than she liked when dancing with near strangers, but he had insisted, and Marian had not wanted to come off as rude. She could have no objection to a dance, even if he was said to be quite the rake.

"I must say, Lady Marian," Mr. Hewitt whispered to her, leaning as close as he could while still keeping the minimum distance apart to perform the dance. "You are quite the sight tonight. Every other lady in attendance must be clawing at their skirts to look half as fine as you."

Marian had no idea what that phrase was supposed to mean. She knew she should thank him for the compliment, but she was having a hard time breathing when all she could smell was the drink on his breath. Clearly, he had had more than most tonight, and it was a wonder he could stand up straight.

"You must have every man in Town barking at your door," Mr. Hewitt continued. His hand slid a little lower on her back than it should, though Marian supposed that was because he was so in his cups.

"I do not know what you mean," Marian said. She tried to keep herself from ending up too close to the man, but he sensed her resistance and pulled her a little closer. She quickly thought over some of the things Will had taught her before she'd gone to the tavern her first night, on what to do if a man became too forward. More importantly, she thought about what Robin had taught her about throwing a punch and using her full strength. She could almost picture the earl holding her arm and waist and standing unnervingly close as he demonstrated the movement. Mr. Hewitt was just as close as Robin had been, but he was far less welcome. She hoped she would not have to use any of her new skills, as causing a scene would only make the matter worse. *Will this dance never end?*

"Pretty thing like you?" Mr. Hewitt's hand slid even lower. "And with a dowry like yours? Makes a man start to wonder how difficult it would be to force your father's hand to make a sale."

Marian felt dizzy, and instinct was telling her to run despite being in the middle of the waltz. She did not want to be anywhere near Mr. Hewitt but could not see an escape as they traipsed around the room, so until she could get away, she tried to imagine the man's face when she and Robin robbed him blind and forced him to leave Town when he could no longer pay his rent.

After what felt like an eternity, the music finally hit its last note, and Marian tried to pull herself away. Mr. Hewitt held fast to her hand. "Please let me go," she said, and her voice was not nearly as strong as she wanted it to be. How did Robin manage to sound so confident all the time? He was not a woman, Marian reminded herself bitterly. He did not have cads like Mr. Hewitt looking at her like he wanted to drag her outside into the garden and find some secluded nook. She tried again. "Release me, Mr. Hewitt."

He twisted his lips into a wicked grin that made her skin crawl, but no one around them seemed to notice her distress. There were far too many people in the room, and another dance had just started up. "Why would I do that?" he asked and took a step toward the nearest door, pulling her with him. He was hoping to compromise her and bring himself a circumstantial marriage!

"Lady Marian?"

Relief flooded through her, and Marian slipped her hand free as Mr. Hewitt focused more on the interruption than his grasp. "Mr. Gisbourne," she said and could have embraced him if they were not in the middle of a ballroom. She hoped he recognized the look in her eyes, however, as he took in the scene.

Mr. Gisbourne looked between the two of them before he rested his hand against Marian's elbow. "You are looking flushed, Lady Marian. Perhaps you need to sit down. Mr. Hewitt," he added and bowed his head. Mr. Hewitt could not possibly misinterpret the fire in his gaze, however, as Mr. Gisbourne turned his polite smile into the subtlest glare.

Mr. Hewitt turned red; he must have sensed the challenge. "Gisbourne," he growled, and then he turned on his heel and strode into the crowd.

"Thank you," Marian said immediately and leaned into Mr. Gisbourne as her strength tried to leave her entirely. "He wouldn't let me go."

Mr. Gisbourne gritted his teeth, his keen eyes still watching Mr. Hewitt make his way across the room. "I noticed. Luckily, Hewitt is a coward, or I might have had to call him out."

A shudder ran through Marian, and it was not unpleasant. A man was willing to duel for her? In fact, Mr. Gisbourne seemed torn between staying at her side and following Mr. Hewitt into the corridor. But another thought crossed her mind, though she wished it hadn't: if she was not so helpless and unwilling to break social structures to protect herself, she would not need a man to fight her battles for her. She wondered if Robin would continue to teach her to fight properly or if she would have to look elsewhere.

"Do you need to get some fresh air, Lady Marian?" Mr. Gisbourne asked, and concern wrinkled his forehead. "Let me take you outside so you can catch your breath."

Though she really wanted to leave the ball entirely, Marian nodded and let him lead her through the still-overwhelming crowd to the back gardens. Several people were already milling about and talking in small groups, but it was much better than the crush inside, even if Mr. Taylor had also sought fresh air and stood deep in conversation at the other end of the terrace. Marian could breathe again, and with Mr. Gisbourne beside her, she was able to swallow her fears and start to find some sense of confidence again. She reminded herself that Taylor knew nothing of her nighttime exploits and would probably leave her alone while he was still wallowing in the shame of being robbed. But Mr. Hewitt . . . How was it that one man could so easily make her feel like she was nothing but a means to a fortune?

"Thank you, Gis," she said again as he lowered her onto an empty bench. Now that she wasn't breathless and her heart had stopped racing, she sounded a little more sincere. "I did not know what to do without causing a scene."

Several people who had also taken refuge in the gardens looked their way in interest, most of them attempting to catch Mr. Gisbourne's attention with a wave or a nod, though not a single one of them was brave enough to meet Marian's gaze. Neither did any of them receive any acknowledgment from Mr. Gisbourne, who leaned against the wall beside her and focused only on her. He certainly seemed a popular man, but Marian was rather pleased he chose to ignore his apparent friends when she truly needed his companionship. He may have been a social person, but she most certainly was not.

"You are far too sensible to understand, my lady," he said, bending his head a little closer to her so he didn't have to fight to be heard over the many conversations around them and the noise of the house filtering through the open doors. "You are nothing like the typical peer, so I doubt you have truly experienced the world. Welcome to high Society, Lady Marian, where most of the women are brainless and the men even more so."

Marian hardly thought that statement was fair; she knew many a person who had plenty to offer, and there was far more variety in Society than Mr. Gisbourne seemed to think. Besides, she had seen a good deal more of the world than he realized, thanks to her recent forays into the shadows of London. But, as if to prove his point, a boisterous laugh echoed across the space, and she and Mr. Gisbourne looked across the courtyard to find a rather large group of men gathered together, all of them apparently fixated on the same thing. A person, most likely, and Marian was about to ignore them when she realized that person was Robin. What was he doing?

He leapt up onto a bench so he was above his avid spectators and bathed in light from the house, and he had such a look of mischief in his eyes that

Marian almost laughed. This was certainly not the calm and collected earl he usually played. "So there I was," Robin said, so much theatricality in his voice that it drew out another laugh from the men around him. Was he drunk? "I was minding my own business, sleeping peacefully and dreaming of that night's splendid supper, when the most odious noise roused me. And I thought to myself, *There must be trouble about!* and took to walking the corridor in nothing but my nightclothes."

This was hardly the sort of talk a man of any rank should have been engaged in while in a public place, and Marian frowned at Robin, wondering how he could be so different every time she encountered him. He had played so many roles now that she wondered again who the real man was.

"And then I saw him," Robin said, and he put on an impressive scowl as he gazed off into the distance and waved an arm. "The illustrious thief. Right there in my house."

"You saw him?" one man asked in amazement. He sounded as if he had never heard a more daring tale, and Marian heartily hoped he was an exception among men. If he could be so easily enraptured by such a worthless story just because it came from an earl, it was no wonder rank played such a significant part of social acceptance.

Robin grinned. "That I did," he said and crouched down so he was closer to his audience. "I told the villain I would not stand for his treachery, and I challenged him right then and there."

"And?" the same man asked.

"And the coward ran."

This third laugh was punctuated by a scoff from Mr. Gisbourne at Marian's side and a grumble that sounded very much like, "Imbecile," though Marian could not be sure. The insult had likely not been meant for her ears.

"Fortunately for me," Robin said, standing up straight again and looking like more of a dandy than he ever had as he casually rested his walking stick on his shoulders, "the poor man had no idea where my true treasure lies, and he got away with only trinkets."

Whispers filtered through the little crowd until one man said, "Are you not afraid he will come back, my lord?"

Robin laughed, and if he had not already entranced his crowd, some of them might have realized there was no real mirth in the sound. It was precisely at that moment that Marian realized what the earl was doing, and she found herself smiling and wanting his little story to end so she could go talk to him and get in on the plan.

"That ridiculous thief is far too unintelligent to search my study," Robin said and smiled as if he had won some enormous bet against an enemy. "He would be foolish to try to get past all my new safeguards now that I know he is stupid enough to come after a man like me."

The man was laying a trap in the best possible way: he was issuing a challenge.

And Taylor was livid. He had paused his conversation to listen in on the ridiculous tale, and his hands were in fists at his sides as he scowled up at the earl. Marian was more than glad she was on the other side of the terrace, far from the man's seething fury. Unlike the rest of the little crowd, he did not seem to much like the attention Lord Huntingdon had garnered for himself.

"We should go inside before we have to listen to any more mindless drivel."

Marian had all but forgotten Mr. Gisbourne standing next to her until his cool voice broke her focus, pulling her attention from the scheming earl to the much less complex baronet's son.

"Oh," she said, trying not to sound disappointed. "Of course." But when she gave Robin one last glance before Mr. Gisbourne led her through the doors, she found the earl looking right back at her with a twinkle still in his eyes and a smirk that made her heart skip a beat.

Robin always had so much expression in that face of his, and as Marian linked her arm with Mr. Gisbourne's, she realized he did not. There was nothing adventurous about the man she walked beside. True, she had known him only a few days, but outside of the day he'd first called on her, he had not broken any rules of etiquette. He had taken her on a drive once—bringing along a maid as chaperone—and danced with her only once tonight so far, as was proper. He dressed well but not flamboyantly, he smiled warmly but had never truly laughed, and Marian had certainly never seen mischief in his eyes. She supposed his propriety would be a desirable trait for any young lady to find in a suitor.

But Marian was not any young lady. She had had her taste of a world outside the high Society to which she belonged, and she wanted more.

CHAPTER *Thirteen*

ROB HAD PROBABLY OVERDONE THINGS at the ball and brought too much attention to himself, but he didn't much care. It had been quite enjoyable, playing the fool, and he could always attribute it to having too much to drink if anyone brought it up and suggested he might not be as calm and collected as he had pretended to be for the last eight years. But it had felt good to let loose a little and garner some real attention for once.

Who would have thought the Elusive Earl would have wanted notice?

The problem was his mother had also taken notice, and she suspected there was something more to his behavior than he wanted her to believe, particularly because he had asked her and Alana to spend the night with a neighbor.

"Are you well, Robin?" She had already asked this question twice since their return from the Middletons' ball, and she hadn't believed him either time.

"Very well, Mother, I assure you." Rob knew she was hoping for the truth, but that was one thing he could not tell her. He hated lying to the woman who had raised him, practically on her own, but it was the only way to keep her safe. He turned to the maid who was packing Mother's valise. "Make sure she has warm enough nightclothes, in case the Shelleys do not keep their fires as large through the night as you do."

"You have never asked us to leave the house to you alone," his mother said from the chaise in her room. "I am convinced you're not in your right mind."

"I am perfectly lucid," he replied, though he would not let himself meet her gaze. She wasn't wrong, and he hardly ever stayed at Huntingdon Manor if his family was not with him. The house was far too big for him alone. But this was for a single night, and surely it was not so strange a thing for him to ask. "I told you, Mother," he said, fighting a sigh. "I have reason to believe the manor will not be safe tonight."

"And what makes you think that?"

Blast it all, would she not just trust him on this? She trusted him with everything else. "This is not something I can explain," he tried. "I just need you to be safe."

"And you?" she asked. "Where will you stay?"

She had already tried to convince him to stay at the Shelleys' with them, but that defeated the entire purpose of the night. He needed to be here, ready to intercept the thief should he choose to try again. Groaning, Rob crouched at his mother's chaise and did his best to look like the young boy she had never been able to deny. "Mama," he said gently.

"It is far too late to leave the house," she said in return.

"I have already spoke to Mrs. Shelley, and she is more than happy to—"

"You are keeping something from me, Robin." Mother put her thin hands on Rob's cheeks, forcing him to hold her gaze. Rob had never thought he looked much like his mother, who was thin and angular and fair. He had taken after his robust sailor father. But they shared the same eyes. In the firelight, her green eyes seemed almost gold as she tried to steal his secrets with her gaze.

And Rob was nearly ready to give in when a cough broke them apart.

"There are rumors the thief will be in the neighborhood tonight," Alana said in the doorway. She did not have much expression in her face, but her eyes pierced Rob with much the same intensity as their Mother's had just done. "I think Robin is intelligent to send us away, just in case."

"You do?" Rob and their mother said at the same time.

Rob had known it would be difficult to convince his mother to leave the manor, but he had thought it would be even harder to get his sister to comply. She was too intelligent for her own good, and he had expected her to put up a fight and demand explanation.

A smile played at Alana's lips as she glanced between them both. "I do," she replied. "You know how much he hates being alone, so he wouldn't suggest we leave if it weren't important. Right, Robin?"

He stared at her, trying to read her surprisingly blank expression. He didn't often have trouble reading his sister, and the fact that she seemed all too aware of his attempts—her growing smile proved that—brought a knot to his stomach. Did she know something she was not supposed to? Whatever secrets she might have had, she was clearly just as reluctant to share them as Rob was his. "Right," he muttered.

She met his stare with one as equally searching as his own, almost like she was trying to decide if her suspicions were correct. "So," she said after a painfully long moment, "I do believe we should be getting on, Mother. We don't want to be keeping Mrs. Shelley up too late, after all."

With both children against her, their mother let out a weary sigh and allowed Rob to lift her to her feet so she could follow the maid who carried her things. "Sometimes I do not understand you," she said, though Rob honestly could not decide if she said it to him or to Alana, and she was out in the corridor before he could ask.

Alana waited for a moment before she followed, the same searching look back in her eyes, and then she patted Rob's arm and cheerily said, "Don't stay up too late, Robin!" as she made her way downstairs to the waiting carriage.

And while Rob very much knew he would have to confront her and try to figure out how much she thought she knew, he had far too much to worry about at the present time. His sister would have to wait.

He had a thief to catch.

Rob sighed and turned his oil lamp a little brighter. His research generally kept his interest well, but tonight proved difficult for him to concentrate. With how little he had slept the night before, he really should have better planned his trap and laid it for a different evening. But the Middletons' ball had been the perfect setup, and he suspected Mother had really only left because the thief had targeted Huntingdon Manor the night before. Otherwise, he might never have been able to convince them to leave.

But in order to confront the thief, he had to stay awake. He couldn't risk dozing off here in the library and missing the man, assuming he had actually caught wind of Rob's carefully planned challenge. Hopefully, Rob had drawn enough of a crowd for the word to spread properly.

But it was barely midnight, and the city was still too lively after a ball like that for an attack to happen within the next couple of hours. And the house was so quiet.

"Pay attention, Robin," he muttered and slapped himself in the face to wake himself up. It worked, though it didn't improve his mood much.

Turning his focus back to the papers in front of him, he resumed the task he had set himself to after Mother and Alana had left. If the thief was indeed among the Quality as he had guessed, that narrowed his list of suspects down considerably. The man had to be fairly young, as well as fit, and he was of a similar height to Rob, which made the list even smaller. He could cross off a few names, men Rob knew to be of a good sort and unlikely to take up thievery, even in a crusade for the poor like Rob had.

Currently, Jason Taylor was at the top of that list, but there were still a lot of possibilities, which was why he needed to catch the thief tonight. At the very least, he needed to observe more of him.

Rob took a deep breath, holding it in his lungs as he rubbed exhaustion from his face. How had he managed to never get tired over the last year? All this time, sneaking into the houses of his peers in the middle of the night had rather invigorated him over draining him, but now he simply wanted a moment's peace. Just one day without another name added to his list of targets. One day without worrying about John or Will. Or Marian.

Now, *there* was a reason to be exhausted. From the very moment he'd first caught her in that tavern, he really hadn't been able to get her out of his head, and it was getting ridiculous. He had barely spent any time with the woman, and yet he found himself revisiting their every encounter and wondering how a young woman like her could have come out of the life she had. She was far more aware of the state of the world than most of the upper ten thousand, and she had an ambitious nature Rob had seldom seen. She was unlike any lady he had met since becoming the earl.

She was far more beautiful than any lady he had met before. Inside and out. And that was presenting a problem.

When he should have been laying his trap the entire evening, he had spent much of the Middletons' ball watching Marian smile for every man who came within a few feet. He had hated every minute of it.

A gentle knock made Rob realize he had closed his eyes and was beginning to dream about Lady Marian and her inability to climb through windows. Particularly about how he didn't much mind that lack of skill when it gave him an excuse to get close to her. "Enter," he grunted and tucked away his notes in a nearby book.

"Pardon the intrusion, my lord," the butler, Hoskins, said as he opened the door and stepped inside the dim library. "But there is a young woman here to see you, and she was quite insistent."

Rob frowned. "It's after midnight, Hoskins," he said. And why wasn't the butler asleep already? The household knew better than to think they had to stay up when he did.

Hoskins very nearly scoffed but kept his emotions to himself. "I am aware, my lord. She threatened to stay the night on the doorstep if I did not alert you, so I thought it best to bring it to your attention."

Rob couldn't fathom why anyone would be so determined to speak to him this late at night, and curiosity brought him to his feet. If nothing else, he had to get rid of the girl before the mimic thief started his approach on the house. *Assuming the man took the bait*, Rob thought again, yawning as he followed Hoskins down to the back entrance.

It wasn't entirely odd for the lower class to seek him out—most of his staff had come off the street, and word tended to travel fast among the serving class—but it was the lateness of the hour that baffled him most. Surely a girl would be intelligent enough to come during the day instead of wandering about the city at night. If it was that girl from Mr. Taylor's house, he would simply have to tell her to come back in the morning, at a more reasonable hour. Surely John would have said as much when he went to Taylor's house the day after they robbed him to invite her again to take up her occupation at Huntingdon Manor.

The young woman was waiting for them just inside the back door, and she looked up as Rob and his butler approached.

He nearly swore but stopped himself and replaced the word with her name, though that was hardly better. "Mari—" Thankfully, he cut himself off so it sounded like he had simply said, "Mary." She had done her best to mask her appearance, but he would have recognized the spark in her eyes anywhere.

"You know this girl, my lord?" Hoskins asked, sounding somewhat skeptical.

Marian put on an impressively innocent smile. "I know it's mighty late, my lord, but you said I could come if ever I needed a job." Her accent was just as impressive as her expression. She had likely been practicing over the last week, though that was hardly cause for praise. No matter how pleased with herself she looked.

Rob coughed when Hoskins looked at him as if silently daring him to confirm the girl's outlandish tale. "Of course," he said, though he didn't quite manage to sound indifferent. "It must have slipped my mind, but you are most welcome. Hoskins, you can go to bed. I will take her to the kitchen and see what we can do for her."

Hoskins looked ready to cry falsehood—he wasn't wrong—but Rob leveled him with a seldom-used glare that convinced the butler to bow and leave the pair of them alone.

The second he no longer had an audience, Rob grabbed Marian by the arm and guided her down the corridor until they reached the library, which would remain empty the rest of the night. He couldn't risk their being over-heard or caught in a compromising position. Though he trusted his staff, it was far too much to ask that they keep quiet about something as scandalous as entertaining a young woman in the late hours of the night.

Once inside the library, and with the door closed behind him, Rob pressed Marian up against a wall and held her there by the shoulders so she could see exactly how angry he was with her for being stupid enough to come. "What do you think you are doing?" he growled. "Do you have any idea how much danger you've put us both in by coming here unannounced?"

The room was still dim, but the oil lamp illuminated her eyes as she looked up at him without an ounce of fear. "You're planning to catch the thief tonight," she said, as if he didn't know his own mind. "I want to help."

Rob snarled a bit and moved in closer, leaning his hands on the wall on either side of her head. He wasn't used to being threatening, but he tried his best. "I do not need your help," he said. "If I did, I would have asked your cousin or John."

In fact, young Russell had learned of a possible target for the thief, and he and John had gone out to keep an eye on one Mr. Smith, who had apparently made himself quite a few enemies at the ball that night, many of whom were on Rob's list of suspects. Rob would have preferred to have his associates here in the house, but necessity meant he would have to lie in wait for the thief on his own.

Marian's expression hardly turned into the fear he'd hoped for. Rather, she smiled up at him and looked downright beautiful, even in her maid's clothes. "I am not afraid of you, Robin Loxley," she said.

Rob tensed at the sound of the nickname on her lips. He was not supposed to enjoy it that much. Neither was he supposed to look down at those lips and wonder what it would be like to kiss the smirk right off her face. He stared at her, frowning as he tried to think of an argument she would not be able to reason against. But he had none, and the longer he stood there, with his hands on either side of her head and that wicked grin of hers tempting him to do something rash, the more in danger he was of losing any willpower he'd thought he had. Somehow this woman had the power to persuade him to do things he knew he shouldn't, like take her out thieving and spend half his focus at the ball watching her dance with Geoffrey Gisbourne and the rest of the *ton* instead of concentrating on his plans.

"You're not afraid of me?" he whispered and leaned closer.

"Not in the slightest," she said. And then she punched him full in the stomach.

It was not a particularly strong hit since she was trapped against the wall with little room to move, but it still caught Rob off guard and nearly knocked the wind out of him. Grunting, he curled up a little out of instinct, which was just enough for Marian to slip out from under him. And while he was proud of her for getting herself free, he was not about to let that smirk of hers continue. Wrapping an arm around his stomach, he pretended to be more hurt than he was and turned around slowly, his eyes locked on hers. He waited until she lowered her defensive hands, and then he lunged.

She almost got away from him, which was impressive, but Rob caught hold of her wrist and twisted her arm up over her head, pulling her in against his chest. She stomped on his foot. Rob let go, but before she got out of reach, he swept his throbbing foot into her legs and knocked her off her feet and into his arms. She tried to twist herself free, but he pinned her arms to her sides and growled as he held her in place.

It wasn't the easiest way to keep a hold on her, but he rather enjoyed looking down at her with her glaring up at him. Plus, they were only a couple of inches apart, and this position gave him a good view of her stunning eyes. "Not bad," he said and was alarmed to find himself a bit out of breath. She had put up more of a fight than he'd realized.

Marian tried one more time to struggle, then huffed a sigh. "Will you let go of me?" she said.

Rob reluctantly set her upright and let her pull out of his arms, though he took hold of her hand so she couldn't get far. It was time to be serious again. "Marian, it is too dangerous for you to be here tonight. I've already sent my mother and sister to stay the night with a friend, and I can't let you—"

"You'll find I am more stubborn than you, Robin," Marian said and gave him a scowl that set him on edge. She was becoming far more distracting than she had a right to be, and that would only lead him to make rash decisions. Like ignoring his rational side and kissing her until he couldn't think anymore. What in heaven's name was wrong with him? When had his teasing turned into truth?

Rob shook his head and dropped her hand before he lost control completely. "Very well," he said, knowing it was a terrible idea. "But if I give you an order, you will obey it. No matter how little you might want to do it. Do you understand?"

She cocked her head and seemed to be scrutinizing him. "That is a high price, my lord," she said calmly. "What if you tell me to do something I simply cannot?"

She was pushing the boundaries, seeing how far she could go before he snapped, and Rob liked her all the more for it. Too many women were content to accept what life had given them, no matter how little. Marian was not. From an outside perspective, she had everything she could have possibly wanted—money, rank, beauty—but she would never be content, especially when she knew how fortunate she was compared to the rest of her sex.

The urge to kiss her grew even stronger, which was nothing short of ridiculous. He had to concentrate, and she certainly would not return the sentiment, given how she had reacted to his other advances. All of that pretending had probably tarnished her view of his affection, and now he would have to pay the price. She would likely truly injure him if he tried to kiss her.

Sighing, he crossed to the fireplace and added wood to the small fire now that it was not him alone. Marian would likely get cold if he did not. "We'll wait here tonight," he said softly. "My study is directly above us, and there is a loose floorboard that is impossible to miss unless you know it's there. Unless he truly is a ghost, if the thief comes tonight, we will hear him."

Marian snorted a small laugh. "Do not tell me you believe in ghosts as well," she said.

He had never been more relieved to hear someone was intelligent enough to know spirits weren't real, at least not in the way everyone else seemed to believe. "I am not Mr. Gisbourne," he said and scoffed. "I believe in what I can see. Now, sit."

He did not miss the quick little salute Marian gave him as she approached him. "Yes, sir," she said, amused by his gruffness as she grinned.

A shiver ran through Rob, the sensation far from unpleasant. But enjoying her presence this much would only distract him. He needed to have a moment away from her. Clear his head. "I need to make a show of going to bed," he said as she settled herself in one of the armchairs in front of the fire. "Before anyone gets the idea that I regularly converse with serving girls late at night. I'll be back soon. Stay here and be silent, or all of this could be ruined."

She nodded but said nothing, her eyes boring deep into him as she watched him in the growing firelight.

Rob cleared his throat and left the room before he let his eyes linger on her for too long. This woman was going to be the death of him someday, but as he made his way upstairs to his chamber—tromping his boots so he was heard—he found he quite liked the idea of his predictable life being turned on its head by the likes of Marian Russell. If there was anyone in the world he could stand to lose control to, it was her.

CHAPTER *Fourteen*

AFTER AN EXCRUCIATING LENGTH OF time that felt like hours but was really only twenty minutes or so, Rob crept back downstairs to the library, stopping only to make sure the study door was still locked and he hadn't somehow missed the thief. He had spent most of that time pacing his room, and though half of him hoped the evening had simply been a dream, the other half was desperate to find Marian still sitting in that armchair by the fire.

He really could not account for his sudden affection for the lady. He had interacted with her only a few times, and none of those interactions had gone particularly in his favor. They seemed eternally at odds with each other, no matter which character either of them was playing. And after all of his teasing, he had ruined his chances. Unless he could get to know the real Marian Russell, not the lady, nor the aspiring righteous thief, and he could be his true self, Robin, the boy who had lost his life at eighteen, there was little chance their tentative relationship could ever improve. Was that even possible? To be himself? It had been so long that he was quite convinced he didn't know who that was anymore.

Even if he could remember, was it even someone Marian would like?

He found her still in the same chair, her legs curled up beneath her as she read a book in the firelight. She looked younger that way, though she wasn't old to begin with. Only eighteen. She had scarcely been a part of the world, and already she wanted to try to save it. There was something special about this woman, and Rob would do whatever it took to keep her safe.

"Do you mind?" he asked, keeping his voice soft so he didn't startle her.

She looked up. "I do believe this is your house, my lord. You may sit wherever you'd like."

Whether or not that wit was the true Marian or simply a part of her lower-class persona, Rob most certainly enjoyed it. Settling himself in the other chair by the fire, he took a slow breath and suddenly found himself at a loss for words. He never ran out of things to say, something which had always driven his mother mad when he was a boy.

Thankfully, Marian filled the silence when he could not. "Do you think he will show up?" she asked, closing her book. "If he was here only last night, he might be more cautious than before."

Rob had considered the possibility. "If he truly announced the Bernhard theft, the fact that I did not make any public admission outside of bragging to a few of my fellow peers will likely have attacked his pride. He failed to get anything of value yesterday, and now he thinks there is a loot worth the risk of trying again."

"And what do we do when he comes?" she asked next.

"I mean to catch him."

Her smile was small, but it seemed to warm the room. "And what if you can't catch him?"

Rob couldn't help but smile back at her, even though she was questioning his skill. That was another thing he liked about her; she did not take care to avoid offending him at all costs. She said what she thought, and she was confident in her opinions. Too few ladies could say the same. Maybe it was her rank that gave her that confidence, but Rob suspected it was simply Marian.

"I can catch him," he said with a little laugh.

"I hope you are right," she replied, "or it will be up to me to make up the deficit."

"Deficit?"

"Indeed."

"Lady Marian, you truly enjoy slighting me, don't you?"

Grinning, she pulled herself into a tighter ball on the chair and rested her head against the wing of it as she gazed at Rob with her perceptive eyes. "I think you've spent a good deal of time forgetting yourself," she said after a moment's study. "Everyone needs to be cut down now and then. Reminded we are all human."

"And how did you come to believe such a thing?" Rob asked. He found himself leaning closer. True, they were speaking in hushed tones so as not to disrupt the silence of the house, but he could hear her without issue. He simply wanted to be closer. He wanted to know everything there was to know about this woman, and he could not do that from so far away.

They had had a conversation similar to this when they had gone out for that drive soon after they first met, but Rob had managed to make a mess of that discussion rather quickly. He hoped he could keep in her good graces longer this time. When Marian said nothing and simply watched him, he amended his question a bit. "Surely there was something," he said, "a moment that made you realize your fortune in life did not extend to the masses."

Frowning a bit, Marian nodded. "I am an only child," she said. "I had Will nearby, but more often than not I was left to myself. My governess was impossibly old and slept through most of the day, so I learned to teach myself the ways of the world, mostly through watching my parents." She shifted in her seat, as if uncomfortable, and then she sat up entirely. "One of the maids, my abigail now, took pity on me and became a friend when I didn't have one, and through her I learned about the way most people live. And I could not ignore what I saw all around me. Her younger sister died of starvation not two months ago because the family's various wages were too poor, and I knew I could no longer turn a blind eye."

"So you became Mary the maid and chose to get a job at a tavern?" Rob said, raising one eyebrow a bit. A tear slid onto Marian's cheek, and it was taking all of his self-control not to reach forward and brush it away. "I confess I haven't figured out what you hoped to accomplish with that."

Marian swiped her own tear away. "I probably didn't think it through very well," she confessed. "Will never liked the idea, though he was kind enough to help me. But like I told you before, I wanted to see if my maid's situation was unique or if the whole world is like that. I wanted to know what it felt like not to have the luxury of spending all of one's time making social calls and dancing at balls. I wanted . . ." She paused and shook her head. "Never mind."

Rob sat forward. "Please tell me."

Sitting up and letting her feet touch the floor again, Marian met Rob's gaze and let her vulnerability show in her face. "I wanted to be someone who wasn't Lady Marian," she admitted.

Rob knew that feeling well. He had become the Elusive Earl simply out of necessity. He could not have survived if his entire life were to be for public consumption, and if he could have, he would have spent his entire life in the country. He had his responsibility to the House of Lords, however, and to his sister, who deserved to find her own happiness. And now there was the question of Marian.

There was a high chance she would never give up this crusade of hers, much like he could never give up his own, and she was far too young to do it on her own. She would get stronger over time, but Rob had seen things while amongst the poor that he could not forget, no matter how hard he tried. The life of the lower class was not an easy one, though most managed to bear it with a smile, for which he was grateful. But could he really bring her into his little fold of law-breaking sheep? It was dangerous enough bringing someone like Will Russell into it, considering he was set to inherit a good deal of money and influence. All of that, minus Marian's dowry, would go to a distant relation if anything happened to him, and Rob knew there were few good men among the upper class. Losing Russell, aside from losing a friend, would tip the balance to benefit the selfish of the aristocracy.

"I never wanted to be an earl," Rob said, though he wasn't sure where the thought had come from. As Marian leaned forward a bit, he swallowed the instinct to shut his mouth and decided he had best just say what was on his mind. There was no need to protect himself from this woman, and if there was any way he could make her feel like she wasn't alone, he wanted to do it.

"I remember those rare moments I had with my father," he said, "when he wasn't off at sea, and he would tell me about what it was like to grow up among the wealthy. He left his life behind when he met my mother, and he never once regretted it. To him, my grandfather and my uncle were a different sort of people from us, the kind who could not see beyond their own importance. I didn't want to be anything like that, and I was always just Robin Loxley."

"How old were you when you became the earl?" Marian asked softly.

It felt like a lifetime ago, and those eight years since had been the longest of his life. "I was eighteen," he said and dropped his gaze to the floor. "Old enough to know what I had been thrown into but young enough to think I might have a way out of it. How wrong I was." And while he felt the tension in his shoulders ease a bit as he admitted how reluctantly he had taken on his mantle, he knew he needed to show Marian exactly why he was telling her his history.

Sitting forward a little more, Rob met her eyes and held them in his gaze. "I know how it feels to want something more for your life," he said. "I spent six years trying to use my money and influence to help the poor, and I spent six years becoming more and more frustrated because my status and fortune could do little to help those around me who were suffering."

"And that is why you became a thief?" Marian guessed.

Rob shrugged. "I hadn't planned to be a thief," he said. "I had spent so much of my youth stealing that I had seen only the hurt it caused, not the benefit to anyone but myself and my family. But then . . ." He hadn't spoken of this day to anyone, not even to his family, but suddenly the words were on his lips before he could stop them.

"Before I found John and took him in," he whispered, "he was part of a group of boys who looked out for each other on the streets. A brotherhood. I could not employ them all, as much as I wished I could, but I sent John to check up on them now and then and make sure they weren't getting into too much trouble. Two years ago, he came back from one of those excursions, and . . ." Rob's chest felt tight, and he took a slow breath to try to clear the emotion from inside him. It didn't help. "John has never been much for showing emotions," he said, "so when he came back to the manor sobbing, I knew something had gone horribly wrong. He couldn't even . . ."

His words stuck in his throat, and it wasn't until Marian took his hand in her warm fingers that he somehow found his voice again. He wished he could see her clearly, but the anguish building up inside him was threatening to spill from his eyes. But with her quiet strength, he was able to finish his story.

"Two of the boys had been caught stealing from a lord, and the man exacted his own justice. One boy was already dead, shot through with a pistol, and the other . . . I did what I could for him, but he died in John's arms. All because he was hungry. And no matter how much it hurt to watch the boy go, seeing how deeply it wounded John made me realize that someone had to tip the balance of the world's scale. Someone had to remind the rich and powerful that they were no more important than the orphans rummaging in the streets for scraps."

John had never been the same since that night. The already quiet boy had become a blank slate, and Rob treasured the moments he could get him to smile or—heaven bless it—*laugh*.

"Someone has to save this world, Marian," he said and blinked to clear the tears from his eyes so he could see her.

She brushed her thumb across his cheek. "I want to help," she said. "You should not have to do this alone. But . . ." Frowning, she wilted in her chair as she seemed to think about what she was saying. "Do you think I could really make a difference if I tried? I know there is little chance I could be like you, but I want to try, Robin. I have to try."

Rob wanted so badly for her to succeed that he nearly shouted an emphatic, "Of course you could make a difference!" But he went with something softer, something he hoped would return some of the confidence he loved about her. "You are unlike any lady I have ever met, Marian Russell," he said. "And I've met a good deal of them. If anyone can learn to champion the less fortunate and give them better lives, you can."

Marian smiled, tears in her eyes, but not of sadness. She leaned a little closer; Rob shifted as well, and he felt she could see into his soul as they gazed at each other. Her eyes were so bright and alive, pulling him ever closer. He'd meant what he said about her being unique, and he feared he would never meet anyone who could measure up to this darling woman. He wanted her to stay in his life forever. But how could he possibly tell her something like that?

Before he could say or do anything, a soft whistle reached his ears. "It's Russell," he guessed and crossed to the door, pulling it open just enough to see out into the dark corridor beyond.

Just as he predicted, Russell waited just outside the door and was quick to slip into the library when Rob stepped aside. He stopped immediately upon seeing Marian and looked about ready to get angry with her, so Rob thought it best to step in.

"Where's John?" he asked.

Russell gave his cousin a good scowl, then turned to Rob to report. "He broke into Smith's house and learned from the servants that he is completely broke, something Smith's friends and associates know well. Our thief likely won't go after him when there is nothing to gain. I told him to wait a little longer, just in case, but I wanted to see if I could help here."

"Good man," Rob replied and clapped him on the shoulder. "I'll take every soldier I can get."

"Including Marian?"

Rob narrowed his eyes, wondering how the man couldn't see how much Marian had done to help them so far. "Every soldier," he repeated.

Marian let out a little gasp, the kind of sound that made Rob's breath catch in his throat, but when he looked back at her, she had a falsely innocent expression on her face as she returned his gaze. Rob couldn't decide if he wanted to pull her up into his arms or get into a match of fisticuffs with her. That fire in her eyes was driving him mad, and it really was going to be the death of him if he wasn't careful.

"Well," he said, though he wasn't sure what to say. They were stuck waiting for their thief to show up, and he was not about to resume the conversation he had been having with Marian. That was not one he needed Russell to be a part of. "I suppose we could—" He stopped when the ceiling above them creaked.

"He's here," he said, instantly on the alert. "Stay behind me," he told Marian, "and for the love of all that is holy, do not engage him, no matter what may happen. He cannot discover you, Marian."

She nodded, which was enough for him, and as Russell made his way to the main staircase, Rob led the way out into the dark corridor and to the servants' stairwell. With Marian on his heels—thankfully silent—he reached the next floor up and slowly made his way to the study. The thief was quieter this time— Rob hadn't heard a sound since that initial floor creak—but he was not about to think that meant there was no one there. Any thief with an ounce of pride would not have been able to resist an invitation like the challenge Rob had issued.

As Russell arrived from the opposite direction in case he'd had to head off the thief, a gentle hand touched Rob's elbow as they neared the study, and he reached back until his fingers met Marian's. Her hand was cold, and Rob wished there were more light coming in through the window so he could look back at her and reassure her with a smile that everything would be all right. But he hoped a squeeze of his hand would suffice.

"One," he whispered, just loud enough for Russell to hear as the two of them got ready.

"Two," Russell replied with a nod of his head. Rob released Marian's hand.

The study door was barely ajar, but it would be enough for them to push it open and attack the thief before the man realized he wasn't alone.

"Three."

Rob was the first one through the door, and though the room was almost completely dark, he found the thief quickly and easily as the man looked up from the desk drawer he searched. Rob jumped forward and grabbed him around the middle, trying to get hold of both arms, but he missed as the pair of them flew toward a bookshelf. The thief shoved himself free right as they hit the shelf, but Russell was there in an instant, fists flying. But the thief was fast and strong and threw Russell—a skilled soldier—to the ground in only a moment.

Rob leapt over Russell and ducked beneath a fist before he threw his shoulder into the thief's stomach and knocked him into the wall. The thief grunted and kicked his knee up into Rob's gut. Rob ignored the pain but ducked down again just as Russell returned and threw a punch into the thief's jaw. Rob caught hold of one arm, and Russell grabbed the other. The thief tugged Rob off-balance and knocked his head into Rob's. Rob wobbled backward, vision swaying, as Russell let out a strangled cry as he flew over the desk and crashed into the bookshelf. And though Rob was dizzy and fighting to stay upright, he saw the thief dart toward the door.

Toward *Marian*.

He dove toward the thief, grabbing him by the elbow and using his momentum to shove him into the wall again. Taking hold of one arm, he pinned it behind the thief's back and pulled up high enough that the man grunted in pain. "Finally," Rob breathed, ready to figure out who had been causing him so much trouble.

"Loxley!" Russell shouted.

The sharp sting came a second later, so acute in the side of his gut that Rob stumbled back in surprise, not entirely sure what had just happened. All he knew was he was suddenly in more pain than he had ever been in in his entire life. His hand slid down to his side, and he was alarmed to find what felt like the handle of a knife sticking out from just below his rib cage. That wasn't supposed to be there. And though a thought told him he should leave it exactly where it was, he grabbed it and tugged, looking down at the blade that glistened red just as the thief darted away. Rob reacted instinctively, throwing out his arm to try to stop him as he staggered, and the knife in his hand collided with the man's leg.

The thief stumbled but vanished.

Rob collapsed.

"Loxley!"

"Robin!"

Rob looked up into two sets of matching hazel eyes, but he turned his focus to Marian. She was beautiful.

CHAPTER *Fifteen*

ROBIN WAS ALIVE. FOR NOW, that was all Marian could stomach to think about.

It was almost five in the morning, and she knew she needed to head home before her parents woke up, but she couldn't bring herself to leave Robin's side. The physician who had arrived in record speed when Will sent a footman to fetch him had assured her cousin that the wound was rather superficial and Robin was fortunate the knife had not hit any organs. Marian had listened to it all while anxiously hiding in the dressing room to avoid raising questions, and it had taken all of her power not to burst into sobs of relief. Robin's housekeeper had been diligent in supplying clean rags and plenty of water, John had mustered a veritable army of fellow servants to protect the house from any further attacks, and Will hadn't left his post at the bedchamber door for even a moment.

Eventually, when the staff all left the room with the doctor, Marian settled into a chair at Robin's side and prayed he made it through. It was not a proper place to be, at a man's bedside, but she didn't want to be anywhere else. Even with Will promising he wouldn't abandon Robin, Marian couldn't leave, and she sat there for hours.

If he would just wake up, she would be able to breathe again. If he would just open his eyes and give her a smile . . .

"I'm scared, Will," she said quietly as she held one of Robin's cold hands between her own. He looked so pale, and he seemed to barely breathe.

Will was settled on the floor in the corner, and as he had for the last few days, he looked completely exhausted in the glow of the fire. "He is going to pull through," he said, though he didn't seem to believe his own words. "Loxley's strong."

Strong or not, the man had been *stabbed*. Strength could only do so much.

"It is my fault this happened," Marian said and gave Robin's hand a squeeze.

Will frowned. "Mari."

"No, it is. I turned up here without invitation, and I distracted him when he should have been making a plan. Instead, he was making sure I stayed safe." If she hadn't come to the house and forced him to let her stay, he might have been able to focus more on the fight and keeping himself unharmed.

Sighing, Will shook his head but seemed too tired to move anything else. He was in no better shape than Marian and badly needed to sleep. "You are not the one who stabbed him, Marian," he said.

She could not argue that point, but it did not alleviate her guilt. She turned her attention once again to the earl. "Why will he not wake up?" she asked.

"He lost a lot of blood," Will said quietly. "I saw it in my soldiers often. He just needs time, and before we know it, we will have the Elusive Earl back, right as rain."

Marian hoped not. There had been something different about him down in the library. No teasing, no joking. He had been fully serious, like he had shed all his masks and been simply himself. She had felt more comfortable talking to him than she had since meeting him, and she had not wanted the evening to end. She liked *that* version of him. The man who had not been nearly as self-confident as she usually saw him. He had pretended to be sure of himself, but Marian had seen beneath that facade easily, almost as if he had wanted her to see beneath it. Was it possible there was a version of Robin Loxley that did not make her want to slap him the moment he opened his mouth?

"You should get home, Marian," Will said, struggling to push himself up to his feet. "You'll be missed if you're not there for breakfast."

Her will to leave was even weaker than before, though, and she clasped Robin's hand a little tighter. "I can send a note to Millie, instructing her to tell my mother I am ill."

"And when your mother comes up to check on you, as she always does when you are unwell?" He put his hand on her shoulder. "You need to go. I'll look after him, and I'll send for you when he wakes up."

"Assuming you're awake yourself," Marian replied, but she did force herself to stand. She was no good to Robin half dead, and there was little more she could do that the doctor had not already done. It wasn't like she could protect him, either, so she knew she had no excuse to justify staying there at his side until he woke up. Not a good excuse anyway. "Promise me you will let me know of any change . . . good or bad," she said.

Smiling a bit, Will pressed a kiss to her forehead before he nudged her out of the room. "I promise," he said. "Promise *me* you will get some rest. Loxley will kill me if he finds out I let you stay up all night fussing over him."

With a heart of lead in her chest, Marian slowly made her way through the eerily quiet corridors of Robin's house. It took all her power not to picture the thief coming out of any of the many rooms she passed, and she wrapped her arms around herself and picked up her pace, almost scurrying down the stairs. The thief had been prepared against the chance of being caught, and he had not been afraid to defend himself by any means necessary.

And they were no closer to discovering who he was. Marian had tried to get a good look at his face as she hid beyond the door, but it had been too dark. Robin and Will had both been busy fighting, and the only thing Will had been able to offer was a guess that the thief had a history of getting into fisticuff matches, which was hardly anything to go on. Marian's only hope was that Robin had injured him enough that he would think twice about stealing anytime soon.

She thought perhaps it was Jason Taylor, given the way he had been glaring at Robin at the ball, but surely the man would be intelligent enough to realize other people would have seen his animosity as well. Could he really be so careless?

Upon reaching the ground floor, Marian realized she had no good way to get herself home. She was dressed as a servant, and the only way she had managed to stay in Robin's room to begin with was by hiding from anyone who might have seen her. If she tried ordering a carriage, she would simply be laughed at, and if she tried to use her real name, no one would believe her. She would likely have to walk home, though it was still dark enough outside that the thought filled her with dread. John and his little troop of makeshift soldiers were protecting the house, but what if the thief was lying in wait just out of sight? What if he saw her leave the house and went after her?

John, Marian realized. She should find John. She had only spoken to the boy once during the night, but she suspected Robin's valet knew exactly who she was since he hadn't questioned her presence when he came to check on his master and tell Will of his plans.

Luckily, she did not encounter anyone as she snuck outside and went to the place she had last seen the valet before he began his watch. As she hoped, she found him sitting in the branches of the big English oak that sat behind the house. "John?"

He glanced down only briefly. "How's Rob?" he asked. John, she had learned during the night, was not one for skirting around difficult subjects.

"He is still asleep," Marian said. "But the doctor was hopeful when he left. Have you . . . ?" She could hardly bring herself to ask the question. "Have you seen him?"

"The thief?" John shook his head, then slipped from the tree, landing just a foot from her. "You'll be needing to go home?" he guessed. "Sun's coming up soon." Robin was right when he had said John didn't show much emotion, and Marian felt her heart ache for him. She had seen him laugh when he was with Robin at the Bow and Crown, but there was no expression on his face now. He was probably too worried about his master.

"Yes," Marian said, though reluctantly. "I wish I could stay, but my family will be concerned if I am not there when they wake up. I will return as soon as I possibly can."

John nodded once, then whistled, the sound short and clear. When another young man around his same age appeared, seemingly out of nowhere, John muttered something to him, and the young man darted off. "Jim'll fetch you a ride home."

Marian could have cried, and she couldn't resist the temptation to pull John in for a hug that he most definitely did not appreciate. Still, she needed the human contact, so she held him as long as she thought he could stand. "You're a good man, John," she said.

He lifted one corner of his mouth in an attempted smile as he took a step back, probably in case she tried to hug him again. "I owe everything I've got to Rob. If something happens to him, don't know what I'll do. And he likes you, Lady Marian," he added, almost as an afterthought. He *definitely* knew who she was, then, though her rank didn't seem to bother him. "Don't go being hard on yourself for this happening. It weren't your fault."

Before Marian could say anything, the sound of a horse caught her ears, and she turned just as John's friend appeared from the darkness on a rather large animal.

"Your ride, my lady," John said with a nod toward the horse.

Her eyes went wide. "My what?"

"Fastest way to get you anywhere," the rider, Jim, said, and even in the dawn light Marian could see his amused smirk. "Hop on up."

Even if John knew she was the daughter of a marquess, he clearly did not understand why she was opposed to sharing a horse with a strange young man she didn't know. She wasn't dressed for riding, sidesaddle or otherwise, and sharing a seat with someone was another thing entirely.

"Is there not a carriage or something?" she asked weakly. If someone saw her . . .

"No time," John said matter-of-factly. "I'll help you up."

Next thing she knew, she was sitting in front of a young man who smelled like the street and was clinging to his arms as he rode across London. By the time they finally reached her home and Jim helped her down, she knew she looked an awful mess, but she thanked him and hurried to the servants' door without considering what he might think of her. If John trusted him, she would have to trust him. She silently thanked Millie for leaving the door unlocked and slipped inside, going as quickly and quietly as she could and hoping she didn't run into anyone on the way.

Marian had told Millie not to wait up for her, but she hoped the girl would be ready to get her presentable enough to go to breakfast without raising questions. Her anxiety, however, would not be as easy to hide behind attire as her exhaustion, and she could hardly breathe as she finally reached her door and stumbled inside.

"My lady!" Millie squeaked the moment she saw her and nearly tumbled out of the chaise she sat in. Clearly, the maid had not slept much either.

As guilty as Marian felt for causing her maid distress, she knew there was little time for making amends. "I need to get ready for breakfast," she said and practically fell into the chair in her dressing room.

"My lady, there's blood on your dress."

Marian looked down and felt sick at the sight of it near her waist. That must have happened when she was trying to stop the bleeding in Robin's stomach while Will ran to send for the doctor. "It isn't mine," she said, though that was hardly a comfort to the girl, who rapidly ran trembling fingers through Marian's hair, trying to undo knots that had formed during the ride across town.

"I have your morning dress laid out," Millie said, and her voice shook as vigorously as her hands.

Marian bit her lip. Neither of them seemed to be up to the task this morning, and pretending that nothing was wrong with her was going to be difficult at best. There was no use. "Millie, you must tell my mother I am ill. I need to lie down and rest for a bit before I go back, and I don't have the stomach for food this morning."

Millie froze. "Go back?" she gasped. "But—"

"He needs my help, Millie." Marian hadn't told her abigail who the thief was, but Millie had heard enough through the grapevine to know he was a man who served people of the lower class like her. Surely she would understand.

Slowly nodding, Millie finished combing through Marian's hair, then grabbed a nightgown for her instead of a day dress. "Her Ladyship will be comin' up to check on you if I tell her you're not well," she said with a frown.

That much was true—illness was the only circumstance in which her mother gave her any real attention—but one look at herself in the mirror and Marian knew she could easily look the part. She was terribly pale, and since she hadn't slept a wink, she looked positively ghastly. "As long as she doesn't send for a doctor," she muttered. Especially if, by some chance, Mother sent for the same doctor who had attended Robin, Marian's secret would never make it through the day. She would never be able to stop herself from asking for more information about Robin.

"I'll get this clean before anyone notices," Millie said, folding Marian's bloodied dress into a tight wad and tucking it under her arm. "And I'll go alert your mother that you're not feeling well."

"Thank you, Millie," Marian said, grabbing the girl's hand before she left. "You have been such a wonderful friend over the years." She knew that sounded like a goodbye, but she couldn't think of a better way to say it. It would be goodbye only if something went terribly wrong.

Millie gave her a warm smile, then hurried away.

As much as Marian wished she didn't have to sleep, she was exhausted, and she made her way to her bed and slipped beneath the covers. For the first time, the mattress didn't feel as soft as it should, and the blankets were not as warm. It was as if the bed was telling Marian that she did not deserve such comforts because she had not been able to protect Robin when he needed her. She wasn't strong enough to fight off a thief, nor was she brave enough, so she had watched a good man get stabbed and now had to wonder if he would ever wake up. If she had been a man, Marian could have stopped the thief, and then she would not be lying in her bed feigning illness so she would not get caught sneaking out of the house and pretending to be something she wasn't.

Within fifteen minutes, her mother entered her room and began fussing over her, as Marian knew she would. "Are you feverish? Do you have a headache? You look pale, darling, and your hands are freezing. Is that maid of yours keeping your room warm enough? Perhaps we should find you a different—"

"No," Marian said quickly. "No, I like Millie. My room is warm enough." Her hands were cold because they'd been holding onto Robin's all night and had just ridden through the cold London streets atop a horse. "I am simply tired, Mother. I think I should sleep late this morning."

Mother didn't leave until she had had some food brought up—making absolutely sure her daughter didn't require a doctor—and Millie had returned to help care for Marian. But as she was stepping out of the room, she paused in the doorway. "Maybe I should cancel my social calls today," she said thoughtfully. "I feel as if I have not spent much time with you since we've been in Town."

Any other day Marian would have enjoyed time with her mother, *craved* it, but she was far too worried about Robin to feel even the slightest desire to keep the woman around. "Please," she said and offered a smile from beneath her covers. "I wouldn't want to keep you from your friends. Go out and enjoy yourself. I have Millie here if I need anything."

Millie nodded emphatically from her seat in the corner, where she was fixing a pair of Marian's stockings. "I won't let anything keep Lady Marian from getting her rest, my lady," the abigail said.

Finally satisfied, Lady Waverly sent one last worried look over her daughter, then left the room, closing the door behind her.

Marian immediately sat up and threw her covers off.

"What are you doing?" Millie asked in alarm.

"I need to go back," Marian said and slipped out of her nightgown so she could dress properly. Now that it was daylight, she would have to visit Robin as Lady Marian, and she hoped she would not run into any trouble by being out on her own. Maybe she would bring Millie with her since the maid was already half-informed about the whole ordeal, but that would only put Millie into danger if something went wrong.

Millie rushed to help her, though her lips were tight with disapproval. "You really should rest, my lady. You didn't get a minute of sleep last night, and—"

"And my friend might be dying," Marian interrupted, and those words brought her to a pause. Robin might be dying. No matter what the doctor said, there was always the chance something could go wrong. Maybe the injury was worse than it had looked. Maybe he had lost too much blood. Maybe the thief would come back to finish the job when he learned he had not been fully successful.

Swallowing tears, Marian took a deep breath and tried to stay strong. "I have to go check on him, Millie. Please."

The maid still frowned, but she agreed with a little nod. "Very well," she said, "but you can't go just yet. You have to wait until Lord and Lady Waverly are out of the house."

There was truth to that, though Marian could hardly stomach the idea of waiting around while Robin suffered from his wound.

As soon as she helped Marian get dressed, Millie went downstairs with strict orders to return the *instant* the marquess and his wife were gone from the house. Marian paced her room as she waited, trying to convince herself that everything would be well. And if it wasn't?

If Robin really died, and he was no longer able to continue his crusade to rob the rich and give to the poor, Marian would just have to take his place. She and Will. She would practice being quieter and learn how to pick locks, and she would have Will teach her how to fight until she was no longer afraid of what might happen if she encountered an enemy. With or without Robin, the less fortunate needed an advocate.

But no matter how many times Marian told herself she was strong enough to do it, she knew it would never be the same without Robin the thief there to silently laugh when she made a mistake.

Her heart ached at the thought of a world without Robin, and she sank into a chair and forced back a new wave of tears. She told herself over and over again that he would make it through, that he would always be there to lead their little band of thieves. He would teach her how to fight and pick locks and put on a mask no one could see through.

She could use one of those masks right about now, seeing as she was sure even a stranger on the street would recognize in her expression the heartbreak she was barely keeping below the surface.

"My lady?" Millie finally returned to her chamber after almost an hour. "Your parents have just left."

"Good. Thank you, Millie." Marian rearranged her pillows beneath the covers once more—she hoped her mother would be out for most of the day, but Marian wanted it to look like she was in her bed—and then she took a fortifying breath. "I'll be back when I can. Please cover for me if you have to."

"They took both the carriages, my lady," Millie replied, and she looked positively miserable about the fact.

Marian, however, was not about to be stopped by the lack of a carriage. She would walk if she had to, though she was sure she could hire a coach easily enough once she got outside. "I'll get my own way," she told Millie.

"Do you need me to come with you?" the abigail asked next. She followed close on Marian's heels, likely nervous to let her go out on her own again. "A lady should not be—"

"Oh no," Marian gasped, stopping Millie with her outstretched arm. She stared down to the entry, where Jones had just opened the door to let in Mr. Gisbourne. Her heart picked up pace until it felt like it might beat out of her chest. "I forgot I agreed to go out for a drive with Mr. Gisbourne."

With everything that had happened with Robin, she hadn't even given a thought to the ball yesterday, nor the final words Gisbourne had said to her as he'd helped her into her carriage behind her parents: "Until tomorrow, my dear."

"Lady Marian is unwell," Jones said—Marian made a mental note to thank him later—"but I would be most willing to bring her a message if you have one, sir."

But then Gisbourne looked up, likely just out of reflex, since he could not have expected to see her, and his lips curled into a smile when he caught sight of her. "It appears she is feeling better," he said and bowed his head to her.

Marian knew she couldn't pretend to be ill now that he had seen her fully dressed and on her way out. It wasn't that she did not want to go driving with Mr. Gisbourne, but she was so entirely focused on Robin that she could hardly concentrate on smiling back at him. But could she really refuse to join him when she had already accepted?

"What are you going to do, my lady?" Millie whispered and took hold of her hand, offering her strength that she badly needed.

Marian squeezed back as she took another deep breath. "I will do what I have to," she said and fixed her smile on a little stronger. Even if Robin was in danger, there was nothing she could do about it. Will was with him, and John, and she trusted them to look after him. She would simply have to keep the drive as short as she could.

Descending the stairs with shaking limbs, Marian used every bit of strength she had to pretend everything was perfectly normal. "Gis," she said when she reached him. Familiar heat spread through her face as he bent to kiss her fingers, but it no longer brought a smile to her face. She merely felt nauseous, and she hoped her lack of breakfast would keep her from being truly sick.

Mr. Gisbourne smiled at her, but the expression quickly turned to concern. "You look unwell, my dear," he said. "Are you very ill?"

She could so easily say yes, and he was a good enough man that he would leave and let her go about her business. But that was the problem. He was a good man. There were so few of those that she could not bring herself to hurt him. "I am simply tired after the ball last night," she said and linked her arm with his. "I am happy to see you, Gis." Perhaps he could be a comfort to her in this difficult situation, even if she couldn't tell him what was troubling her.

He pulled her close as he led her outside. "I hoped," he began but faltered when they reached his gig. He cleared his throat and tried again. "I wonder if you would permit me to take you out without a chaperone, my lady. There will be plenty of eyes in the park, but I want to keep you for myself as much as I can."

The heat in Marian's cheeks doubled, and her first instinct was to run back inside and hide in her bedchamber before she figured out whether all of this was truly her new reality. Mr. Gisbourne wanted to court her. She'd guessed as much, but the way he waited for her response, with so much uncertainty in his bright eyes, told her he had no intention of leaving her side if she allowed it.

Did she want to allow it? She was only eighteen, after all, and marriage was a big decision. It was likely one of the few decisions she could make in her life, and even then she would have only half a say. Her father would get the other half. Mr. Gisbourne was a good man, she thought again, but was he the sort of man she could grow to love?

"Lady Marian? I hope I was not too bold."

"No," she said and tried again to look as if nothing were amiss. She sent a nod to Millie, who reluctantly closed the door and left her alone. "No, I think that sounds nice." It wouldn't be the first time she had gone on a drive unchaperoned since her first interaction with Rob the earl had been just the two of them. But this felt infinitely more intimate. More intimate than anything she had felt with Robin. Unless she counted last night . . .

Mr. Gisbourne helped her up into his gig, then followed after her and took the reins, his wide smile speaking volumes of his happiness. He was an easy man to like and even easier to please, apparently.

Only when they were on their way to Hyde Park did Marian realize the vehicle had only the two seats. "You knew I would say yes to going unchaperoned?" she asked in surprise.

"I hoped," he corrected. "I want all of London to know I have been smitten."

Marian should have welcomed that comment. She should have enjoyed it. True, Mr. Gisbourne was only the heir to a baronetcy, but he was wealthy, intelligent, well-liked, and good-natured. A fine match for anyone. She knew she would not find his equal among the peerage. So why did she sink lower in her seat as Mr. Gisbourne seemed to grow taller with satisfaction?

Because she *had* found his equal—his superior, in fact—and that man was currently suffering from a stab wound.

"You are very quiet, my lady," Mr. Gisbourne said, putting his hand over her clasped ones.

Marian looked up at him and felt her strength crumbling beneath the compassion she saw in his eyes. Did she trust him enough to share her burden? She wanted to, and she leaned into him, hoping to find some strength.

He responded by pulling his horse to a stop, even though they were nowhere near the park. "Lady Marian," he said, his voice low with concern.

Her careful calm broke, and she fell against him as a sob seemed to tear itself free. He wrapped an arm around her shoulders, and she took hold of his other arm, desperate to keep from falling apart entirely. "I'm so scared," she whispered into his shoulder. What if Robin didn't wake up? She couldn't explain how she felt so connected to him, but she was. If she lost her earl, her thief, she didn't know what she would do.

Mr. Gisbourne held her for a long while, rubbing his hand along her arm to comfort her. She felt surrounded by his hold, like he would do anything to protect her, but she didn't want to be there. No matter how much he might have cared, and how much she cared for him, he was not Robin.

When her tears calmed a bit, Mr. Gisbourne gently pushed her away and used his thumb to wipe her tears from her cheeks. "This is about Mr. Hewitt, isn't it?" he asked.

Mr. Hewitt? In light of everything that had happened last night, Marian had all but forgotten about the man who had tried to drag her from the ball. Compared to watching a man she deeply cared for bleed out onto the floor, Mr. Hewitt was a trivial matter. And yet something had changed in Mr. Gisbourne. Something dark in his eyes, which were usually so kind.

And instinct told her to lie.

"Yes," she said and dabbed at her eyes with the handkerchief he offered her. "He was such an awful man."

Mr. Gisbourne's usually soft gaze turned cold. "You do not deserve attentions like that," he said almost to himself. Then he took a breath and brushed his thumb across her cheek again. "Come. I'll take you back home, and we can go driving tomorrow if the weather holds. I would hate for you to be subjected to the *ton* when you are distressed."

"Thank you," Marian whispered, and she tried her best to remain comfortable with the man beside her despite everything within her telling her that something was off, even if she didn't know exactly what it was. Something in the way he was sitting so stiffly?

When they arrived at her house and Mr. Gisbourne jumped down from the gig, his leg nearly gave out beneath him.

Marian froze. "Are you injured?" she asked him as he reached up to help her down.

Something dark flickered in his eyes. "An old hunting accident," he said after a pause. "It often pains me when it's looking like it might rain."

Marian forced herself to smile, even though her gut told her he was lying. Why else would he avoid her gaze? "It is not too painful, I hope," she said. His injured leg was the same leg Robin had wounded on the thief last night. Taking Mr. Gisbourne's hand, Marian did everything she possibly could to look as natural as she ever had, hoping he thought she believed his lie. If he did not . . .

Offering his arm again, he led her to her door and placed a gentle kiss to her hand when the door opened for her. "I hope you feel better soon, my lady," he said. "And do not be afraid of men like Hewitt. You deserve to have the world fall down at your feet, and I will make sure you get everything owed to you in life."

As Marian watched him return to his gig with a bit of a limp in his step, she did not doubt his words. Something told her Mr. Gisbourne would do whatever it took to make her happy.

And that terrified her.

CHAPTER *Sixteen*

ROB NEEDED TO FIND THE thief. He had never needed anything more in his life, and the fact that he still hadn't figured out who the man was made his blood boil in his veins. Surely there was something he had missed. Some clue that would make everything else fall into place and point him in the right direction. But he had been staring at his list for hours, a list that had not grown much smaller since adding military service as one of the possible qualifications. He didn't even know if that was an accurate assessment. All he knew was the man was a skilled fighter.

There were too many selfish and cowardly men in this blasted country, and Rob knew the list would likely only grow unless he found the worst one of them all and put a stop to his rampage.

If he could just breathe . . . Rob groaned as he shifted in his chair, glad that Mr. Russell had agreed to go upstairs and rest for a few hours, though he had done so reluctantly. The man had been hovering over Rob ever since he'd woken up, as if there was more to his injury than a simple knife to his gut. Rob would live, and he needed Russell to be alert.

John had been harder to convince, and the boy was now fast asleep in the other chair in the library, where Rob had taken refuge to avoid Mrs. Keller bursting into tears every time she checked on him in his bedchamber. John was likely too young to be kept working late hours like he had been, but Rob knew there wasn't much he could do to stop him. The young man was loyal to a fault and would probably never leave Rob's side, even if ordered. Rob smiled at him despite being annoyed that he would not go to his bed to sleep.

Taking a slow breath so he didn't risk the chance of coughing—he had done that earlier and thoroughly regretted it—Rob returned to studying his list of suspects, though it was starting to look like gibberish to him. He had been staring at it for too long. Why couldn't he just figure it out? If he had gone to Eton as a boy instead of working the sheep fields, maybe he would have been intelligent enough to have discovered the man's identity by now, but Rob could not shake the feeling that he was simply missing something. That last piece of the puzzle.

A shout reached his ears from the entrance hall, and Rob lifted his head, glad to have an excuse to set his list down. Perhaps it had not been a shout, per se, but the voice had been loud enough to reach him clear in the library, which meant whoever it was, they were not being particularly quiet.

Groaning again as his body protested the movement, Rob pushed himself up to his feet and wrapped an arm around his rib cage as he slowly made his way to the door to see what was going on. He rarely heard shouting in his house, though Alana had done a fair bit that morning when she'd arrived back home and demanded to know what he had been doing when he got stabbed—so the sound was certainly cause for investigating.

Thankfully, his sister had agreed it was best if she and Mother kept away until this dreadful business was over, though she'd left again with the promise of a lengthy conversation when she returned. It was probably time to confide in her, though something told him she would not be as surprised as he hoped.

Upon reaching the edge of the entrance hall, Rob could hardly stand anymore, and he had to lean against the wall and take a few steadying breaths before he could really focus on the heated argument happening in the doorway. He knew he should not have left his bed, but he had never been a homebody in his life, and sitting still was not in his nature. He was strong enough. He hoped.

Hoskins was refusing someone entrance, and she was having none of it. *She.* Rob brightened when he recognized Marian's voice. Hoskins was putting up a good fight, but Marian was holding her own, and a lesser man would have cowered beneath her attempts to threaten him. Rob was eager to see who came out the victor.

"You are being unreasonable!" Marian said through the mostly closed door.

"I am being no such thing!" Hoskins replied, a little out of breath. "Now kindly—"

"Lord Huntingdon will—"

"My master is not admitting—"

"If you do not let me in this door right this minute," Marian growled as she wedged her boot between the door and the frame, "I will slap you so hard that . . . that . . ." Apparently, she wasn't prepared to finish that particular threat.

"Let her in," Rob said, deciding he had best stop the argument before Marian tried to break down the door or physically attack Hoskins.

Hoskins glanced back at him in surprise. "My lord!" he said, though his words came out in a grunt as he struggled to keep the door closed against Marian's attempts to open it. "You should not be up. The doctor was very clear that no one should—"

"Let her in," Rob repeated.

Hoskins reluctantly complied, stepping back just as Marian attempted another push through the door. Because she met no resistance, she stumbled inside and nearly fell to the floor, but she was quickly steady on her feet again and staring at Rob, her face pale and worried. "You're alive," she breathed.

Was that worry for him? Rob made to take a step but instantly stopped himself before he collapsed. He silently cursed his body for failing him, but to his delight, Marian hurried over to him and put her hand on his arm.

"Why are you out of bed?" she asked, likely trying to look stern but far too relieved to manage it.

Rob simply grinned and wished he could stand without using the wall for support. What did it matter if he couldn't find the thief when Marian was looking at him like that? "You look tired," he said and reached out a hand to brush his fingers along her cheek.

A tear slipped from her eye as she took hold of his hand as if she wanted him to stay near. "I was so worried," she said, closing her eyes.

Apparently, Russell hadn't been lying when he said Marian had not wanted to leave his side, and Rob could hardly bring himself to believe it. For a man who had not realized how much he truly cared for her until yesterday, he was becoming more deeply entranced by this woman every moment he was with her.

"I am quite well," he told her and adjusted his hand so he could rest his palm against her cheek. She leaned into his touch, which was rather encouraging. "Nothing a few days won't fix."

Shaking her head, Marian pulled away as if she needed to have some distance between them in order to speak. "What if something had happened to you?" she asked. "What would I have done then?"

She looked so alone standing there holding her arms around her middle that Rob momentarily forgot how weak he was and took a step toward her to comfort her. He couldn't even take that one step without sinking to the ground, barely catching himself on his knees and moaning in pain as the landing jarred every sore spot in his body.

"Bad idea," he growled to himself, but then Marian was there at his side and lifting his arm over her shoulders. *Maybe not such a bad idea after all.*

"You should not have left your room," Marian scolded. She tried to lift him—he tried to help—but the pair of them remained there on the floor. Rob didn't think it was all that bad, considering he hadn't been quite this close to Marian since their little skirmish the evening before, and he rather enjoyed her warmth, but Marian frowned and looked around for help.

To Rob's surprise, Hoskins had disappeared. Rob had expected the man to hover and make his silent disapproval clear. For once, the butler had apparently decided he did not know better than Rob and had returned to his other duties. But despite how much that pleased him, Rob knew that made his and Marian's situation difficult. He could hardly keep himself breathing properly, and there was little chance Marian would be strong enough to lift his weight on her own.

Taking a painfully deep breath, Rob whistled the best he could—he was usually better at it but was far too distracted currently—and waited only three seconds before John appeared from the corridor and slid to a stop in front of him.

Rob glared at him. "You're supposed to be sleeping," he said.

John gave him a searching glance, then smirked ever so slightly. "You're not supposed to be on the floor," he replied. "You'll be wanting some help, then?"

"Yes," Marian said before Rob could express his frustration. "Please. He cannot stand on his own, and he's too heavy for me."

John grabbed Rob's other arm, not nearly as gently as Marian had, and hoisted him up. "You're eating too much, Rob," he said.

Rob would have replied if he wasn't using all his concentration to keep most of his weight on John's shoulders instead of Marian's as the pain in his side threatened to make him pass out. He had to stay awake. Otherwise, he would lose time with Marian, and that was far from what he wanted.

"Where?" Marian asked, a little breathless as she and John practically carried Rob deeper into the house.

Rob tried to walk along with them, but he was so tired that his legs weren't doing what he told them. *Useless legs.* "Library," he said. Aside from fetching his notes on the thief (and wishing he had sent John to do that), he had been avoiding the study all morning. There was something macabre about being in the same space where he had lost a good deal of his blood. Mrs. Keller had only been able to clean it so well, though he imagined she would keep at it until the room was spotless again. No one in the house wanted a reminder of what had happened.

It took them a long time to reach the library, and Rob was grateful when his companions lowered him into a chair so he could stop holding his breath against the pain. "Thank you," he said to John before he turned his eyes to Marian and hoped she understood that his gratitude for her went deeper than it did for John. In fact, he rather wished John weren't there. The last time Rob had sat in this library with Marian, things had been leaning in a direction he did not want the boy to witness. If her concern was any indication, Marian would not object to a continuation of that conversation.

"Robin? What's wrong?" Marian knelt in front of his chair and took hold of his hands. Whatever she saw in his face, it worried her.

Rob tried to smile, though he was too much in pain and far too distracted by thinking about what might have happened last night if Russell hadn't interrupted them. "I am perfectly well," he said, though it came out as a grunt and with a grimace he couldn't stop. Even Marian calling him Robin was not enough to help him ignore the nastier effects of being stabbed.

Holding tighter to his hands—almost too tight—Marian frowned as she looked up at him. "What were you thinking?" she asked, and now there was a sharper edge to her voice, much like when she had fought against Hoskins. "You should not have even sat up in bed, and now you are wandering around the house? The thief might not have killed you, but you are going to do the job yourself if you're not careful."

Rob wanted to take a nap. He wanted to lean forward and kiss Marian more. Ignoring the sharp sting of pain in his gut, he pushed himself closer to her with his elbow and pretended John wasn't in sight, even though the boy was standing in the doorway with a mischievous grin on his lips. "It's almost like you care," Rob said to Marian with as good a smirk as he could manage.

Marian leaned away from him. Disappointment added to the pain in his abdomen, and Rob fell into the back of his chair. Had he read her wrong? Yes, he realized when she started to cry. He had most definitely read her wrong.

"Marian?" he said. "Marian, what's the matter?"

She spoke so quietly that he would not have even heard her if he hadn't leaned forward again. "I know who the thief is."

That sentence hit Rob harder than he would have thought, given how important that knowledge was. But it was in the way Marian shared her little bit of news that Rob felt sick to his stomach. Marian knew who they were looking for, but how had she discovered him?

"Marian," he whispered as fear sent his heart pulsing faster in his chest. It was someone she knew. Someone she had trusted. "Gisbourne," Rob guessed, and he did not need her nod to confirm that truth.

Geoffrey Gisbourne was most definitely on Rob's list, but he had not let himself think too hard on him. No matter the signs, Rob had thought he was too biased against the man to trust himself on that account.

"How?" he asked as his memory brought him back to the night before. He had never gotten a good look at the thief's face, but he could piece it together well enough and come to the same conclusion now that he had a second witness. The man was well-off and intelligent and had the build of a natural fighter. And there had always been something off about him, as if his smiles hid a darker countenance.

Marian gripped Rob's hands as if her life depended on it. "We went out driving this morning," she said.

They had done that before, but Rob sensed something different about this particular drive. "Alone?" he growled.

Nodding, she apparently didn't feel the need to say anything in response to that comment and simply continued. "When he climbed down from the gig, his leg would not support him. He said it was a hunting accident, but—"

"He was lying." Rob sent a glance at John, who understood what he wanted and hurried from the room to fetch Mr. Russell. He was their strongest man in case they had to act before Rob was healed. "Why would you go out with him unchaperoned?" he asked, though that was hardly important now, not when they had the information they needed to protect the city from the villainy of the mock thief.

As if she only just realized she was holding his hands, Marian frowned down at their fingers clasped together, then released him so she could move to sit in the chair opposite him. "I did not know he was the thief until we were already out," she said, as if confused by his question. "What should that matter? I have spent far more time with you unchaperoned."

That much was true, but "Going out at night to steal from the villains of London is not the same as spending a drive with a man who is courting you," Rob said.

"One could argue my time with you has been far more intimate," Marian replied, and then her face turned pink.

Even when she was snapping at him, Rob was enchanted, and he decided he was well on his way to falling in love with her, though he had no idea how.

If he hadn't just been stabbed, and if the city wasn't currently under attack by a man who was more dangerous than they had originally realized, Rob might have asked Marian how she had so easily put him under her spell.

"We can't let Gisbourne keep hurting innocents," he said, though reluctantly.

"Gisbourne is the thief?" Russell replied from the doorway. "*Your* Gisbourne?" he added when he reached Marian's side.

Her Gisbourne? Rob did not like the sound of that, though it should have worried him that he was more bothered by the idea of a man like Geoffrey Gisbourne courting Marian than he was by learning Gisbourne was the thief. He attributed his misplaced disgust to sheer exhaustion after the events of last night.

Marian nodded, which was not a denial about her ties to Gisbourne.

The pain in Rob's chest deepened, but he did his best to ignore it. "Now that we have our enemy," he said, "we have a greater chance of stopping him."

"He goes to White's fairly often," Russell suggested.

Rob shook his head. "We cannot call him out in public, or he will likely make a connection between us and the original thief."

"Which is accurate," Marian said, though quietly. She kept her eyes on the floor at her feet and looked particularly downcast.

Rob, however, had no idea how to lift her spirits, especially when he could barely lift a hand.

"He might go out to steal something again," John said.

"Undoubtedly," Rob said. "He does not have nearly the same level of fame as me, and that will hurt his pride until he knows he is the best thief out there."

"Or until he has taken out the competition," Marian said, even more softly than before. "If he is brave enough to attack a man like the Earl of Huntingdon, he will not be afraid of his rival thief."

Rob nodded as his thoughts flew around his head, trying to fit into place and give him a clear path of where to go from there. "We just have to get ahead of him," he said, tapping a single finger on the arm of the chair; he couldn't manage much more than that but needed the movement to think properly. "We need to figure out where he is going to strike next and stop him before he can."

Aside from that, the biggest problem was actually stopping Gisbourne. It wasn't enough to catch him in the act, considering that would incriminate the rest of them as well unless they had a good excuse for wandering the city in the dead of night. No constable would believe them to simply be out for a stroll and happening upon the thief. There had to be a way to make the man get *himself* caught. Without definitive proof through legal means, there was no other way to ensure he was cut off from doing his misdeeds.

"But how are we supposed to figure out where he will go?" Russell asked. "His attacks have been random."

"There has to be a pattern," Rob said, still thinking hard. "He is cleverer than I would like, so he would not steal from just anyone. He would either need to be provoked or encouraged."

"He went after you 'cause you're fairly flush in the pockets," John said with a shrug. "But the dress woman? She's not."

"Neither was Tilby," Russell said.

That was when Rob noticed something change in Marian. It was subtle, as if she hadn't even realized her own thoughts connecting, but she sat up a little straighter. Frowned a little deeper. And there was no mistaking the horror that slowly darkened her brow as the answer to this mystery came to her at the same time it did for Rob.

"Me," she whispered and looked up at him with wide eyes. "I am the pattern."

Rob badly wished to tell her she was wrong, but his thoughts on the matter had slid into their proper places and left no room for argument. "Gisbourne saw you on the street the day you talked to Mrs. Bernhard," he said with a sigh. "And I would guess you were upset."

"I was worried about her family," she said.

"You danced with Mr. Tilby," Russell said and put a hand on her shoulder to offer some support as the weight of this realization pushed her deeper into her chair.

If he had had the strength, Rob would have taken her up in his arms to protect her from the guilt that was likely building inside her. This was in no way her fault.

"I danced with Tilby just after I would have danced with Gis had he not been called away," she said. "With Mr. Gisbourne, I mean," she corrected.

Rob's heart felt a good deal lighter suddenly. "And then there was me," he said and smiled at Marian. To his utter delight, she smiled back, and yet again, he wished the two of them were not joined by their companions. If it were just her, he could tell her how beautiful she looked when she was gazing at him like that. He considered telling her anyway.

John and Russell were good-natured men who understood the importance of a happy life; surely they could not fault him for falling for a young woman like Marian. Rob wished his timing had been better though. It was difficult to concentrate on love when he was trying to catch a dangerous thief while half dead.

He would do better to focus on one before he gave in to the other. "We need to make a plan," he said and rose to his feet so he could go to his study to get any information he could find on Geoffrey Gisbourne.

All three of his friends protested the motion at the same time Rob got too lightheaded to stand and collapsed. Thankfully, Russell caught him before he hit the floor, but that didn't make the impact any less painful as Russell's arm pressed into Rob's injured side.

"Are you out of your mind?" Marian nearly shouted the question as Russell helped Rob back into his chair. "You can't go jumping up and pretending you weren't stabbed last night!"

Though he knew it did not paint him in the best light, Rob slumped in the chair and considered sliding down to the floor, where he wouldn't have to hold any part of himself up. How could a little knife make his body so blasted tired? He had never felt so helpless in his life.

"We don't need you going and getting yourself killed, Rob," John said angrily. Though he had offered up little to the conversation so far, he clearly felt the need to take a stand on this point. "We all know you're strong, but even God rested on the seventh day."

Rob chuckled, though it hurt to do it. He had a lot of reasons to like John, and that list seemed to grow the longer the boy was in his service. "You're edging close to blasphemy," he warned with a grin.

"Don't go to church anyway," John shot back.

"Let *us* keep an eye on Gisbourne, Loxley," Russell said, and he touched Rob's shoulder before he returned to Marian's side.

Marian glared daggers at Rob and looked ready to physically hold him in his chair if necessary. He was sorely tempted to try to make her do just that. But then a new thought crossed her mind, and her indignant anger vanished, replaced by fear and alarm that stole the color from her lovely cheeks.

"Mr. Hewitt," she said.

Rob felt sick to his stomach as that name brought to mind several accounts he had heard about the man. There were plenty of lecherous men in the world, but Hewitt was among the worst of them. Rob had been meaning to go after the blackguard for a while now, once he had a clear reason for it. "I know him," he said.

"And so does Gisbourne." Marian visibly shuddered, and if Rob had been able to move, he would have marched straight to Hewitt's house and beaten the man to a pulp. Whatever he had done to Marian, he would pay for it. Eventually. When Rob wasn't dying.

Crouching down to be at eye level with his cousin, Russell spoke gently, for which Rob was grateful. Marian was agitated enough as it was. "Why do you think Gisbourne will go after Mr. Hewitt next?"

Another tear slipped down Marian's cheek, driving Rob positively mad as he sat there useless, but she brushed it away herself. "I danced with Mr. Hewitt last night," she said, almost timidly. "Gis—Mr. Gisbourne rescued me before Mr. Hewitt could try to do anything truly terrible. He asked about Mr. Hewitt on our drive this morning, and he was not happy. He was frightening."

Blast it all, Rob didn't care if he was dying—Marian needed someone to hold her, and Mr. Russell was too much a buffoon to notice. But the instant Rob tried to move, Marian's eyes snapped up to him and turned hard.

"If you move so much as a muscle, Robin Loxley," she said as she stood, "I will go find myself a knife and stab you again."

If Rob hadn't been in love with her already, he most certainly was now. She wasn't very good at being confident about herself, but when it came to looking after others, she was as fierce as any man Rob had ever met. "Marian Russell," he muttered.

She ignored him and turned to her cousin. "Do you know where Mr. Hewitt lives?" she asked him.

"No, but it should not be hard to find out." With a little nod of his head to the room in general, Russell slipped out into the corridor and vanished.

Marian turned next to John, who snapped to attention like the most diligently trained soldier.

He never acts that way for me, Rob thought with a slight frown.

"We need to keep an eye on Gisbourne," she said, "in case he might be up to something else tonight. But be back here before it gets dark. We'll have to make a plan."

As soon as John was gone, Marian focused her strong gaze on Rob, who couldn't help but smile at her despite the glare she was giving him. "And you," she said.

"Me," he replied and reached for her hand. He was positively thrilled when she took hold of his fingers, even more so when she briefly closed her eyes and blushed a pretty pink color. "What task do you have for me, my lady?" he asked, and then he pulled her close enough to kiss the back of her hand.

Her breath shuddered from her lungs, and she watched him like she was trying to understand why he would be acting the way he was. "I need . . ." She swallowed.

As carefully as he could, Rob pushed himself up to his feet without letting go of Marian's hand. It wasn't easy, but he wanted to be level with her. He wanted to brush his fingers across her cheek and watch her blush rise. He wanted to tell her that she was just as important to him as the others. More so. And he could not do that with words. He bent low, and he gently tipped her chin up until their noses brushed.

"What do you need?" he whispered, only a breath away from touching his lips to hers.

He could not bear the distance anymore. Her pull was too strong, and he crossed that last little bit and kissed her. And, to his utter relief, she slid her hand up to his neck and kissed him back. *She didn't hate him.* He pulled her closer, flush against him, and the pain in his body seemed to disappear because she fit so perfectly in his arms that it was like she filled in all the holes and made him something more.

He had fallen completely for this woman.

But no matter how fiercely he wished he could keep standing there with her in his arms, his strength gave out, and it took everything in him not to fall over as he broke the connection between them and tried to breathe again.

Marian's eyes glistened with tears, and she pressed her palm to his cheek. She was so entirely beautiful, and Rob felt he could see into her soul as they stood there in silence. She was afraid. Of what, he did not know, but he hated to think she had any fear at all, because he was supposed to protect her. She needed him to protect her.

As if she knew his thoughts, she shook her head. "I need you to stay alive," she said, and then she ran.

And Rob didn't move. Partly because he couldn't but mostly because Marian ran. Because she did not want him. And that was more painful a wound than any knife could inflict.

CHAPTER *Seventeen*

HE HAD KISSED HER. MARIAN had barely been able to hold herself together, and Robin had kissed her. And what had she done? She'd *run*. Of all the idiotic things she could have done, that was by far the worst. It wasn't like she was afraid of him. Not anymore. More than once she had imagined what it would be like if he'd actually kissed her instead of simply teasing that he would. She had never been kissed before, and she had thought if anyone could do it well, Robin could.

She'd been wrong.

He hadn't kissed her well. His kiss had been absolutely *perfect*. She could not even imagine anything being better than standing there in his arms and knowing he felt something for her. He hadn't said as much, but she had seen it in his eyes. Those beautiful, bright, expressive green eyes of his had said everything words never could have. Robin *loved* her.

And somehow she had fallen in love with the man in return, and she didn't know when or how.

"So why did you run?" she asked herself as she paced her dressing room and waited for Millie to return. It was nearly ten o'clock at night, and Marian had left Robin—run from Robin—nearly twelve hours ago. She had spent the day holed up in her room so her mother would assume she was still feeling poorly, and she had spent every single minute of those hours thinking about the earl.

She knew exactly why she had run. She had run because she was terrified by how strongly she felt for him. It had come out of nowhere, and it was maddening not having a clear picture of her own feelings until twelve hours ago, but she could not deny that was what she felt. He made her feel warm inside, like she was strong and capable, like she could actually do something to help the people around her. He made her feel like there was more to her than a pretty face. He did all of that without saying a word.

And now she feared she had wedged an entire continent between them by running away from those feelings that so frightened her. What had Robin thought when she left? Surely he had decided she felt nothing for him since she had given him no evidence to the contrary, and now she was stuck pacing her room and hoping she would get the chance to explain it to him. He had opened up to her in the library before everything took a disastrous turn, and she wanted to do the same. She wanted to look into those beautiful eyes of his and try to tell him everything she felt. Would she get the chance?

Marian had spent last night at his bedside worried she would never see those eyes again, and then she had found him half dead in his house, and that fear had only grown. He may have been awake and acting like himself, but that knife had cut deeply. He had been so pale, and while she knew it would take time for him to heal, she had seen something lurking beneath his skin. She couldn't explain it, but as she traced a single path around her dressing room, her whole body trembled with the fear that he was not as well as he pretended to be. That was why she hadn't found the courage to go back yet. What if she returned to Huntingdon Manor and found the house shrouded in mourning?

Don't think that, she scolded herself. Will would have told her if something was wrong. But it was difficult not to wonder and imagine the worst.

A soft knock on the bedroom door brought Marian to a pause, and she hurried over to it and whispered, "Who is it?"

"It's Millie, my lady."

Marian opened the door just wide enough to let her abigail inside. "Did you get one?" she asked, a little breathless.

Millie's hand shook as she pulled from beneath the folds of her skirt the knife Marian had sent her to find. It was small, but Marian could see that it was wickedly sharp. Not unlike the one that had pierced Robin's side less than a day ago. It was a good deal better than the penknife she had stolen from Taylor, though she prayed she would not have to use it.

"I don't like this, Lady Marian," Millie whispered and appeared more than relieved to hand the knife over to her. "This one sounds too dangerous."

It likely was dangerous, but that was the point. After what she had seen in Gisbourne's eyes that morning, Marian genuinely feared for Mr. Hewitt's life. Tying the knife around her waist with a bit of brown ribbon, she quickly examined her appearance in her mirror before deciding there wasn't much else she could do. She had dressed as a man again, this time securely pinning her hair beneath her cap, and she had dirtied up her face a bit so she would hopefully be unrecognizable. If Mr. Gisbourne really was their thief, he was far more likely to realize who she was than a stranger would be, so she had to take every precaution.

"Have Lord and Lady Waverly gone to bed?" Marian asked as she smiled a bit at her reflection. Maybe she didn't have much experience, but she felt she looked the part, and that gave her some much-needed confidence.

"Yes, my lady. Twenty minutes ago."

Marian frowned. Her parents would probably still be awake for some time, but she couldn't afford to wait much longer. "And the horse is ready?" she asked.

Millie nodded. "Mr. Russell is waiting outside."

If Will was waiting for her, that meant she couldn't dawdle anymore. It was time to see if she was as tough as she hoped she was, because nothing about tonight was going to be easy. She had to focus, for Robin's sake as well as her own.

By the time Marian got outside, a chill had settled deep into her chest that had nothing to do with the cool night air. She couldn't decide if she was anxious because things might go wrong or if she was nervous because they could not *afford* for things to go wrong, but her heart pounded as she hurried to where Will waited with the horses. She could hardly breathe.

"How's Robin?" she asked first.

Will helped lift her into the saddle, and then he put a hand on her leg, which helped settle her nerves just a little. With a kindhearted soldier like Will at her side, she didn't have as much to fear. He would look after her if anything went wrong.

"He was asleep when I left a few hours ago," he said, and his usually quiet voice was even softer than normal. "John will know more." As he hefted himself onto his own horse, he glanced around the quiet street. "Are you sure you want to do this, Mari? John and I can—"

"Yes," she said, as much to herself as to her cousin. No matter how frightened she was, she could not leave the plan short a man. She could not abandon Robin when he needed her most. "I need to do this."

"John will meet us at Hewitt's," Will said and nudged his horse into a slow walk. "He said Gisbourne conducted his business as usual and went to bed early tonight."

"Probably so he could go out without notice," Marian said. She gripped the reins of her own horse tightly and was grateful Will had taught her to ride astride one summer, much to the dismay of her mother. If she had been seen riding sidesaddle while dressed as a man, someone would most certainly have taken notice.

Hewitt did not live far. They reached his house in ten minutes and left the horses a ways down the block, in a little square of trees where they hopefully would not attract notice. It was still early yet, and some people would be out and about until it got later.

John arrived within a few minutes and greeted the both of them, though he didn't meet their eyes. Leading the way, since he had more experience in thieving, the boy followed the line of town houses. He walked casually so as not to draw attention, as did Marian and Will just behind him, but as far as Marian knew, they were not seen before they arrived at their hiding place just across the street from Mr. Hewitt's door.

"Thief will have to come this way to get around back," John said as he hid himself in the shadows. "Or if he goes for the front door, we let him inside so he can't run, and then we'll need to cut him off 'fore he can make a getaway."

"I will take the front entrance," Will said. The two of them must have talked through the plan earlier, when Marian was stuck eating dinner with her parents and pretending everything was well and she was simply tired. Not for the first time, Marian envied Will's bachelorhood freedom. Her only options for leaving the house were social calls and dressing as a maid or a man to sneak out.

"I've got the back," John said.

Then both of them looked at Marian, who pulled her eyebrows together. There were only the two entrances to the house; did they expect her to simply wait around as a lookout?

Will frowned, but it was not because of her building anger. "You will be inside the house," he said to her and didn't seem to like the idea.

Inside?

"You'll have to flush him out," John explained. "Scare him into running."

A chill settled at the base of her spine, but Marian tried to look confident. "I can do that," she said. Could she? That would put her in the same place as Gisbourne and at an even greater risk of being recognized than she already was. But there was logic to the plan. She would never be strong enough to stop Gisbourne if she were waiting at one of the entrances. Will was a soldier and a good fighter, and she suspected there was a lot more to John than what she could see on the outside. If she was going to help see this mission through to success, being inside the house was their best option.

Putting a hand on her shoulder, Will gave her a look that was full of concern. "Marian," he whispered, "you don't have to. We can handle this, and you can go see how Loxley is faring while you wait."

As tempting as that was, Marian was determined to help Robin, no matter how much it frightened her. But just as she was about to tell Will as much, she caught an expression on John's face. He might have been shadowed in his hiding place, but there was just enough moonlight that she saw something akin to pain flash across his eyes.

"John?" she said.

The boy immediately put on a confident expression that she might have believed if she hadn't seen the worry there a moment ago. "Gis could be here any second," he said, his voice rough.

Marian inched a little closer and put her hand on his arm. "John, is something wrong with Robin?"

He clamped his jaw shut and shook his head.

That did not make Marian feel better in the slightest, and she looked at Will, wondering if he knew something she didn't. But Will looked just as concerned as she felt, which was not a good sign.

"John?" he said.

"Gisbourne," John replied and nodded toward the street.

Sure enough, there was Geoffrey Gisbourne. Though he wore rough clothing and kept a hat low over his head, he still walked with a swagger and an air of confidence that a lower-class man would not possess so easily. His blond hair stood in stark contrast to his dark clothing, and when he turned at the door to glance around the street and make sure it was empty, the moon lit up the profile of his face.

Marian's stomach seemed to be twisting itself into knots as she watched him quickly pick the lock to Mr. Hewitt's door and slip inside the house. "And to think I considered him," she said, the words tasting bitter.

"Everybody makes mistakes," Will said with a grim smile, and then the three of them hurried across the street.

John slipped around back while Will hid himself as best he could in the shadows of the house, and Marian paused on the doorstep to take a quick breath and tell herself she could do this. She *had* to do it. For Robin. For the innocents Gisbourne had hurt. For herself.

"If you run into trouble," Will whispered to her as she took hold of the doorknob, "whistle as loud as you can. We'll come. Otherwise, we'll give you five minutes before we come in after you and help flush him out."

Marian knew she could trust them to keep her safe, and she pulled open the still-unlocked door before she could talk herself out of being brave.

The house was dark and quiet around her, and though some moonlight came in through the windows, Marian could hardly see anything. How had Gisbourne known where to go? Putting her hand against the nearest wall and moving forward at as quick a pace as she could manage without running into anything and making noise, she repeated everything Robin had taught her in her head. It wasn't much, but it made her feel like he was right behind her, walking her through every step.

Marian paused when she reached a staircase and closed her eyes, listening to the stillness around her for any sign of Gisbourne. Where would he have gone? It was not a large house compared to some, but there were still more rooms than she had time to search. Wasting time wandering around would make it harder to catch him, so she had to focus and find him before he finished stealing from Hewitt.

A floorboard creaked above her, only the slightest sound but enough to give her a direction. With one hand still against the wall and the other gripping the knife at her waist, Marian hurried up the stairs and tried to keep her heart from pounding so fast. It was beating so loudly in her ears that she thought maybe Gisbourne would hear it too.

If you're scared, Robin had told her, *you have to remember why you are doing it. Who you are doing it for.*

Pausing at the top of the stairs, Marian blinked away a tear that blurred her already compromised vision, and forced herself to take a slow, deep breath. Then she pictured Robin. The way he smiled when he was trying not to laugh. The anger that sparked a fire in his green eyes when he saw someone being hurt. She imagined how he would look at her when she returned successful. How he would take her hand and tell her how proud he was. How he would take her into his arms and kiss her like he had before, like he actually felt something for her that ran deeper than camaraderie.

She imagined him whole and well. After tonight, they could steal from the ones who deserved it again. The two of them. But they could only do that if they stopped Gisbourne from hurting innocent people.

She finally felt herself calming, and Marian took one last deep breath before she found her wall again and pressed forward, listening hard for any sign of the man she needed to drive from the house. He couldn't be far now. Just a few more steps, and . . .

"Hey!" A vicelike hand wrapped around her wrist and tugged so hard that her shoulder popped and sent a wave of pain through her. Marian gasped and twisted, trying to free herself, but her sudden captor pulled her against his chest and wrapped a strong arm around her. "I hoped I might catch myself a thief tonight," he said.

Mr. Hewitt!

Marian tried to struggle free, but he was far larger and stronger than she was, and her panic returned full force as he pulled her back toward the stairs, where a lit lantern sat waiting. How had she not noticed the light behind her?

"You may be just a pup," he growled in her ear, "but you'll hang for this, mark my words. You picked the wrong man to rob, boy."

Hewitt adjusted his hold as she kept struggling, but when his hand swept across her as he fought to get a better grip, he froze. Marian's fear turned her whole body to ice.

"Not a boy," Hewitt said with an eagerness that made Marian's stomach drop, and then he slammed her back against the nearest wall, knocking her cap from her head, and wrapped his hands around her arms to pin her in place. In the dim glow of his lantern, the hunger in his eyes was clear as day as he looked her over with interest. "Maybe I won't send you away just yet," he said and leaned in close enough that she could smell the sourness of his breath.

Marian was in trouble, but every attempt she made to free herself just brought Hewitt closer, and she couldn't get enough air into her lungs to whistle for help. Will and John wouldn't come for her until it was too late.

"Please no," she whispered.

Hewitt simply sneered and moved in for a kiss.

"The lady said no," a different voice said, and something slammed into Hewitt, knocking him to the floor and taking Marian with him. She landed hard, her already sore shoulder screaming at her, but she ignored the pain and scrambled away from Hewitt as Gisbourne loomed over the man with hatred twisting his face into something frightening. "You're despicable," he spat down at Hewitt. "Going after anything that moves."

Before Hewitt could say anything, Gisbourne kicked his boot into the man's gut. "What do you have to say for yourself, Hewitt?" he growled, but he kicked again without letting the man get a breath.

Marian wanted desperately to run, but she was frozen to the spot, watching in shock as Gisbourne slid to his knees, grabbed Hewitt by the collar, and punched him in the jaw, in the nose, anywhere he could land his fist. Hewitt wasn't even fighting back—maybe he couldn't—and Marian realized with horror that Gisbourne was likely going to kill the man with his bare hands.

Then Gisbourne pulled out a knife.

"Gis!" she shrieked.

He froze on the instant, his knife hovering just over Hewitt's chest. Marian had no idea if he recognized her voice or if he was simply shocked to hear his name, but he didn't move for so long that she slowly reached out her hand and touched his arm. He immediately turned to her, his eyes wide as he took her in.

"Marian," he whispered, almost as if he didn't believe his own eyes.

"You can't kill him, Gis," Marian said, and her words came out in a breath. Though her fingers shook, she kept her hand on his arm in case she had to try to stop him from murdering Hewitt. "Please," she added when he remained motionless as he stared at her.

Finally, he swallowed and glanced down at Hewitt, whose shirt was still clenched in his fist. "He was going to attack you," he said.

A chill ran through Marian at the coldness of his voice. "But you stopped him," she said. She struggled up to her feet, then took hold of Gisbourne's arm with both her hands. A gentle tug brought him standing straight as well. "You stopped him, Gis. It's over now." Could she take the knife from him, or would that trigger his anger? Marian didn't know how he would react, but she knew she did not like the sight of the blade in his bloodied hand. She had to do *something*.

Gisbourne was so tense that his knuckles were white, and he barely breathed. His focus was still on Marian, at least, but she couldn't be sure how long it would be.

"Let me take the knife," she whispered. With one hand she reached up and touched her fingers to his jaw, and she ran the other down his arm to his wrist. Slowly. Carefully. "You don't need it anymore," she said.

"He would have hurt you." The man was terrifying. There was nothing but anger and surprise in his eyes, and he hadn't relaxed for even a moment, not even beneath her touch. If she made a false move, there was no telling what he might do.

"Gis?"

"Marian!" Will suddenly appeared at the stairs, John right behind him, and Will's face was white as he took in the scene.

Gisbourne reacted quickly, grabbing Marian around the waist and pulling her up against him. A second later, he had replaced the knife with a pistol and pointed it at Will. "You stay back," he warned.

Will was intelligent enough to stay where he was, and though his eyes jumped to Hewitt's still form on the floor, he kept his focus on Marian. "No one else has to get hurt," he said, lifting one hand in a gesture of peace. "Just let her go, Gisbourne."

But Gisbourne only held her tighter to him. "I am the only protector Marian needs," he said.

Tears pricked at Marian's eyes, and she didn't know what to do. Gisbourne said he was protecting her, but his hold was so tight that she could hardly breathe. "Let me go," she whispered.

"I will keep you safe," he replied.

Could he not see how much he was frightening her? She trembled like a leaf in his grasp and could hardly stand up straight as she tried not to imagine what terrible things he might do to her if she did not escape his hold.

Will swallowed, fear in his eyes. Fear and something else.

Then she saw John, whose eyes were full of tears, and Marian's fear shifted. "Will?" she whispered in horror.

"So your precious thief has found himself some pawns," Gisbourne snarled. "And you're one of them, Marian?" He pulled Marian a step back, farther from the men at the top of the stairs. "I should have known. That idiotic earl has fooled London long enough, but no more."

Marian's heart sank into her stomach. Gisbourne knew who Robin was?

"Did he sneak into your room late at night as well, my lady? Is that why you're so enchanted by him? Unfortunately for you, silly girl, I do believe I killed him. But I would not waste my tears on him, Marian. He's not worth it."

Marian did everything she could to sound strong and unafraid, though she could hardly manage it. "You didn't kill him," she said. "He survived, and he is never going to let you get away with this."

"Marian." Will's voice broke. Why was he looking at her like that?

Then she caught sight of John's face again, and she realized the boy was full-on crying now. She couldn't say she knew John well, but she had never seen him show emotion like that. Robin had said he wasn't very expressive. Only when— Everything inside her seemed to turn to ice, and she was so dizzy that she thought she might faint.

"No," she whispered. It couldn't be true.

But Will nodded once and looked on the verge of crying himself.

Gisbourne laughed. "So I did kill him? Excellent. That leaves me without competition in every regard, now, doesn't it?"

"Let her go, Gisbourne," Will said, but Marian barely heard him. Her ears were ringing too loudly as she processed the news, unwilling to believe it until she had proof.

But she did have proof. It was on John's face, in the tremor of Will's voice. In the lump in her chest where her heart should be.

Robin was gone.

In her eighteen years, Marian had felt plenty of grief. She'd cried with Millie when her sister died, and she'd said goodbye to her grandparents when they'd gotten too old to keep living. She had even cried over Will when he enlisted, fearing she would never see her cousin again. She had passed lonely summers and watched her mother grow distant, and she had felt the sting of not being enough to make any difference in the lives of the less fortunate.

But this? This was a hundred times worse. She thought she might never breathe again as the pain of heartbreak struck her like a knife to the chest. She had *loved* him. And she hadn't had the chance to tell him. No, she had been angry with him and accused him of being less than he was. She had given him every reason to think she cared nothing for him, and now . . .

She would never get the chance to tell him. She would never get the chance to spend her life discovering the real man behind the facade. She would never . . .

Marian might have screamed if she could breathe, but all she could do was lean into Gisbourne's hold and pray she woke from this nightmare.

"You will pay for his death," Will said, his voice distant.

Gisbourne laughed again, and he was loud enough that somebody shouted downstairs, raising the alarm. The household was finally waking up, and in mere moments someone would arrive upstairs and discover their master beaten to a pulp on the floor with four thieves standing over him. They needed to leave.

What was the point?

"You'll never be able to prove anything, Russell," Gisbourne said, and he tightened his hold on his pistol as he pointed it at each man in turn. "Who would believe a lesser son over me?"

He spoke the truth, and Marian could see that Will knew it too. Like Marian, her cousin was barely holding himself together.

But it was John who spoke, his voice small and thin. "You murdered a good man, Gisbourne," he said. Though Gisbourne chuckled, John set his jaw and added, "You'll be haunted for that, mark my words."

And then, to Marian's horror, Gisbourne touched a kiss to the base of her neck, sending a wave of nausea through her. "Come with me, darling, and I can protect you. There is no point in keeping company with thieves and their little ghost stories. You're worth far more than that."

Marian shuddered beneath his intimate touch, but her repulsion sparked something else inside her, and she realized she was just standing there and acting helpless. No one was coming to save her. Robin hadn't taught her to fight for nothing, so she took a breath and told herself that he was gone and she needed to be strong. He had died to protect her and the rest of London, and she would not let his sacrifice be in vain. She wasn't some silly girl with no brains or value outside of her fortune, and the world still needed a protector.

So she had to find Gisbourne's weakness. She would never overpower him in a test of strength, and he would shoot Will or John if she made any sudden attempts to get away. As with any opponent, she had to go after him where she knew it would hit the hardest. Just like he had.

"Gis?" To her surprise, she sounded far less panicked than she felt.

Gisbourne leaned closer, and though he still pointed his gun at Will, he turned his head to her so his nose brushed her hair. "Yes, my love?"

One more deep breath, and Marian felt like she could do anything. Her fingers found the knife at her waist and ever so slowly pulled it from the ribbon holding it in place. "I . . ." She needed a moment longer to free the knife, so she carefully turned in his hold until she was looking up into his eyes. He could have been a good man, she thought, if he had learned to have his heart in the right place. If he had recognized the reason behind what Robin had done.

"Gis," she said again and leaned up on her toes so her mouth was only an inch from his. Her knife was finally free, and she smiled. She smiled in the way Robin would have smiled when he had his enemy right where he wanted him. "I hope you get everything you deserve," she said.

She stabbed the knife into his hip, and Gisbourne fell back with a hiss of pain, crashing into a painting that fell over the top of him when his weight knocked it from the wall. Marian didn't wait to see how badly she had hurt him but rushed forward and grabbed Will's hand, pulling him into the closest room and shouting for John to follow. She went straight for the window and shoved it open.

"Go!" she shouted.

John practically leapt from the window, landing cleanly on the ground with a roll before he was back on his feet. Will paused, but when he caught Marian's glare, he followed, though he stumbled a bit when he hit the ground. Marian was not quite as confident as she had been a minute ago, but she could hear footsteps on the stairs and Gisbourne moaning, so she knew she could not let herself hesitate. She slipped one leg over the edge of the window, then the other, and she grabbed onto the windowsill as she lowered herself down as far as she could before she dropped. She lost her balance when she landed, but Will caught her before she fell, then pulled her after John, who was already halfway across the street to where the horses waited.

Marian didn't look back at Hewitt's house until she was on her horse and heading out into the street behind Will and John. Flickering lights glowed from most of the windows, but so far, no one had gone outside to chase after the intruders. Neither could Marian see Gisbourne anywhere in the darkness. Had he gotten away, or had Hewitt's servants caught him?

John led the others back to Marian's house, taking a roundabout way just in case they were followed. The city looked different as they went. Darker. The night air seemed to press in around Marian and make it difficult to breathe, but she knew that was her own heart desperately trying to tell her it couldn't be true. He couldn't be gone. But no matter how hard she tried to distract herself by focusing on everything but her thoughts—the movement of the horse beneath her, the smell of the dirt in the street, the muted sounds of hooves as if the horses knew the need for secrecy—all she could think about was Robin.

By the time they arrived at Aspen House, all the energy that had filled her while leaving Hewitt's house was gone. She was simply numb.

"I'll look after the horses," Will told her after he helped her dismount. "John and I will watch the house tonight to make sure you're safe."

Marian turned to John, determined to tell him to go back to Huntingdon Manor and see to everything there, but the boy was already hunkering down in the shadows of the stairs. Maybe he didn't want to go back home now that his master and friend was . . . Marian couldn't bring herself to even think the word again. She was trying to be strong, but a girl could only do so much.

She could not, however, leave the night on such a gloomy thought, so no matter how much she was hurting, she squared her shoulders and spoke before Will left for the stables. "This is not over yet," she said. Both men gave her questioning looks, so she nodded to emphasize her words. "Robin may be . . . gone . . . but Gisbourne is not. If he got away, that means we have another fight coming. Besides, there are still people who need our help. We cannot abandon them when we still have the power to make a difference."

The smallest of smiles appeared on John's face, and Will stepped forward and put his hand on her shoulder. "Rob would be proud of you," he said quietly.

Marian hoped so. Robin was the best of them all. "We need to keep together," she said. "None of us can do this alone, so we are going to have to rely on each other to get through all of this. We *are* Robin."

Will took a breath. "We are Robin," he repeated.

"Robin," John muttered from his hiding place.

And though it was not going to be easy to carry on from this point, Marian knew she would never be able to go back to the life she had known before she'd met Robin. She had changed, and she would do everything she could to change the world right along with her.

CHAPTER *Eighteen*

AFTER SOBBING INTO HER PILLOW for most of the night, Marian slept for only a couple of hours before heartache woke her at dawn. She was tempted to play sick again, but doing so a second day in a row would surely convince her mother to send for a doctor, and that would only complicate things. She hoped keeping herself busy would keep the pain at bay.

She needed to find out what had happened to Gisbourne anyway, and the only way to do that was to find the morning paper or maybe even go straight to the source. There was no better way to get information than to ask the women of London.

"Good morning, Mama," she said as she entered the breakfast room. She had spent as much time as she could making herself look healthy and refreshed so she could avoid questions, and Millie had told her she would never guess anything terrible had happened last night. She hoped her abigail's word rang true for the rest of the household.

Her mother glanced up only briefly, as she was focused almost entirely on her food. She had not read the paper yet, Marian guessed. Her father was there as well, and he had the paper in his hand, though he had only just begun to read.

Marian lowered herself into a chair and did everything in her power to keep from fidgeting. She had to act as natural as possible, but the waiting without knowing was not going to be easy. "I am feeling much better today," she said to break the agonizing silence.

"That's very good, dear," Father said.

The room fell into silence again.

"Is there any noteworthy news?" she asked after as long a pause as she could stand.

Mother glanced up again. "You do not generally care for the news of Town," she remarked, lifting one golden eyebrow in surprise.

Marian nearly winced but held her expression neutral. "I just thought I should take more of an interest now that I am out in Society," she said casually. "Though, I have a lot to learn, I know."

Mother smiled, reaching across the table to put her hand over Marian's. "You are young yet," she said. "I have no doubt you will grow into your role as a lady quite nicely."

That was high praise from a woman as refined and revered as the Marchioness of Waverly, but Marian hadn't gotten any answers yet, and she could hardly swallow as she sipped her tea. It was probably too early for the papers to know anything yet, so she would do better to seek information elsewhere.

"Are you making any calls this morning, Mother?" she asked.

Once again, Lady Waverly looked up in surprise. "I thought you hated making calls," she said as Father peered over the top of his newspaper to surreptitiously listen in. "Oh, but you are trying to become more involved, of course." She waved her confusion away and continued. "In fact," she said, "I am due to visit Mrs. Thornton within the hour. She has had a terrible head cold these last few days, so I thought I might—"

"Any other calls?" Marian asked impatiently. Mrs. Thornton was nearly eighty years old and most certainly would not be privy to the latest gossip. She needed good, quality news. She needed to know if Gisbourne had been arrested or if he was out there now, waiting for the best moment to strike and ruin her forever. She doubted he would let her carry on now that she knew his secret.

Mother frowned, clearly thrown by Marian's eagerness, and it seemed she could not find a response this time as she eyed her daughter with curiosity and confusion.

"Perhaps you should let Marian take the lead, my dear," Father said, then ducked behind his paper again, as if afraid that his comment might upset the calm of the morning. But he had one more thought to add. "Did you not say just yesterday you were keen to see how she fares on her own?"

Marian could not stop her mouth from gaping open, and she turned to her mother, trying to understand how Father could think his wife of all people would ever be interested in what Marian did during the day.

But, to her complete surprise, Mother smiled and replied, "I did say that, didn't I? You do spend so much time on your own that I have been curious about how you go about your day."

It had been years since Mother had paid the least bit of attention to her daughter outside of making sure she continued to grow as a proper lady, and even then she had become far less attentive, to the point that Marian sometimes forgot Mother was nearby at all. Mother interacted with Will far more than she did with Marian, and she had done so for years. Ever since Father had become a marquess. "I didn't think you cared," Marian said before she could stop herself.

Her mother had been about to grab her water glass, but she knocked it over as if startled and fixed an alarmingly hurt expression on Marian, completely ignoring the water soaking into the linen on the table. "Didn't think I cared?" she whispered and glanced to her husband, who slowly set his paper down with a similar expression. "Of course I care!"

Marian had no idea how to react to that response, and a myriad of emotions seemed to wrap around her heart and squeeze it tight. She was already barely keeping herself in one piece after last night's horrible events, and this unexpected declaration was not helping anything. Beyond those rare moments when Marian was sick, her mother never fussed over her like she used to, and yet the idea that her mother didn't care about her day-to-day seemed as preposterous to Mother as the notion that Marian could take over as marquess when her father died.

"What?" Marian whispered, and to her dismay, tears built up in her eyes. If she started crying now, she worried she would never be able to stop.

"Why would I not care?" Mother asked. She reached out a trembling hand to her husband, which he took with a frown. "Marian, there is nothing in the world I care about more than you."

None of this made any sense. "But . . ." Marian swallowed. "But you hardly pay me any attention. You let me go wherever I wish, and you hardly seem to have a preference in the man I might marry. I could be roaming the streets at night, for all you know, and you would hardly speak against it."

"Well, that is a bit ridiculous," her father said, and there was one of those elusive twinkles in his eyes. He was teasing her, and though that should have made her angry, it nearly brought a smile to Marian's face. She had missed this side of her father. "You are far too sensible to do something like that."

"If you had not grown up as well as you did," Mother said, "I might have worried more for you, but . . ." Her voice was weak. Small. Apparently, she had taken Marian's words far harder than her husband, as if they had cut her right to her heart. "I have never been prouder to be your mother, Marian Russell."

Marian did not have the words to respond. Her parents weren't inattentive; they trusted her. But surely they would have praised her choices more if they truly thought she was doing well in life. Wouldn't they?

"I doubt you remember your maternal grandmother," Father said with a smile.

Marian shook her head. Father's mother had died shortly after her husband, and she had been a kind woman, if perhaps set in her ways. But her other grandmother? They'd never spoken of her, and Marian had always wondered why.

"She would have said your eyes were too brown," Mother said, and she snorted a laugh in a way Marian had never seen before. Mother was always so collected and refined, and a laugh like that was, well, not. "She likely would have told you to change them to blue."

Marian frowned. "But that is impossible," she said, though she was pretty sure her mother knew that.

"Nothing was impossible to Lady Blatham," Mother replied. "I am half-convinced I came out with blue eyes because she willed them to be so."

While this information was intriguing, Marian had no idea how it related to the topic at hand. Why would Father have brought up Lady Blatham when they would do better to explain why Marian had been so wrong about how much attention they paid her?

"I don't understand," she said finally, looking between her parents and silently begging them to clarify.

Reaching across the table again, Mother took Marian's hand and gave it a squeeze. "My mother was a horrible woman," she said as casually as if she were telling her about the weather. "She spent her every waking minute telling me how I needed to act. What I should say. What to wear. When I had my first Season, she was always just a step behind me, whispering into my ear to stand up straighter and not to touch anything because I would dirty my gloves. Everything was dictated by Lady Blatham. I am enormously fortunate that the man she chose to be my husband was a loving man"—she sent a smile to Father, which he returned—"but if I had been given the choice—any choice—I might have picked a different life for myself than to be raised by such a woman. It was no way to live, and I never wanted that life for you. When you became old enough, I wanted you to make your own choices."

Marian blinked, and a tear slipped onto her cheek to match the one that slid down Mother's. Could it be true? It was almost too much to believe, but . . . but it would explain everything. How she was able to go wherever she wished, as long as she had a chaperone, of course. How she was able to befriend Millie when a maid was hardly a suitable companion. How they didn't seem to care about Mr. Gisbourne being only a baronet's son when any other parents in their situation would demand a more advantageous match.

Overwhelmed, Marian wrapped her arms around herself and fought to breathe before she fainted. If she had never discovered Gisbourne's treachery, they never would have stopped her from choosing him. And, as terrifying as that thought was, she loved them for it.

"You care," she whispered, and suddenly Mother was pulling her to her feet and wrapping her in her arms. Father joined in, the three of them locked in an embrace in the middle of the breakfast room, and it was almost enough to quell the ache in her chest.

Marian feared it would take far more than a figurative family reunion to fix that particular hurt.

Eventually, though Marian had no idea how long she stood there in her parents' arms, they separated, and she couldn't help but smile as her father muttered some excuse and left the room, brushing tears from his cheeks as he went. He was a good man, and after some of the men she had met over the last several days, she realized she was infinitely blessed to have him for a father.

"You know," Mother said gently, "I think we need to spend some more time together. It seems I do not know you as well as I thought."

"I know how you feel," Marian breathed, still warm from her parents' embrace. Clearly, she had misread everything about her family, and she badly wanted to correct that mistake.

Brushing her own tears away like her husband had his, Lady Waverly fixed on a happy expression and said, "What would you say to a day of shopping, my darling?"

"I would love that," Marian said. Anything to distract her from the misery lurking just beneath the surface of her contentment. But then she frowned because the thought of traipsing around Bond Street with all the rich and powerful made her stomach hurt. After everything, she needed to be around people who didn't flaunt their circumstances. "Could we go to Cheapside?" she asked. When she got wide eyes in return—the marchioness had likely never been to Cheapside—Marian scrambled to find a good excuse that wasn't the truth. "I feel as if I have been through all of the usual shops, and I am hoping for a change of scenery. It could be fun."

If she had to hazard a guess, Marian was pretty sure her mother was realizing she knew her daughter even less than she thought. To Lady Waverly's credit, however, she smiled and nodded. "Of course," she said. "It sounds like a grand adventure, and I have always wondered what I might be missing. As soon as you are ready, we can—"

"I'm ready." Heat blushing her cheeks, Marian bit her lip and did her best to explain. "I can imagine the crowds will only grow later in the day." She needed the distraction *now*. Hopefully, in the chaos of the common London street, she would be preoccupied enough that she wouldn't imagine Robin lying cold in his bed.

A shudder ran through her. That sort of thinking would not turn out well for her, and she scolded her heart for choosing pain over the wonderfully good memories she had of her thief. She had his legacy to carry out, and she couldn't very well do that if she was bogged down by sorrow. No, she had to stay strong and be the woman Robin had believed she could be. *"If anyone can learn to champion the less fortunate and give them better lives,"* he had told her, *"you can."*

Marian wanted so badly to believe it that she took a strengthening breath and held it in her lungs for a moment. She pictured Robin's warm smile, and a wave of calm swept over her.

"Well," her mother said, "I suppose we could get an early start, if that is what you want."

"It will mean more time with you," Marian added, and she managed a very real smile. She truly did want more time with her mother. They would have much less to do together now that Marian was grown and as she went about living her own life. And when she eventually married?

Perhaps she would never marry. Knowing how it felt to truly love someone, she wasn't sure if she could ever be content with anything less. And the odds of her finding someone as worth loving as Robin Loxley? It would be better if she resigned herself now to a life of spinsterhood. Her dowry was plenty large for her to support herself and then some. Besides, what husband would allow her to take over Robin's legacy? Either she would have to remain single forever, or she would be forced to keep secrets and sneak around.

The choice was easy. In order to be the sort of woman who made a difference in the world, Marian would have to be alone. She would never find another man like Robin.

"Jones," her mother said as they found the butler in the entry hall. He snapped to attention as she took Marian's hand in her own. "Order the carriage and tell Lord Waverly we will be in Cheapside. My daughter and I are going out for a much-needed mother-daughter day."

Marian smiled. The distraction would do her good, and tomorrow she would be brave enough to move forward on her own.

CHAPTER *Nineteen*

CHEAPSIDE WORKED BETTER THAN MARIAN could have hoped. Not only were there so many people wandering the street that they could hardly walk without being jostled about, forcing them to focus on their feet and their destination, but the shops themselves were far more diverting than either of the ladies could have guessed. Marian found a charming bonnet in a little shop wedged between a cobbler and a dressmaker, and her mother was rather caught off guard by how cheaply she could purchase all of her embroidery needs when she wasn't in the high-end stores of Bond Street.

There was plenty to keep them occupied until noon, and they stopped in a little tearoom for a break, laughing at the way they had piled up so many purchases in their carriage that they would have a difficult time fitting inside when it was time to return home.

It felt like things used to, before Mother had taken a step back to allow Marian her independence, and she had had no idea how much she'd missed her mother until she was strolling down the street arm in arm with her. She had very nearly forgotten she was in secret mourning, and the afternoon ahead welcomed her heart with open arms. She was stronger than she'd realized, and she would treasure these happy moments for the rest of her life.

"Lady Marian."

Marian stopped dead in her tracks, the blood rushing from her head and leaving her dizzy. How had he found her?

"Mr. Gisbourne!" Lady Waverly said brightly, and the two of them shared bows. "What a pleasant surprise. I hardly thought I would recognize anyone down here in Cheapside."

Gisbourne attempted a smile, but it did not reach his eyes. He was far too tense to feign his usual carefree nature, his fingers gripping a walking stick until his knuckles were white.

Marian hoped that was because she had injured him enough last night to make it difficult for him to walk.

"I must confess I stopped by Aspen House this afternoon," he said. "Lord Waverly told me where I might find you, and I am fortunate to have come across you."

Marian wondered if her mother would listen if she told her the truth. If she said Gisbourne was a murderer, a thief, a scoundrel, would Mother believe her? "Why would you want to find us?" she asked, trying to sound as icy as her heart felt. Forgetting about what had happened to Robin had also meant forgetting about the perpetrator, and she couldn't believe she had gone half a day without wondering if he might appear. He had already proved how easily he had tracked her movements across the city, so what should make today any different?

"Lady Marian," her mother scolded. "That is no way to greet a dear friend."

Even without the man's nefarious secrets, Lady Waverly barely knew Gisbourne. Certainly not enough to call him a dear friend. "I think we should be getting home," Marian replied, but her tug on Mother's arm did nothing.

"Oh, I think we can spare a few minutes," her mother said with a scoff.

"I am feeling tired, Mother."

"Nonsense. You have hardly done anything for days."

"But I—"

"Whatever is wrong, Marian?"

"If I might," Gisbourne interjected, and Marian shuddered at the sound of his voice. Only twelve hours ago he had had her wrapped in his arms, determined to drag her out of Mr. Hewitt's house to who knew where. She could still feel his breath, as if he were restraining her now. "Perhaps I could have a moment to speak to you, Lady Marian."

They were in the middle of the street, surrounded by people hurrying past and barely avoiding collisions with each other, and it was for that reason only that Marian said, "Very well."

No matter what he might say, she would make sure he understood that she would never, under any circumstances, converse with him after today. In fact, she hoped she could find a way to rid London of the man for good.

Approving of Mr. Gisbourne and his false manners, Lady Waverly wandered off to the nearest shop to look in the window, near enough to still be a chaperone but far enough not to overhear her daughter's conversation.

As soon as they had a bit of privacy, Gisbourne took a step closer to Marian, and she was pleased to see the grimace that crossed his face as he did.

Between her knife and Robin's, they had most assuredly done some damage to the man's leg. He had escaped Hewitt's house, yes, but at least he hadn't done so unscathed.

Clearing his throat, Gisbourne made sure no one was listening in, then said, "Someone saw you." His voice was low and soft, far from the menacing tone he had used last night, but Marian did not believe his gentleness in the least. She knew his true nature. "Leaving Hewitt's house last night," he added when Marian did not react. "They recognized Mr. Russell and made the connection to you. They are coming for you, Marian."

She frowned. "They're coming for me?" What did that mean? Was she to be arrested? Sent to Australia like a common criminal for doing nothing wrong? It was Gisbourne who had killed a man. But she knew better than to think she was safe when he knew her secret like he did. Swallowing, she tried not to show her fear in her face. "Who was the witness?" she asked. "You?"

Gisbourne took another step toward her but froze when she flinched. He was afraid she would run, no doubt. "Marian, I would never—" He paused, his eyes locking onto something behind her. But only for a moment. Blinking, he shook his head and continued. "Your cousin hasn't been found yet, but it is only a matter of time. He will be ruined, Marian. And I do not want to see the same thing happen to you. I won't see you diminished in any way, and this—"

"Why are you telling me this?" Marian asked. "If you do not want me arrested, then tell whoever it is you think is coming after me to stop. I have done nothing wrong."

"You were in a strange man's house in the middle of the night."

Marian had been in several strange men's houses at this point, and she was rather proud of the fact. Unless Gisbourne managed to send her to prison, she would do it again. "This conversation is over, Gisbourne," she said and turned to rejoin her mother.

Gisbourne grabbed her arm. "What about your family?"

Marian tensed and turned her head to face him again. What about her family?

"What will happen to them when the constable comes for you? I—" He paused again, frowning as he tracked the movement of something in the crowd.

Marian glanced behind her, but there were far too many people to guess what he was looking at. "Let me go," she demanded.

He only tightened his hold. He was right, and he knew it. Her father was important to the House of Lords, but would anyone listen to him once they found out his own daughter was a criminal? High Society looked to her mother as an example of grace and prestige, and one of her biggest joys in life came from being someone to look up to. If Marian let herself be destroyed like this, if she accepted her fate as a criminal, her parents would be utterly ruined.

"Are you willing to drag your parents down with you?" Gisbourne asked. "I can help you, Marian. I can . . ." He trailed off, focused on the crowd yet again, and he even took a step before he remembered himself. What was going on? "I can argue against the claim that you were at Hewitt's and tell them you were out on a midnight stroll with me. I will swear to your innocence. You may have gotten lost following that Loxley imbecile, and your reputation will undoubtedly suffer from these accusations, but I am willing . . ." He narrowed his eyes, his focus still behind her. "I am willing to marry you anyway."

Marian's stomach clenched as anger flashed through her. "Marry me anyway?" she repeated. Did he really think that declaration would appeal to her? "There is nothing in the world that could induce me to take your hand," she said, and her voice came out stronger than it had been all day.

Gisbourne's hesitant smile fled from his lips immediately, and he returned his full focus to her. "What?"

Marian tried to tug her arm free again, but she was stuck. "You killed my friend," she said. "You've ruined my cousin. You're nothing but a criminal dressed in fancy clothing, and you think a lifetime of misery and fear is worth not being arrested?"

"Marian, listen to yourself."

"No, *you* listen to me."

Gisbourne growled. "You would have joined yourself to that idiot of a man? A common *thief*?"

"A thief who steals to help those in need is far better than a man who does it for his own entertainment," Marian said, and she hardly cared that they were still surrounded by people rushing past. She doubted any of them were really paying attention to her. "He was ten times the man you are."

"You don't realize what you're throwing away," he said roughly. "I am offering you the chance to—"

"I know what you're offering," she spat. "I don't want any of it. I would rather spend the rest of my life in a prison than ever set eyes on you again, Geoffrey Gisbourne. You—"

"No!" he growled, but not at her. Several passersby glanced his way in alarm, but he wasn't focused on any of them. Whatever he *was* looking at, it must have disappeared, because his gaze shifted back to Marian. Mostly. He kept shooting glances into the crowd, as if searching for something. "Marian,

I—you're not real!" He raised his free hand, and Marian jerked back when she saw the pistol in his fingers.

"Gisbourne!" she cried, but his grip on her arm remained firm.

A woman passing by saw the weapon as well and let out a scream, and within moments, the whole street erupted into chaos. Marian fought to free herself but was buffeted by people trying to get out of range, and she would have been knocked to the ground if not for him keeping her upright. Women screamed, men shouted, and Marian searched the crowd for her mother or anyone else who might help her.

Gisbourne seemed to think she was in danger—she was—and he pulled her close against his side and staggered backward into the middle of the street, clearly unaware that the danger was him. "I killed you," he snarled toward one of the shops. "I killed you!"

The volume of the announcement made the crowd still in fear and grow quiet, as if the words had had a magic effect on the people trying to get away. And the sudden silence made it easy for Marian to hear the response.

"You certainly tried."

That was when Marian saw him, and a flame burst to life in her chest.

Several people shifted, creating a break in the crowd. But one man stood his ground at the edge of the street, his arms folded and looking for all the world as if nothing were wrong in the least.

"Robin?" Marian whispered, her heart pounding. Was he a ghost, come back to haunt Gisbourne? But she didn't believe in ghosts, and he looked far too real as the sun shone down over the buildings and gilded his brown hair with streaks of copper. He looked so *alive*.

"I suggest you let the lady go," Robin said. "Unless you're hoping to get stabbed a third time."

"Are you a specter?" Gisbourne asked. His hand shook as he pointed his gun at Robin, and Marian feared he might shoot without meaning to. He could hit any number of the people in the crowd. "You shouldn't be here."

Robin's confident smile grew. "That's what happens when you kill a man, Gis."

Marian wanted to run to Robin and make sure he was real before her heart broke anew, but Gisbourne's grip had gotten so strong that her fingers were going numb. But she couldn't just stand there helpless, and there were too many people nearby. Someone was going to get hurt, and that would be on her head. She had drawn him here, and every crime he had committed up to now had been for her.

"You must have something on your conscience if you're seeing me," Robin said, and he slowly unfolded his arms, dropped his hands to his sides, and stepped forward once. Then again. His eyes never left Gisbourne, even as whispers started up in the crowd. "You've already confessed to murder," he continued, "but maybe an apology would make you feel better."

Marian tried to make eye contact with the nearest man in the crowd, silently begging him to get as far as he could. But he was too focused on the impending confrontation to even pay her any notice. So were the two women next to him.

Now that Robin was closer, Marian realized he was still incredibly pale, and though he appeared to be fully well, there was a shallowness to his breath. He may have been alive, but he was far from whole, and she suspected he was barely holding himself upright and would not be able to keep up his ruse for long. She had to do something to help him.

"What are you looking at?" she said as loud as she could as she involuntarily trembled in Gisbourne's hold. "There's nothing there, Gisbourne."

Robin's mouth twitched.

Gisbourne growled. "He is right there," he said and pointed at Robin with his pistol.

Even if Robin hadn't actually smiled, she still felt the effect of it, and she had to force herself to sound afraid instead of overwhelmed with happiness. "Who?" Marian asked. "I don't see anyone. Gis, you're frightening me."

The people in the crowd had started frowning, glancing between the two men as if questioning their own vision. Apparently, Marian's influence was still strong, even if there was a high chance no one in Cheapside knew who she was. She must have looked the part of someone who should be listened to, and she would absolutely take advantage of that.

Her tactic must have been working already, because Gisbourne adjusted his grip on his pistol, but he shook so hard that it was a miracle he hadn't accidentally fired his weapon already. "If I shoot you," he said, sending a wave of terror through Marian, "you'll go away. You'll vanish like the spirit you are."

"Then, shoot," Robin said. He spread his arms wide and moved even closer, and Marian nearly cried out and begged him not to. He was making himself more of a target. But he was also shielding one or two more people from becoming victims since Gisbourne was less likely to miss him. It was the likelihood of hitting Robin that Marian did not like. She would not survive his dying again.

She twisted as much as she could, finally catching someone's eye. The woman blinked, as if roused from a trance, and frowned at Marian. "Move," Marian whispered, begging her to understand.

Thank the heavens the woman nodded and looked for the best way to get out of the line of fire should anything go wrong. The woman touched the arm of the man next to her, pulling him out of the same fixation, and their attentions seemed to ripple through the nearest people. They slowly shifted to the sides, not so far away that they couldn't keep watching but no longer directly behind Gisbourne. Across the way, the crowd behind Robin followed suit and left a clear path.

"Either you'll kill me in reality and pay the price," Robin continued, and his eyes glistened with pride, even though he hadn't looked away from Gisbourne's face, "or you'll appear as a madman shooting at nothing. Or you can put down your gun and let one of the Runners arrest you for attempted murder."

Two men in matching coats suddenly pushed through the crowd between Robin and Gisbourne, their keen eyes taking in the situation and their pistols drawn. One of them frowned at Gisbourne and muttered, "I'd hoped you were jesting about the madness, Huntingdon."

Gisbourne tensed, suddenly realizing he was not, in fact, the only one who could see Robin standing there in the street. "You're alive," he snarled and shoved Marian forward to give himself plenty of room.

She barely managed to stay on her feet, and though sharp pain shot through her freed arm, she could see Gisbourne's fear rapidly shifting into unbridled anger. Robin would never be able to react in time. Not injured as he was. Gisbourne was already steadying his aim. "Gis, no!" Marian shouted and leapt toward Robin to block him from the bullet that didn't come. She turned, her heart racing.

Gisbourne hesitated for only a moment when his eyes locked with hers, but he lifted his gun again and pointed it right at her chest.

The gunshot was louder than Marian expected, and she waited for the pain to hit. But it was Gisbourne who cried out, his suddenly empty hand covered in blood as he gripped it tight with the other. He snarled and lunged for her, but Robin darted in front of Marian with a gun of his own pointed at Gisbourne's heart.

"Take another step toward her, and I will kill you," Robin warned. "I promise I will not miss."

Gisbourne seemed torn, his body jerking forward a little as if he was about to try again, but it was a comment from one of the Bow Street Runners that ultimately held him in place. "I would listen to the man," the Runner said. "I've never seen someone make a shot like that. It's a miracle he hit you and not the lady."

Marian shuddered, frozen to the spot as she tried to comprehend what had just happened.

Clutching his injured hand, Gisbourne snarled at Robin again, then turned his attention to the two officers. "Why are you just standing there?" he asked. "I told you—"

"You told me one William Russell killed Lord Huntingdon and robbed Samuel Hewitt with the help of Lady Marian," the second Runner interrupted. "Imagine my surprise when the Earl of Huntingdon stepped through our door this morning, perfectly alive."

"Mr. Russell was with me all evening," Robin said, and he pocketed his pistol. Though he looked calm and casual, Marian could see the tension still rippling through his body. How long would he be able to pretend he was all right? "I was injured the other day," he continued, "and Russell was keeping me company. My whole staff can confirm it, as can my considerably lighter purse; the man is deucedly good at cards. And if you ask Lady Marian's maid, I am sure you'll find the lady was in her bed all night, exactly as she should be."

"Of course she was," a deep voice that made Marian jump replied. Her father pushed his way through the crowd, John at his heels, and wrapped Marian in his arms as if to protect her from the motionless Gisbourne. "It would be preposterous to think otherwise," he added, his voice thrumming through his chest into Marian's cheek. She clung to him, tears threatening to escape from her eyes now that she was no longer in danger. When was the last time Father had held her like this? Like he wanted to protect her from the world? Robin must have sent John to fetch him, and she loved him all the more for it.

"Of course," the taller of the two Runners said.

"I think Mr. Gisbourne is not quite right in his head," replied the other. "If he so easily believed he was looking at a ghost."

"I am not mad," Gisbourne muttered, but there was no strength to his words. He simply stood there, his eyes on the ground as his defeat settled on him. Based on the growing whispers of the crowd, there would be few people in London who would not know the morning's events before long. Whatever friends Gisbourne might have had, he surely would not keep them after this humiliation.

Stepping forward, each officer took hold of one of Gisbourne's arms and tugged him back toward Bow Street. "Let's see what to do with you," one of them said, and they disappeared into the crowd that parted just long enough for them to pass.

"Huntingdon," Marian's father said, and he waited until Robin looked over.

Robin glanced at Marian briefly, a smile in his eyes, but he kept his attention mainly on the marquess. "My lord?"

"I owe you my daughter's life," Father said. "You risked your own to save her. How can I ever thank you?"

As much as she cherished being held by her father, Marian's arms ached for Robin, and she met his gaze, hoping he understood how incomprehensibly happy she was to see him. She had hardly grasped the fact that he was even alive, and she wasn't sure she could believe it. Not until she touched him.

"With all due respect, my lord, she saved my life first," Robin said, and then he smiled in a way Marian had never seen before. It was the sort of smile that said a million things, things she didn't understand but desperately wanted to. It was the sort of smile she could spend a lifetime trying to fathom.

Thankfully, the crowds had had their fill of entertainment for the day now that the excitement was over, and the streets filled with chatter again almost on the instant as the people of London returned to their chaotic shopping.

And Marian couldn't handle it anymore.

Pulling free of her father's hold, she threw her arms around Robin's shoulders and gasped, "You're alive" as he matched the embrace, holding her so tight that it felt like he was holding her together. It was hardly the sort of embrace they should be sharing in a public place, but Marian hardly cared. She had her Robin back.

"Gisbourne never would have believed I'd died if you and Will didn't," Robin said quietly, and he rested his head on top of hers. "I'm sorry for John's lie, my love, but it was crucial." *My love.* He fit so perfectly around her, and Marian didn't want to leave.

There, at Robin's side, she felt whole again.

"Marian." Her mother's voice came out as little more than a breath, but Marian broke away from Robin just enough to see her pushing her way through the crowd with Will right behind her. The poor woman was as pale as a sheet, and based on the dust on her skirts and the way Will kept a hand at her back, Marian guessed she had not endured the confrontation consciously. Before her mother could find any more words, she fainted into Will's arms, confirming Marian's thoughts.

Though Marian expected him to shake her in anxiety and call for help, Lord Waverly simply sighed and picked his wife up with the ease of a man who had done it before. "Thank you, William. I will take her to the carriage," he said.

"I think it is a good time for all of us to return home for the day. Huntingdon, I should like to have a word with you. When you're ready." And he winked at Marian before stepping into the foot traffic of Cheapside, followed closely by Will and John.

Marian immediately fell back into Robin's hold, determined to stay there as long as she possibly could.

He grunted and sagged a little against her. "Still got stabbed two nights ago," he reminded her with a chuckle. "Perhaps we should follow your father's advice before all of London realizes what they could be witnessing. We've already fed the gossip mills enough, don't you think?"

Marian hardly cared. Robin was alive, and he was holding her, and all was right again. She wouldn't have minded if all of London appeared on the street and watched as she brushed a stray bit of hair from Robin's brow.

"Is it too much for me to say I love you?" she asked. It was easy to admit, particularly standing there in his warm hold. And she was not about to miss her chance again. "I don't know what I would have done without you."

Robin grinned and touched his forehead to hers as if drinking in her nearness. "From what I heard," he replied, "you would have done splendidly. The poor still would have had a savior."

"I suppose I should leave that up to you now," she said and sighed. She was no good at the whole thievery thing. Not as good as Robin, anyway, and she only seemed to get him into trouble. All this madness with Gisbourne had started because of her, because he'd wanted to protect her.

Despite the little audience, Robin brushed his lips against hers in the tiniest of kisses. It was small, but it was enough to make her shiver with pleasure. "What would Robin the Thief be without his Maid Marian?" he whispered.

Marian grinned and took him by the hand, leading him to the waiting carriage before they really caused a scene.

CHAPTER *Twenty*

ROB SAT AT HIS DESK, the oil lamp turned low and the house quiet around him. He was reading a report sent to him by one of the tenant farmers he looked after, but he had read the same sentence three times already and taken in none of it. He liked helping his tenants and providing them with decent livings, but sometimes documents like this drove him straight to boredom. There was only so much time he could spend reading about crop projections before his eyes drifted to the window and his hand began to itch.

Once a thief, always a thief.

He would do better to just go to bed and resume his perusal in the morning, when he did not have the moon calling him out to the streets. He was tired enough.

Just as he made to rise from his chair, the cool blade of a knife slid beneath his chin, and he grinned. She was really getting good. "I didn't hear a thing," he said. Quick as a flash, he grabbed hold of her wrist and twisted himself free so he could stand.

She countered and slipped out of his grasp, brandishing her knife. Marian glared at him with all the ferocity of a tiger in India, everything about her lithe and agile. Even if he tried to surprise her, she would be quicker. Heavens, she was beautiful.

"Bravo," Rob said and offered polite applause. She was definitely getting better. "But now I know you are here, so how will you . . . ?" He paused as she raised a purse of coins, which to his knowledge, had been locked in the desk all night. The desk where he had been sitting for some time. "Impressive," he offered when he really wanted to say the woman was astounding.

Over the last year, she had learned enough and trained enough that she was a force to be reckoned with, and he couldn't help but beam at her.

"You should be impressed," she said, and a fire gleamed in her eyes. "I had a good teacher."

Rob slowly moved closer, backing her up against the wall despite her knife. "It sounds to me like your teacher is good at what he does," he said, his voice low.

As Marian reached the wall and had to stop, she grinned and touched the tip of her knife to Rob's belly. "He is," she said. "There is no one better than John."

That was as much as he could take. Grabbing her wrist, Rob pushed the knife out the way and moved in close so the two of them were only a few inches apart. "John," he repeated, trying to sound angry. The spark in her eyes made that rather impossible. "Now, Tuck, that is the sort of talk I will not tolerate in my house."

"Then, it is a good thing it is my house as well, is it not?" Marian replied, and she crossed the last bit of distance between them and pulled Rob in for a kiss that left him warm from his head to his toes. She was remarkably good at completely disarming him with those lips of hers, though Rob had yet to complain. He simply pulled her into his arms and relished in her nearness.

"A lady of the house can say whatever she wants," Rob agreed, though he wasn't sure he managed the words very clearly. He was far too busy tangling his fingers up in her hair and marveling as always at how well she fit in his arms.

Kissing him again, Marian smirked, then pulled a hat over Rob's head, tilting it at just the right angle. "Well, come on," she said. "These rich people are not going to rob themselves. Will and Alana are waiting downstairs."

He frowned. "Do you really think this is necessary anymore?" he said. "You already spend all day persuading your peers to be better, and you do far more good as Marian than I do as a thief." And while he was enormously proud of her, the fact that she had been dismantling the darker parts of polite Society from the inside out made him feel rather useless.

But Marian smiled at him and wrapped her arms around his neck. "Where would be the fun in that?" she asked and teased a kiss against his lips. "Not all of them are listening to reason, and you should have heard the way Mrs. Bennett was talking to her footman this morning. I half expected Miss Young to suggest she and I seek out the notorious thief and provide him with evidence for a new target."

Rob's eyebrows flew high. Marian and Miss Young had struck up a friendship several months ago, and they and Alana were so often together that he wouldn't have been surprised if the young lady knew about their nighttime adventures. "She is still sympathetic to the lower class, then?" he asked. He never would have guessed it, though he might have learned it sooner if he had ever given the lady a chance.

"She is not the only one," Marian replied, and she adjusted his hat again, as if he might have to hide his face in his own house. "More and more are learning that kindness benefits not just the poor but themselves as well."

"I do believe they are becoming intelligent enough to follow the example of the illustrious Lady Huntingdon," Rob replied, and he couldn't help but grin, just as he always did when he called her that. He liked it nearly as much as calling her Tuck. "You, my darling wife, are incredible."

"I learned from the best," she replied and kissed him so deeply that his head spun. "From the man I love with all my heart. Now, hurry and dress in something appropriate before you make your sister wait too long. She is eager to show you how quickly she can pick a lock now—I think she may be better than you!" She slipped away and disappeared through the door with a laugh that echoed in Rob's chest like a ball of light bouncing around inside him.

Oh, but how he loved that woman. He paused and leaned his back against the wall as he contemplated the utter bliss that was his life.

Geoffrey Gisbourne had long since been sent to Australia for the safety of others in London and would not grace good Society for many years, if ever again. His sister was happy and well, as was his mother. True, the city was plagued by a band of merry thieves, but thanks to their efforts—both at night and during the day—the upper classes had begun to figure out the best ways to avoid becoming targets, and the *ton* had become a generally nicer bunch of people.

And Rob's wife daily gave him the sort of smile that could give a man life. She was everything he could have hoped and dreamed for in a partner, and he would cherish her goodness and selflessness forever. Some things were worth fighting for, and Marian would always be at the top of that list.

ABOUT THE *Author*

DANA LECHEMINANT HAS BEEN TELLING stories since she was old enough to know what stories were. After spending most of her childhood reading everything she could get her hands on, she eventually realized she could write her own books, and since then she has always had plots brewing and characters clamoring to be next to have their stories told. A lover of all things outdoors, she finds inspiration while hiking the remote Utah backcountry and cruising down rivers. Until her endless imagination runs dry, she will always have another story to tell.

Dana loves connecting with readers and talking books!

Website: www.lecheminantbooks.com

Facebook: @authordanalecheminant

Instagram: @danalecheminant